Praise for the Adventures of a Young Sailor series

PRISON
SHIP

"Adventure fans will not be disappointed with the daring rescues, shark attacks, espionage, and heated battles that fill the pages of this historically accurate and vastly entertaining sequel." —*SLJ*

"Those who enjoyed the first of the series will be enthralled with this adventure-packed second book." —*VOYA*

"*Prison Ship* is a great story about survival and justice. . . . The reader feels like a mate of Sam's." —*VOYA*, teen reviewer

"Readers who prefer their wooden decks awash in blood 'and worse' will not be disappointed. . . . Voracious fans of the nautical genre will happily sign on." —*Kirkus Reviews*

"Readers will be absorbed in the day-to-day life of young Sam, and his vivid tale will keep them on edge. . . . Not for the faint of heart, this novel is a brilliant introduction to the likes of C. S. Forester's classic 'Horatio Hornblower' saga." —*SLJ*

"Fans of the *Master and Commander* series or movie will enjoy this seafaring adventure. Sam is an engaging narrator who includes tremendous detail about daily life aboard ships." —*VOYA*

"Sam leads an exciting and dangerous life as a powder monkey. . . . A gripping adventure story on the high seas." —Travelforkids.com

Books by Paul Dowswell

Adventures of a Young Sailor
Powder Monkey
Prison Ship
Battle Fleet

Adventures of a Young Sailor

PRISON SHIP

Trilogy

Paul Dowswell

BLOOMSBURY

Text copyright © 2006 by Paul Dowswell
Illustrations copyright © 2006 by Peter Bailey
First published in Great Britain by Bloomsbury Publishing Plc in 2006
Published in the United States by Bloomsbury U.S.A. Children's Books in 2006
Paperback edition published in 2007

Published by Bloomsbury U.S.A. Children's Books
175 Fifth Avenue, New York, NY 10010
Distributed to the trade by Holtzbrinck Publishers

The Library of Congress has cataloged the hardcover edition as follows:
Dowswell, Paul.
Prison ship : adventures of a young sailor / by Paul Dowswell. — 1st U.S. ed.
p.   cm.
Summary: After being framed for cowardice in a sea battle, fifteen-year-old Sam and his friend
Richard are sent to Australia, where they must fight for their lives in the outback.
ISBN-13: 978-1-58234-676-2 • ISBN-10: 1-58234-676-3 (hardcover)
1. Australia—History—19th century—Juvenile fiction. [1. Australia—History—19th
century—Fiction. 2. Great Britain—History—19th century—Fiction. 3. Napoleonic
Wars, 1800–1815—Fiction.] I. Title.
PZ7.D7598Pr 2006   [Fic]—dc22   2006007275

ISBN-13: 978-1-59990-156-5 • ISBN-10: 1-59990-156-0 (paperback)

Typeset by Dorchester Typesetting Group Ltd
Printed in the U.S.A. by Quebecor World Fairfield
1 3 5 7 9 10 8 6 4 2

To
J & J
the Morpeths
and
the Catons

Sortedam Lake

CITY WALLS

COPENHAGEN

CITADEL

Sand Bank

CITY WALLS

Battery
Crown Battery

A Sand Bank

DANNEBROG

DANISH FLEET

ELEPHANT

BRITISH FLEET

Middle Ground
Sand Bank

Outer Deep

THE BATTLE OF
COPENHAGEN
April 2ND 1801

Contents

I went to sea to find adventure.
I faced storms and battles, but nothing could
prepare me for the journey which followed.
Sent to the far side of the world for a crime
I didn't commit, I became a prisoner,
thousands of miles from everything I knew.
I was only fifteen.

CHAPTER 1

HMS *Elephant*

It was half past three in the morning. I was lying in my hammock, gently swaying with the swell of the sea. Coarse woollen blankets kept me warm, as did the stifling fug of two hundred sleeping men, crammed down here on the lower gun deck of HMS *Elephant*. It reminded me of the clammy warmth of a stable packed with sheep and cattle.

I had slept deeply since midnight; through the snoring, the sleep-talking, the hacking coughs that most of the crew had, even through the half-hourly chime of the ship's bell. I was dreading the four o'clock bell. That would be when I would have to tear myself away from my comforting cocoon and face the raw, biting cold of the North Sea in winter.

In blizzard and high winds the Navy still requires a man to climb frost-covered rigging, to haul himself above the deck while his hands turn blue and clumsy in front of his eyes, and to scrub the icy deck with the wind whistling through his meagre shirt and trousers. And who in his right mind would look forward to a trip to the heads, to sit in the open air, bare-arsed in a howling gale, as icy waves hurl freezing spray up around the bow of the ship?

In these last calm moments before the day began, my thoughts began to drift. How lucky I had been to escape the wreck of the frigate *Miranda* when she sank off the Cornish coast by Pentherick. I still had only a hazy idea who had survived and who had perished, although I was grateful to providence for sparing my two great friends on the frigate, Richard Buckley and Robert Neville. I had rescued the ship's cat Bouncer too, but left him with the landlord's wife at the Royal Oak in Pentherick. It was a better life being a pub cat – plenty of fuss from the customers and plenty of scraps from the kitchen.

I travelled to Plymouth with Richard and Robert the next day and we were sent at once by sea to Portsmouth and a new posting on HMS *Elephant*. As the three of us stood on the forecastle of the Portsmouth tender, a fierce wind whipped the clothes on our backs. I didn't care. I was enjoying being a passenger and not having to concern myself with sailing the ship. Richard leaned over to Robert and shouted, 'So tell us about this ship we're heading for.' As a midshipman Robert had been briefed about his new posting. Not us. As ship's boys we were just expected to do what we were told, no questions.

'The *Elephant* is a 74 – and most of those seventy-four guns are placed over two gun decks. So she's quite a bit bigger than the *Miranda*.'

'What size crew do we have?' said Richard. He sounded wary. I knew how he felt. Neither of us had been on a ship bigger than the *Miranda*.

'There'll be around six hundred men aboard,' said Robert. 'She's a ship of the line. As soon as we reach Portsmouth we're to set sail for the Baltic. I've been informed that the Danes, Swedes, Russians and Prussians have all banded together against us.'

My heart sank. 'Why's that?' I said. 'Isn't it enough to be at war with France and Spain?'

'Bounders are in a bate about our right to search their ships to see if they're carrying goods for our enemies. We're not at war yet,' Robert said gravely, 'but we might be soon. I wouldn't be too worried about it. None of these fellows are a match for our Navy.'

'These 74s,' I said. 'Are they more dangerous than a frigate?'

Robert wondered. 'I'd say safer. Frigates go looking for trouble on their own. A ship of the line goes out with the fleet, so there's safety in numbers.'

Our conversation was interrupted by another midshipman. 'What ho,' he said, barging past Richard and me to shake Robert's hand. 'You must be Neville. I was told you might be aboard. I'm Oliver Pritchard. I'll be serving on the *Elephant* too.'

With that he placed an arm around Robert's shoulder and marched him away. I overheard him sneering loudly about 'consorting with the lower orders', an observation I'm sure we were intended to hear.

The boy looked a year or so older than Robert, and was both taller and heavier. 'Don't like the look of that one,' said Richard, as we watched the two midshipmen talking together on the opposite side of the forecastle. I had to agree. This Pritchard had a thin, mean face, and one eyebrow almost constantly raised in a challenge or a sneer. His whole body seemed to coil with a fidgety tension. I don't think Robert liked him much either. He was standing slightly away from him, with a cool expression on his face.

We didn't talk with Robert for the rest of that short voyage to Portsmouth. It was a shame. We three all knew as soon as we reached the *Elephant* our easy friendship would have to end. He did pass me on the forecastle though. 'Jumped up little twerp, that

Pritchard,' he said quietly. 'I'd keep out of his way, if I were you.'

We sailed into Portsmouth early on the morning of 22nd February 1801. It was a fresh winter's dawn and when I first saw the *Elephant* the rising sun was glistening on the gold-painted figures that embellished the two great cabins at her stern. The Captain's, on the upper deck, had its own balcony. Beneath it were the windows of the officers' gunroom. I could picture their comfortable interiors and felt a twinge of envy when I imagined how our bare quarters would look.

Robert read my mind. 'We'll make you an officer yet, Witchall,' he said with a grin. 'And you too, Buckley.' Surnames in company, Christian names in private. It was a curious friendship the three of us had.

'Not me, Mister Neville,' said Richard. 'I'll be back in Massachusetts before I'm old enough to be an officer.'

Although he was an American, Richard's family expected the Royal Navy would give him the best apprenticeship for a life at sea. He was destined to command a ship, I was sure. I couldn't imagine I was. Being a grocer's son and a pressed boy, the best I could expect was to get out of the Navy alive.

Close up, I could see how big the *Elephant* was. She sat high in the water with her two gun decks, and a quarterdeck raised above the upper deck. She looked like she packed a ferocious punch.

Going aboard I was struck by the smell of the ship. Several days away on land had given my nose a rest from the sharp whiff of tar, pitch and gunpowder, and the low stench of wet wood, rank bilgewater and several hundred seamen. It took me straight back to my first fearful night on the *Miranda*.

We went through the ritual of having our names entered into the muster book. The ship's captain, Thomas Foley, oversaw the proceedings. I liked him at once. He was around my father's age and six foot in height.

'I've heard reports of your gallant actions on the *Miranda*, Witchall,' he said to me. Turning to one of the ship's lieutenants he remarked, 'Perhaps we have the makings of a midshipman here, Mr Mayhew.'

'Carry on as a powder boy for now,' said the Captain, 'but we shall keep you in mind if a more suitable appointment presents itself. I'm placing you with Thomas Shepherd, James Kettleby and Vincent Thomas on the starboard afterguard watch. You'll know them from your previous posting. Buckley can join you too. You'll all be manning a quarterdeck carronade.'

I couldn't help but grin from ear to ear when I heard Tom and James had survived the shipwreck – although they were years older than me, they had been good friends on the *Miranda*. The towering Welshman Vincent Thomas was from that ship too. I didn't know him so well – other than by my nickname for him, 'Vengeful Tattoos'. His body was covered with fearsome Biblical quotations. It was good to have Richard serving in the same gun crew too. We could keep an eye out for each other. I wasn't sure about being placed on the quarterdeck though. Being out in the open during a battle would leave us dangerously exposed.

We met with Tom and James that dinner time. Hearing the two of them, chattering away in their Cockney and Geordie voices, took me straight back to the mess deck of the *Miranda*. Their faces lit up when they saw the two of us. 'We 'eard you'd got away from the ship,' said Tom. 'Thought you might've slipped the cable, Sam!'

'We both washed up close to Pentherick,' said James. 'Got whisked doon to the *Elephant* the next day, along with Mr Thomas here.'

Vincent Thomas nodded. He seemed friendly enough.

'Middlewych is here too,' said Tom, 'although he's servin' as a lieutenant, rather than first lieutenant.'

Middlewych! I was pleased. The last time I saw him, he was trying to persuade some drunken sailors to take to the waters as the *Miranda* lay breaking up. He was the officer I liked the most.

'Foley seems decent enough,' I said.

James said, 'Aye. Foley doesn't have to act severe. He's proved his worth many times over. They say Lord Nelson thinks well of him.'

I saw Middlewych on deck, supervising the loading of provisions. 'Glad to see you alive, Witchall. I'm sorry I couldn't secure you a better post on the *Elephant*, but the captain knows you're a good lad.'

This sounded promising. I had gone to sea for adventure and advancement that would never cross my path as the shop assistant or school teacher my father wanted me to be. What was it Captain Foley had said – 'the makings of a midshipman'? And after that, a lieutenant! And to think how much I had resented being pressed into the Navy and how I had longed to escape. Now the prospect of becoming an officer was being dangled in front of my eyes.

The five of us former shipmates were all happy to make up a mess, especially as we were now all together as a gun crew. The mess tables were stowed between the guns of the gun deck and set up only when it was time to eat. The gun deck was also where we would sling up our hammocks to sleep.

Our table had room for six, with three on two benches either side. To make up the numbers we were joined that first evening by another seaman new to the ship named John Giddes. He worked as an assistant to the

Purser. None of us would have chosen him as a mess mate, but the officer of the watch bluntly told us he was joining us. Giddes was a lanky, dark-haired man with a narrow face and sullen eyes. He was handsome, I suppose, but had the air of someone caught doing something he shouldn't be.

As we sat down for supper Tom turned and spoke to him. 'Where you from, John?'

'I'm from London, like you,' he said.

'Where abouts?' said Tom, seizing on the opportunity to find out more about him.

'Lived all over,' he said. 'Whitechapel, St Giles, Cheapside. Father was a cobbler.'

'Where did he work?' said Tom. 'I never knew any cobblers with Giddes on the sign.'

'Always worked for some else, didn't he.'

'How'd ye end up here?' said James.

'You're a nosy lot, aintcha?' he said. 'If you must know, they took me off a merchantman bound for Liverpool.'

That was the end of that. What an odd man, I thought.

Talk turned to our duties on the carronade. Tom would be gun captain. Vincent Thomas would sponge out and load. James Kettleby would help move the gun. Richard would help him. Although only a year older than me, he was now judged strong enough to manhandle a cannon, especially a carronade as it was lighter than a long gun. As Powder Monkey I would be running to the ship's magazine deep in the hold to fetch gunpowder when it was needed. Carrying a cartridge box that could blow me to bloody pieces made me shudder every time I thought about it. James added to my anxiety when he said, 'Personally I'd rather be on the gun deck than the quarterdeck. I don't like the idea of being oot in the open. We're too much of a target, especially for any sharpshooters up in the enemy's rigging.'

'We'll have to make do with the job we've been given,' said Tom. He turned to me and told me more about our gun. 'Carronades don't have the same range as the long guns, so we use 'em when the ship's up close to the enemy. They're lighter and smaller so they're quicker to reload. You'll have your work cut out keeping us supplied with powder, Sam. It's a long way from the quarterdeck to the after powder room, so you'll have to run faster than ever.'

Our meal finished we settled into uneasy small talk. Giddes was prickly silence. Vincent Thomas was cheery enough. He made me laugh as he chuntered along in a sing-song Welsh voice that didn't quite go with his massive bulk. But I noticed James and Tom seemed reluctant to smile at his stories.

That first day aboard the *Elephant* seemed a long time ago. Now we were four days into our voyage, pushing through the North Sea after leaving Portsmouth on the second day of March. The four o'clock bell I had been dreading tolled at last, followed by the shrill peep of the Bosun's whistle. All around was frantic activity as we tumbled from our hammocks. My bare feet landed in a puddle of freezing water that had sloshed in through the gunports during the night. James had told me to expect this in rough weather as the deck was only five feet above the waterline. The shock of it brought me fully awake.

Jack Tars are a hardy lot, but most of the crew were suffering from a wretched cough brought about by the cold. Many of these men had recently returned from the Mediterranean, and found this harsh weather a trial. They say Hell is burning hot, but its residents could just as easily be tormented by freezing cold.

Our first duty was to chip from the decks the ice that had formed overnight. So far we had made most of the voyage through thick fog, and today it still showed no sign of clearing. Distracted from my work I peered over the rail and could see nothing ahead but a dense drifting mist. Perhaps this was what Monsieur Montgolfier saw when he flew his balloon into a cloud?

'Bosun, start that man,' barked Midshipman Pritchard, and one of the bosun's mates stepped forward and hit me with his rope. I was so cold the blow barely registered on my numb shoulders, and really, I deserved it. I crouched down again on the deck and began chipping away with the chisel I had been issued.

'Put your back into it Witchall,' snapped Pritchard, strutting by in his thick woollen coat. He came up close and placed the toe of his boot over my hand splayed on the deck. He did not press down hard enough for it to hurt but it was a deliberately insulting gesture. 'If I have to tell you again, I'll have you flogged,' he hissed. I'd been told that the ship's Purser, Nathaniel Pritchard, was his father, and I wondered how far his influence had brought the boy a midshipman's berth.

When the decks were cleared of ice we were mustered to raise the anchors. It was exhausting work, especially with breakfast still three hours away.

Soon after dawn I was called to adjust the main royal and began to climb the rigging in the company of four of the topmen. I looked down on this vast warship, and the fraction of her crew who were scurrying to and fro about the deck. Despite all the hardship, and any lingering resentment about being pressed into the Navy, I felt a great sense of pride. The two hundred and fifty men on the *Miranda* might have made up a village. Here there were five hundred sailors and a hundred marines. The ship had its own chaplain, even its own band. I thought that six hundred souls must make us more of a small town. Robert Neville was right about feeling safer on a 74. She was formidable.

I wondered how we would fare if we had to fight. Only

the incessant cold took my mind off the battle we were sailing towards. I had been in combat barely two months before. Now when I heard the roll of the drum that called us to quarters I could vividly recall the stench of blood and gunpowder, and the screams of the dying. I wondered if this time it would be me who would be torn to pieces by chain shot or gutted in hand-to-hand fighting.

Waiting for the order to drop the sail I strained my eyes towards the land, hoping to see a glimmer of light from a seashore cottage or even a town or village, but the fog was too thick. Close by, I knew, lay the coast of my home county Norfolk. I had heard we were near our assembly point at Yarmouth Roads, where the Royal Navy gathered its fleet to sail to the Baltic. This was as near as I had been to home since I was pressed the previous summer, and all at once I felt a great yearning for its familiar comforts and shelter. Far off in the darkness I heard the sound of cormorants calling to one another, and gannets and auks. Seabirds with nests by the shore. If I were one of them, I could fly in a straight line back to my sweetheart Rosie in Yarmouth, then still further north to Wroxham and home. If I were there now, I'd be tucked up in bed, instead of shivering up this mast, staring down at the grey waters crashing against the ship. The sea was cold enough to kill any man who fell into it in little more than a minute.

*　*　*

On the next day we met up with the other ships of the fleet. Up in the rigging again during a brief break in the fog, I counted over fifty vessels around us. I had never seen so many men-o'-war in one place in my life. Would being part of such a formidable armada make it less likely that I would be killed? The fleet was commanded by Vice Admiral Sir Hyde Parker. I knew very little about him. Much to the men's excitement we were also sailing with Vice Admiral Horatio Nelson. He was aboard the *St George* and all of us hoped that he might pay our ship a visit sometime during the voyage, so we could get a glimpse of him.

We stayed at anchor at Yarmouth Roads nearly a week before setting sail. As we pushed further north rumours swept through the fleet. Our destination, it was said, was to be Copenhagen. Diplomats were there even now, trying to persuade the Danes to give up their alliance with the Swedes, Russians and Prussians.

I came across Robert Neville while I was on an errand to the orlop deck. Down there in the depths of the ship, we had some privacy and he could talk to me without formality.

'It'll come to nothing I'm sure,' said Robert. 'The Danes are allies with the Prussians and the Swedes – two of their greatest enemies! Danes and Swedes fight like cats and dogs. The French won't lift a finger to support the Danes either, although they've probably promised they will, and the Russians can't help them because their fleet is always frozen in at this time of year. I'm sure that as soon as we poke our noses over the horizon at Copenhagen they'll surrender right away.'

This was all very reassuring and I presented this as my own opinion to my mess table later that day. They were all impressed.

'I hope you're right Sam,' said Tom tersely. 'I 'eard we get most of our timber and rope from the Danes and the Swedes. If we're at war with them both, then we'll have a job building new warships.'

The thought of us running out of material to make ships frightened me. As a small boy I had been taught that our Navy protected us from the French, who were our greatest enemies. I knew how narrow the English Channel was, and how, on a bright day, the French coast around Calais could easily be seen from England. I could imagine their leader, Napoleon, standing on the beach looking over to the cliffs at Dover and plotting an invasion. All at once I felt proud to be a British sailor.

John Giddes was still sullen, sipping his grog and shovelling down his pease. 'Cheer up,' I said, 'at least we'll be helping to defend our country from the tyrannous French!'

'Hark at the little hero,' sneered Giddes. 'Are you tellin' me being pressed isn't tyranny?'

James laughed nervously and made a swift attempt at

changing the subject. 'Ye know, ten year or so ago, when the press gangs came roond Newcastle and Sunderland, the sailors in the harbour taverns got together and fought 'em off with their fists. Ye don't often hear aboot that in Portsmouth or London.'

'You're a bunch of hard bastards you Geordies – is that what you're sayin'?' laughed Tom.

'Aye,' said James. 'Not like ye spineless Cockneys!' The pair then began a mock sparring contest.

Then James got serious, and lowered his voice to a whisper. 'I've got me doubts aboot this experdition. Yer Vice Admiral, Hyde Parker, his heart isn't in it. What would you rather be doin' if ye'd just married a bonny young girl like what he has? Pacing yer quarterdeck in a freezing fog or entertaining yer new bride in a big four-poster?'

'But Nelson is sailing with us too,' I said.

'True enough, lad,' said James, 'but he still has to do what Hyde Parker tells him.'

'Maybe the Danes will have quite a fleet waitin' for us?' said Tom quietly. 'Maybe twice our number?' This was all treacherous talk, not for the ears of any passing bosun's mate.

Then John Giddes spoke up. He seemed impatient, exasperated, even. 'Yes but most of the Danish fleet is made up of old vessels. And their crews will be poorly trained, if that. Denmark ain't been at war for the best part of a century. There'll be plenty of volunteers all right – we're out to attack their 'andsome capital after all – but they'll barely know one end of a gun from another.'

We all looked on, astonished. This was the most we'd heard him say so far. And I couldn't help noticing that although he usually talked like a Cockney, occasionally he sounded oddly well spoken.

'So, my friend,' said Tom, turning to Giddes with a new-found respect. 'What did you say you were doing before the press gang got you?'

'Never you mind,' he said, and that was the end of that.

As our voyage progressed the weather steadily worsened. We pressed on through endless fog and put down our anchors every evening. Vice Admiral Hyde Parker, it was said, was wary of travelling at night for fear of his ships colliding. On some mornings we spent an hour chipping ice from the rigging and clearing snow from the deck before we could weigh anchor. During the day, snow and sleet came and went, and the ship's timbers seemed so sodden I wondered that the *Elephant* did not sink. There was no respite from the cold. When we ate and slept, great howling draughts whistled around the ship.

'There's enough of a draught in here to turn a bloody

windmill,' Giddes said. I was sure he wasn't really a Cockney.

Then two and a half weeks after we had left Portsmouth we peered through the snowflakes and could dimly make out a long low sandbank to the starboard bow. This was The Skaw – the northernmost point of Denmark. Copenhagen lay a few days' further sailing to the south. Reaching the coast brought no improvement in the weather. Giddes and Tom continued to argue about the fighting merits of the Danes. We would find out soon enough who was right.

CHAPTER 2

Enter the Admiral

Close to the coast we stopped hourly to test the depth of the sea. Tarrying in these shallow waters made the journey more irksome. I just wanted to fight and be gone. Then, God willing, we could head south to warmer waters. The older sailors had more patience.

'Coast round here's well known for its treacherous shallows,' said Tom at supper.

'Aye,' said James. 'That young bride o' Hyde Parker'd be rather disappointed to find her new husband shot for incompetence when he grounded half his fleet before they even got to Copenhagen.'

'Oh, I don't know,' said Vincent. 'She'd be getting his Vice Admiral's fortune, without having to put up with his amorous attentions. Imagine that – how old is he? Sixty if he's a day. And she's only eighteen I heard. If they shot 'im, I'd bet she wouldn't believe her luck!'

Talk around the mess table turned to what would happen when we reached our destination.

'I reckon we just need to shake a big stick at the Danes,' said Tom. 'That'll be enough to drive them out of this alliance. They'll not want their city destroyed. I'll eat my hammock if there's any actual fightin'. So there's every reason to avoid gettin' grounded. Wouldn't make us look very threatenin' would it?'

Every day fresh rumours reached my ears about the strength of the Danes and their willingness to fight. On March 21 we anchored two or three days' sailing away from Copenhagen and the rumours grew more alarming. Sweden, it was said, had sent a fleet to help defend the city. The Russians had freed their ships from the ice, and were even now heading south to fight us.

What was true and what was not, we would only discover when we arrived at Copenhagen. At night I dreamed of a huge armada waiting there to destroy us. As the prospect of battle looked more likely, the men grew restless. Fights broke out. Tempers frayed. The cold and the tension were eating away at our morale.

*　*　*

On the morning of March 26 I passed by Robert Neville when I was fetching provisions from the hold. 'Lord Nelson, Sam!' he said to me, his eyes alight with excitement. 'Lord Nelson! He's coming to this ship this very day. He's going to be fighting with us here – leading a squadron into battle.'

I couldn't quite believe it. I had never even seen anyone you might describe as famous and the prospect of being on the same ship as our greatest admiral filled me with excitement. 'Why us?' I asked.

'The *Elephant* has a shallower draught than the *St George*,' said Robert. 'He'll be wanting to get close enough to the Danes without fear of grounding his ship. Take a 98 gunner like the *St George* into water that shallow, and you're almost begging to be grounded. This is a secret between the two of us. But don't worry, you won't have to keep it for long.'

Robert needn't have worried about that. Before the forenoon watch was half completed I had been told by three other seamen. 'Well, that'll be something to tell the bairns,' said James.

Nelson arrived that afternoon. We were scrubbing the deck, and the whole ship stood to attention to welcome him aboard. None of us needed telling that the diplomats had failed. No sooner had Nelson joined us than the fleet weighed anchor. As the wind filled the

Elephant's sails a little knot twisted in my gut. So much for all our talk of avoiding battle.

As we sailed on, Captain Foley took him up to the quarterdeck on a tour of inspection. I was surprised to see how small he was. I was approaching my fourteenth birthday but I was tall enough to be able to see the top of his head. He was slight too – a wiry, narrow-shouldered man. If it wasn't for his weather-beaten seaman's face, I would have said he looked more like a dancer than a fighter. But his bravery was apparent to all. His chest was covered in medals, and he bore the obvious cost of his gallant actions, with an empty right sleeve pinned to his jacket.

I recognised his face from likenesses on plates and mugs commemorating his famous victories, but I can't quite put into words what a great honour it was to actually see him.

That evening, at supper, we talked of nothing else.

'I heard that when he lost his arm, he was back on duty an hour after it was amputated!' Vincent said.

James wasn't so easily impressed. 'He's a brave man, to be sure,' he said. 'But he's reckless too. That battle at Tenerife where he lost his arm – some people say he should never have attacked in the first place. The island was too well defended.'

Tom shrugged. 'Can't win 'em all, can you?' He was

obviously proud that Lord Nelson had chosen our ship. 'He sailed on a 74 during the Battle of the Nile – HMS *Vanguard* it was. He knows the right ship to get him into the thick of battle.'

Thick of battle? I didn't like the sound of that. Perhaps having Lord Nelson on board was not such a good thing? 'Here, hang on,' I said to Tom. 'I suppose this means we'll be right in the middle of things, doesn't it?'

'Certainly does,' said Tom. 'Nelson's a man who likes to lead from the front.'

'So we're going to be the front?'

'This is what you call your swings and roundabouts, Sam,' said Tom. 'We get the glory and we get the danger. Difficult to have one without the other. Think of the prize money, though!'

It was exciting to have a real life, flesh and blood hero on board. The whole crew were convinced they would be telling their grandchildren about it. But a little voice in the back of my head kept whispering 'Only if you live to tell the tale . . .'

We had now left behind the open sea and entered the shallows around Copenhagen. The Danes had removed the buoys that marked the deeper stretches of navigable water and we moved forward with caution. In the last days of March we were set to work preparing our own buoys for the channel known as Holland Deep.

On the morning of April 1 the signal was given for Nelson's squadron to weigh anchor. A cheer from the entire fleet drifted across the grey sea. When I heard that sound a rush of excitement swept through me. Here we were, hundreds of miles away from home, about to fight an enemy on their own territory, but the fleet was full of confidence and certain of our success.

We anchored again in King's Deep, a stretch of water a mere two miles away from the city. Richard and I were called up the mainmast to attend the weather topsail braces and we could see the streets and buildings of Copenhagen clearly from high above the deck. The Danes had positioned a long line of ships to form a barrier between us and the city. I counted twenty-five in all. In between the ships were floating batteries of guns. Above the harbour were shore batteries and forts. It all looked formidable. Not only that, but not far in front of the Danish line there was an enormous sandbank, the Middle Ground. In front of that was shallow water which allowed little room to manoeuvre.

But the ships I saw were fewer in number than I expected. Of the Swedish and Russian fleets there was no sign. Perhaps they were coming up behind us, to trap us against the shore? Perhaps they weren't coming at all? I would only stop worrying about them when we were away from this place.

As I looked beyond the defences to the spires and houses of the capital, I began to feel troubled. We had been sent here to fight enemy seamen, who would be trying to kill us as surely as we would be trying to kill them. But we had also been sent here to bombard a city full of ordinary people, and women and children.

Piercing screams cut short my train of thought. I looked across the rigging to see two men plunging from the foremast topsails to the deck.

'What the hell happened?' said Richard, and we both held on to the yardarm a little tighter. I felt sick, and my arms and legs began to tremble. 'Hold tight, breathe deep,' said Richard. I couldn't bear to look down at the deck. I knew a fall from that height would kill a man.

I steadied myself and glanced over to where the men had been working only moments before. The horse – what we called the rope beneath the yard where we rested our feet – dangled in two, twisting in the wind. We could see the frayed ends where it had snapped. 'There'll be hell to pay for that,' said Richard.

I knew neither of the dead men but I learned their names were Henry Dutton and John Colliver. They were given a sea burial that afternoon. A funeral so close to the prospect of action unsettled the men. We stood around the deck in a fierce wind and threatening sky as the chaplain rattled through the service as quickly as decorum would allow. Edward Eaves was the man's name. He was not popular among the crew, but then chaplains rarely were. Word had it he was aloof and indifferent to their troubles. This was his first Navy posting, Robert had told us, and talk among the officers was that he had left his previous parish in a hurry. I didn't really care one way or another. I kept thinking of the battle to come and how those of us who were killed or mortally wounded in the thick of the fighting would be quickly turfed over the side.

That night at supper, Tom reckoned we would fight the next day. While we ate, Middlewych came to our table.

'Captain's asked me to find a crew for a boat to test the water depth around the Danish fleet. Would you men do me the honour of accompanying me?' It was not a request to refuse. I think we all knew it would be better to volunteer than be ordered to go. 'Good. Now wear something dark so you can't be seen.'

We put on every spare piece of clothing we could muster and blackened our faces with burned cork. Middlewych was waiting for us on deck with a party of men ready to winch the ship's jollyboat over the side.

'Before we go,' he explained, 'we must muffle the oars.' We wrapped old cloth around the rowlocks, to stop them squeaking as we skulled through the water.

Middlewych turned to a midshipman and said, 'Go and tell Captain Hardy the boat is ready.'

A minute later we were joined by a distinguished-looking gentleman. 'He's Nelson's flag captain,' James whispered to me. 'He's been with him for the last three years. He's a pretty valuable fellow to be sending out to the tip of the enemy's front line, I must say!'

Also with us was an able seaman named Spavens, who always heaved the lead to determine the water depth on the *Elephant*. He was unmistakable with a long ponytail that hung most of the way down his back, and great mutton-chop whiskers. He had a solidity about him that suggested utter dependability.

The boat was lowered into the water and bobbed gently up and down awaiting our arrival. Icy wind blew over the bay and through our thin clothing, piercing us to the bone.

We set off at eight towards the lanterns of the Danish fleet and the twinkling harbour lights beyond. The cloth worked well enough to muffle the squeaking of oar in rowlock but I wondered if the splash of our oars in the water would give us away? Perhaps the wash of the sea against the side of a ship would mask the noise we made.

We moved forward with great caution. I took the starboard oar nearest to the bow, with Richard on the larboard side. Immediately behind me Spavens stood in the bow of the boat with Middlewych, lowering his lead-weighted measuring rope into the water every few yards. As we crept towards the enemy fleet,

Middlewych recorded the water depth with great care in his notebook. Captain Hardy took his position in the stern of the boat, eyes scanning the Danish fleet for any sign that we had been spotted.

It was a dim night, with a quarter moon that was rarely visible between the thick clouds. Still, I could hardly believe how close we were getting to the enemy. Then, as we rowed forward, my oar struck something solid in the water, making a sharp scraping sound. Middlewych immediately whispered for us to lie on our oars, and the boat carried on drifting forward. We all waited, ears straining into the silence, for any indication that the noise had aroused suspicion in the Danish line. Silence lay deep and impenetrable.

'What on earth was that?' whispered Middlewych.

'It was me, sir,' I confessed.

'Never mind lad, not your fault. Let's have a look.' He peered around the black void that surrounded us. 'Confound it,' he muttered to himself. 'It's blasted ice in the water.'

'We'll just have to press on with greater caution,' said Captain Hardy. Middlewych looked crestfallen. I supposed he felt he should have spotted the ice.

'Men,' said Middlewych. 'We're approaching the Danish fleet, so no noise at all. No talking, no sneezing, no coughing – or we're all dead men.'

As the evening drew on, the cloud above us grew

thicker and the light of the moon was extinguished. This was good. We'd be better hidden in the dark waters.

As we rowed I forgot about the Danish ships and concentrated instead on trying to avoid the ice in the water. The sheer physical exertion of rowing had warmed me a little, and I only began to shiver when we stopped to take a sounding. During these frequent stops I allowed my mind to wander, but my attention was suddenly drawn to the sound of voices coming over the water towards us. Suddenly fearful, I thought it must be an enemy boat come out to attack us. Then I listened harder. This language must be Danish. But the men talking did not sound alarmed. It was more a quiet discussion they were having. There was an occasional laugh or murmur that sounded like disagreement. Amid the babble of this unfamiliar tongue, I'm sure I heard the name 'Nelson'. I wondered how anxious they were about having to fight our most famous Admiral.

We had brought no weapons out with us on the jolly-boat. Only Middlewych and Hardy carried their swords and a pistol apiece. I turned to look and was alarmed to see the bow of a great Danish warship looming above us. I had not realised how close we were to the enemy line. The voices we heard must be guards positioned in the bow. I could not believe Hardy and Middlewych's daring. But surely the enemy could see us? Any second, a volley of musket shots would pepper the boat and kill us all.

My heart began to beat hard in my chest, and my breathing was loud in the silence. Richard looked over with great concern, and raised his index finger to his lips. I could tell by his eyes he was terrified too.

Spavens was making another sounding with his lead. He seemed to be taking forever over it. The gentle babble of conversation above our heads continued.

Spavens finally pulled up the lead and Middlewych signalled for us to head for home. I wondered how he kept his bearings on this inky night, but much to my relief we made it back to the *Elephant* within half an hour.

We climbed thankfully back on to the ship and the boat was hauled aboard. Captain Hardy called for the watch Bosun. 'Extra ration of rum for these fine men,' he said. 'Oh, and sixteen ounces of tobacco between them. Put it to my account.' Then he was gone.

While Richard went to collect our rum, I was sent down to the Purser's quarters to buy the tobacco. His cabin was below the waterline, on the after cockpit of the orlop deck. Richard and I didn't smoke, but the rest of them would be pleased with this bonus. I had spoken to the Purser only once before and didn't like him. The fact that he was Oliver Pritchard's father was part of it, and I could see exactly where the boy had picked up his pompous manner.

Down in the orlop deck just above the hold, only the rats were lively. One scurried close to my feet as I walked through the gloom, trying to remember which cabin door was Pritchard's. Behind me was the midshipman's berth, and hammocks were strung up for those not on duty. Pritchard's cabin was there on the starboard side, close to the mizzenmast, which ran through the ship down to the keel. I wondered if he was asleep and paused to listen before I knocked on the door.

I could hear two voices, both of them slurred and loud. 'So, those two topmen, Dutton and Colliver, they liked a smoke you say?' That was Pritchard. 'Well, I'll put them down for sixteen ounces a piece over the last week.' He gave a cackling, drunken laugh.

'I want a cut of all this, you hear.' That was Giddes. He sounded different - more like an officer in the way he spoke. But it was him, I was sure. He also sounded irritated. 'I'm scratching your back, so make sure you see me right.'

'Don't get too greedy, Mr Giddes. Otherwise a few more of us might find out who you really are,' taunted Pritchard.

'Don't get clever with me, you pompous little arse,' said Giddes. I heard furniture scrape along the floor, and imagined he had lurched forward to grab hold of the Purser. His voice rose in anger. 'You tell them about me, and I'll tell them about your tobacco swindle, and the charges for clothes you take from the wages of dead sailors. That'll go down well with the crew. We can both swing together. Won't that be cosy?'

Pritchard sounded desperate. 'Shut up, you bloody fool. Someone will hear you.'

They stopped. I froze in my step. I thought it would be best to just creep away and get the tobacco tomorrow. But then the door burst open. Giddes stood there glowering.

'What the devil are you doing here?' he said, and dragged me inside the cabin, hand around my throat.

Pritchard was sitting at a small table, one elbow resting by an empty bottle of rum and two glasses. He looked at me with drunken contempt.

'I've just come to buy tobacco – orders from Captain Hardy,' I squeaked out, expecting Giddes to hit me at any moment. He loosened his grip.

''ow long you been there?' Giddes was back to his Cockney accent.

'I just got here this second,' I blurted out. 'I was just about to knock. I didn't hear a thing.'

Pritchard spoke calmly and firmly. 'Let the boy go, Mr Giddes. Let's get him his tobacco. How much did the captain order?'

I stood there shaking while Pritchard bumbled about, looking for the keys to his storeroom. He left the cabin. Giddes glowered.

Pritchard returned with the tobacco and asked my name. He wrote it down carefully in his ledger. 'Samuel Witchall, right? Which watch are you? Captain Hardy will check these records, so you'll be flogged to within an inch of your life if this is a trick.'

As I ran back upstairs, I felt indignant. When a man died at sea, his wages were eventually returned to his family. Pritchard was charging dead men for tobacco and clothing, safe in the knowledge that they would not be around to query these deductions to their earnings. Giddes was helping him do it. And he was not who he said he was. Had they believed me when I said I had only just arrived outside the door?

'Where've you been,' said Richard when I rejoined my friends. 'You look like you've seen a ghost.'

We knocked back our rum. It warmed our frozen bodies and steadied my shaking hands. Then we crept to the gun deck to sleep. Tomorrow, almost certainly, we were going to have to fight.

CHAPTER 3

The Battle of Copenhagen

That night my sleep was constantly disturbed by the sound of ice bumping against the hull of the *Elephant*. The temperature was so cold that when a man carrying a lantern made his way through the deck you could see his breath curling like smoke from his nose and mouth. Water dripped from the low wooden ceiling and condensation settled like dew, chilling me to the marrow.

Breakfast burgoo and scotch coffee never tasted better. I wondered why the body craved sweet things when it was cold. James had told me about a dried fruit and brown sugar delicacy the Scots called 'black bun', which they fried in batter in a deep pan of oil. It sounded just right for a day like this.

As we ate I asked Tom what he thought our tactics would be. He paused between mouthfuls then said, 'We've all seen that row of Danish ships. I reckon we're gonna squeeze up next to them and slug it out. We'll be so close we won't be able to miss.'

I lost my appetite. But James offered me a crumb of comfort.

'We're used to fighting, whereas the Danes aren't scrappers. Whatever happens I'll bet we'll be firing at least twice as quickly as them. So our 74s'll be like 148 gun ships to them. And their 74s, if they've got any, will be like our frigates. I think we'll make short work of it.'

John Giddes looked sceptical and put in a rare word. 'Most of those Danish ships've had their masts taken down. They're probably grounded in the mud, so there's no retreat for them. We might 'ave better ships, better guns and better commanders, but we're still foreigners here. The Danes are fightin' for their lives and for their city so I don't think they're gonna be a walkover.'

Giddes was acting as though the incident last night had never happened, but he refused to meet my eye. I wanted to talk to Tom and Richard about him, and what I had heard, but so far I hadn't had the chance.

* * *

47

Talk around the table dried up. As I finished my burgoo and knocked back the dregs of my coffee I wondered if this was the last meal I would ever eat. After breakfast we were called out on deck so the Reverend Eaves could hold a brief service. I peered through the cold morning light at this short, thickset man in his clerical robes, and strained to hear him speak.

> *Almighty and everlasting God, mercifully look upon our infirmities,*
> *And in all our dangers and necessities,*
> *Stretch forth thy right hand to help and defend us;*
> *Through Jesus Christ our Lord, Amen.*

The words consoled me, although I couldn't help but wonder whether the Danes were reciting exactly the same prayers too, and whether their infirmities, dangers and necessities would be looked upon any less mercifully by the Almighty.

The ship was called to quarters and we scattered sand on the decks to soak up the blood that was sure to be spilt. Richard pointed out that much of our fleet were still at their anchor to the North, and wondered why they were not closer. 'Too many ships, too little space,' I said. I was glad Richard would be close to me in the battle. I liked to think we would be able to look out for each other. I hoped I would not be called upon to throw him over the side if he were terribly injured.

We waited in silence by our gun, growing tense and numb. Being out in the open the quarterdeck was much colder than the gun decks, and I longed to be down there under cover. The wind rattled the netting that had been placed above our heads to protect us from any yardarms that might fall when fighting started. It was an uncomfortable reminder of how dangerous it was out here. My experience of battle had taught me first hand that enemy ships always aimed at our masts and rigging to try to cripple us. And here on the quarterdeck we were also easy targets for snipers up in the enemy's fighting tops – something we had never had to worry about on the gun deck. Worst of all, with all those disadvantages, we were close to the middle of the ship – the spot where the enemy always concentrated his fire. During any battle, I'd heard it said, most of those killed were from the middle of the ship. My eyes began to water in the face of that wind. I hoped no one would think I was crying in fear.

Just after ten o'clock the rumble of cannon fire rolled across the water. The battle was finally beginning and I would soon be able to forget about the wind and the cold. At once we were called over to the larboard guns and waited for our ship to move into action. The harbour guns were flashing in the middle distance, although their shot was falling short. Gun smoke began to drift across the water towards us and catch in our throats.

For the first time, I could see what a battle looked like rather than just hear and feel it. On the gun deck of my old ship, the *Miranda*, we could only tell what was happening by listening to the commands of our officers. Once the firing started, with the roar of the cannons and the ringing in our ears, even that became impossible.

For now, seeing events unfolding from the quarterdeck was thrilling – like watching a forbidden play or hearing a fascinating conversation not meant for our ears. But I also felt terribly exposed. It was like a dream I sometimes had where I stood naked in the congregation at a christening or wedding.

We watched our ships slowly move towards the Danish line. HMS *Edgar* was first to edge forward along a narrow stretch of water in front of the enemy. I did not envy them their task. As soon as she reached the Danes their muzzles flashed in the grey morning light. There was something random and ill-judged about the Danish barrage. Their gunners were obviously not men who had trained every day, as we had.

In reply the *Edgar* unleashed a thunderous, ordered broadside. Splinters flew into the air and peppered the sea, as the first ship in the Danish line was ravaged by her cannon fire. But as the *Edgar* sailed down the enemy line she began to take fire too. Before she dropped anchor in front of the fifth ship in the line, several of the Danish guns had found their target. I could barely bring myself to look as splinters burst from the *Edgar*'s wooden walls. It was easy to imagine the carnage left in the wake of the shot as it tore through her decks. Two more of our ships followed behind the *Edgar* to take up their positions opposite Danish vessels.

As two further 74s followed, disaster struck. On their approach to the narrow channel, they grounded in the shallows. But they carried on firing from where they had halted and their shot was hitting home. Then another of our ships moved forward but she too was caught on the Middle Ground before she could even reach the channel. I wondered if Spavens had taken the wrong soundings on our trip the night before. Now, all of a sudden, the battle was turning against us.

'Let fall' came the order. Our sails filled and the *Elephant* edged forward. It was our turn to brave the fire of the Danish line and I struggled to keep my fear at bay. It was time to stop watching and start taking part. We sailed before the wind and I wondered if we too would be grounded. But the *Elephant* carried on moving forward and we were soon within range of our enemies. Shots from the shore batteries began to scream down around us. They landed fore and aft, throwing up plumes of water or whistling close by the sails and rigging. The fire was fierce but none hit home and we sailed on without damage.

As we approached the Danish ships I began to feel

something close to terror. Standing there in the open, clutching my cartridge box, I expected at any moment to be hit and vanish in a fiery, bloody flash. James could see the fear in my eyes and placed a hand on my shoulder. 'Hold fast Sam, hold fast.'

We reached the first enemy ship and the gunnery officer shouted, 'Fire at will'. Our carronade exploded into life, lurching back on its wooden runner. The 32lb shot made a terrible mess of the quarterdeck of the ship opposite.

'That's why they call it the smasher,' yelled James. No sooner had we fired than Tom, James, Vincent and Richard began swabbing out and reloading. I handed over my cartridge, relieved not to be holding something that could blow me into tiny pieces, and then ran for all my worth down the four staircases that led to the after powder room in the hold. Grabbing another cartridge I stuffed it in my box, screwed the lid down tight and was back before Tom and his crew could fire again.

'Well done Sam,' said Tom. 'Hold fast now, we'll be firing any second.' I could barely hear him over the noise of the guns.

Each Danish ship passed before us, close enough for me to see their crew. Muskets cracked from their masts, and shots thudded down on to our deck. Close by, one of the marines clutched his shoulder and fell backwards, his musket clattering to the deck and discharging its ball.

It buried itself in the wooden rail close by our carronade. I said a silent prayer of thanks. To be shot by one of our own men would have been inglorious.

I thanked God too that we were wearing our dull sailor's slops and not the bright red jackets of the marines. Even through the smoke of battle they made an easy target here on our deck, as did the officers in their blue jackets and gold braid.

Each Danish ship fired its long guns at us as we passed, but the fire was slapdash. Tom was right. The Danes were unskilled in handling their guns. Again our carronade exploded into life. The shot hit home, crashing into the foremast of a Danish 74, causing several men in the fighting top to fall to the deck. Now I could see the work of our gun as it mauled ships and claimed lives with every discharge, I wished again that I was down in the gun deck as I had been on the *Miranda*. But then a sliver of shot landed right at my foot, missing my cartridge box and my toes by a fraction of an inch. That fired me up. 'Give the bastards one from me, Tom,' I said before I ran off to collect more powder.

We passed a dozen or so of their ships, all firing as the *Elephant* moved forward. Then came the order to stop. Across the sea from us was the *Dannebrog*, so close we could see the men on her deck, even through the gun smoke.

53

'She's a 64 by the look of her,' said Tom, 'and she's flyin' the Danish admiral's flag.'

Over the top of the gun port I could see she was a handsome man-o'-war, tall in the water and bristling with cannon along her two gun decks and quarterdeck. She was also badly damaged, having suffered the attentions of the British ships which had passed down their line before us.

My ears began to ring from the sound of cannon fire. I was glad of it as I could no longer hear the screams of injured men. Immediately to our stern was HMS *Glatton*, which I had learned was commanded by the notorious Captain Bligh, but I could barely see her through the gun smoke, nor any of the other ships that fought alongside us.

Our carronade fired constantly and I began to tire of my incessant trips to the powder room. The Danish forces, though formidable, seemed to be doing little damage to the *Elephant*. Perhaps we'd been lucky for now.

The battle continued; more of our ships took up position in front of the Danish fleet. Through the smoke I saw a squadron of frigates pass down the line behind us. Although we pounded her steadily, the *Dannebrog* continued to fire back.

As we fought, Lord Nelson walked up and down the quarterdeck behind us – excitedly urging us on. He seemed unconcerned for his safety, and his courage gave me heart. When a shot hit the mainmasts and showered us with splinters I heard him say to an officer, 'It is warm work, and this day may be the last for any of us at a moment.' Then he laughed and said, 'Mark you, I would not be elsewhere for thousands!' I could not agree. I would have *given* thousands to be elsewhere.

As a musket shot whistled over my head I heard a midshipman rush up to inform Lord Nelson that Hyde Parker had hoisted a signal ordering him to break off the action. I wondered at first how such a signal could be seen, but perhaps the view was clearer atop our masts? 'Thank the Lord,' I thought. 'Let's get away from here before we're all killed.'

I ran to the magazine hoping fervently this would be the last cartridge I would have to fetch for this battle, and by the time I returned we would be calling off the action. But when I got back, Nelson and Captain Foley had come close to the rail by our cannon and I heard almost all of what they said.

'You know Foley,' said Lord Nelson, 'I have only one eye – I have a right to be blind sometimes.' Then he put his telescope to his blind eye, turned it towards Hyde Parker's ship and said, 'I really do not see the signal.'

I had to bite my tongue. I wanted to scream 'Don't be stupid. Do what you have been ordered you to do! What if the Swedish and Russian fleets are coming?' But

I knew such insolence could get me flogged to death or hanged. What had made Hyde Parker make such a signal, though? Whenever I could, I squinted through the smoke to see if there were any more masts on the horizon.

As midday turned to early afternoon the *Dannebrog* began to burn steadily and acrid smoke drifted towards us. I could also see that several of the Danish ships had surrendered. Some burned fiercely. I wondered if their magazines would explode and cause carnage on the neighbouring ship in the Danish line. Aboard the blazing ships the sailors who had survived our merciless barrage were trying to escape by throwing themselves from the gun ports or over the side of the upper deck. Some of our ships had launched their boats to try to rescue these poor wretches. Many of them were badly injured and struggled pitifully in the freezing water. But even as we tried to rescue their seamen the Danes still fired upon us from their shore batteries.

Then the *Dannebrog* struck her colours to surrender. All at once I began to breathe a little easier and allowed myself to hope I would come out of this battle alive. We were ordered to stop firing, and I sat down on the carriage of the carronade to drink some water. I realised with a twinge of guilt that Lord Nelson had been right not to withdraw. He had sensed, far earlier than me, that we were winning.

Bosuns' whistles peeped as some of the *Elephant*'s boats were lowered to cross over the narrow stretch of water between us and the *Dannebrog* to help the men who were trying to escape a fiery death. But as they approached they were fired upon with muskets. Lord Nelson, clearly angered, ordered us to start firing again as soon as our boats were out of danger. Vincent Thomas loaded grapeshot into the maw of our carronade and we peppered their deck.

Just after the carronade discharged, while my ears were still ringing, I was thrown to my feet by a violent explosion. When I got up I could see enemy shot had hit the quarterdeck between two guns just down from us and men from the crews were lying dead or dying. They were swiftly picked up by their comrades and thrown over the side. Most of those were beyond caring, but one of them, almost sliced in two by grapeshot, was a young boy who had been powder monkey to the gun next to us. He was clutching at a gaping hole in his belly, trying to stop his insides pouring out, and livid fear danced in his eyes. When they picked him up he started yelling, 'Mother, help me! God help me! Mother, don't let them do this to me . . .' The marines hesitated, then their sergeant came over and shouted at them: 'He's a goner. Let him go over and finish him.' They swung the boy as they threw him, which must have hurt him terribly and he screamed all the way down to the water.

I had seen many men die horribly in battle, but this was the worst. That could have been me, howling in agony for my mother. A lieutenant on the quarterdeck swiftly reordered the gun crews from whoever was left alive. Richard was told to act as powder monkey for the carronade next to ours. He was handed the leather cartridge box that the dead boy had been using, and flinched when he saw there was blood all over one side of it.

'I'll show you the drill,' I shouted. 'Whatever happens, keep the lid firmly down. Now follow me.'

We sprinted down the stairwell and ran through the middle of the upper gun deck to the stern. The noise was deafening, the heat unbearable. Then another ladder took us to the lower deck and immediately down to the orlop deck beneath the waterline. From there it was just a few steps to the after powder room. No one else was outside, not even the marine who usually stood guard there. 'Sometimes you have to wait with several powder boys,' I said, 'sometimes not. We're lucky this time.' Then I called for a cartridge and a hand appeared through the wet curtains that shielded the men inside from flying sparks. Richard did the same. As I made sure his lid was screwed tight, Oliver Pritchard came running up to us.

'You two, drop your boxes and follow me now,' he

said. We looked at each other in puzzlement, but an order was an order. He said, 'Quickly, down the ladder to the hold.' We did as we were asked. He did not follow. Instead he stood at the top of the ladder and shouted, 'Macintosh, come here at once.' Then he turned to us and drew his pistol. A marine, bayonet on the end of his musket, arrived at his shoulder.

'Caught these two trying to hide in the hold,' he said to the soldier. 'Lock them in the bread room and make sure they stay there.' He tossed the soldier a key and marched off.

'But we were ordered down here,' said Richard.

'And we need to get back to the quarterdeck with our powder,' I shouted.

The marine waved his bayonet at us. 'Shut up or I'll run this through the pair of you.'

We were bundled into the store room and left there in the dark. 'What will our crews do without us?' said Richard. He sounded scared. I felt utterly bewildered.

It was bizarre being in the heat of battle one moment, then the next being locked away from it all at the bottom of the ship. My heart was beating fast and I was bursting with energy. I just had to sit there in the dark with the stifling smell of mouldy bread in my nostrils.

There beneath the waterline we could still hear the muffled discharges of the guns, and more clearly, from the orlop deck above us, the screams of men brought down to the ship's surgeon.

'What the hell is this all about?' Richard said angrily. It was too dark to actually see him.

I began to think more clearly and grew suddenly afraid. Of what I was not quite sure, but I knew we were in terrible trouble.

'I didn't tell you about last night. We've not had time to talk,' I said. 'You know I was gone a while fetching that tobacco. I overheard Nathaniel Pritchard and John Giddes arguing. They were both drunk, and were talking about charges for clothes and tobacco they would take from dead men's wages.

'And then, when they were quarrelling, Pritchard said something to Giddes about him not being who he says he is.'

'Well, we all thought that,' said Richard. 'So who the hell is he?'

'I didn't hear that much –' Then I understood in an instant what was happening to us.

'Oh Jesus Christ help us,' I wailed, crushed by a terrible certainty.

Richard was alarmed. 'What? What is it?'

'Last night – Giddes came to the door. Caught me standing there. I said I'd just arrived and didn't hear a thing. That must have given me away. Now Pritchard has got his son involved, and they're trying to set us up.'

'Why me?' said Richard. His voice seemed angry, even

accusatory, as if it was my fault.

Now I felt angry with him. 'Oh, I don't know. Maybe it was because you were here with me just now, maybe they thought I'd tell you anyway. They'd know we were friends.'

Silence fell between us. The battle above our heads was winding down. Only occasional cannon fire could be heard and no one was screaming on the surgeon's table. It was so dark in there neither of us could see our hands in front of our faces.

Richard spoke again. 'So what happens next? We get court-martialled. If we're lucky, we'll be flogged, probably severely. If we're unlucky, we get hanged from the yardarm.'

CHAPTER 4

Condemned

We listened to the rest of the battle from our lonely prison. The ships' guns were silent, then they started up. Shot screamed in from ashore, then stopped. We heard shouted commands and clattering against the hull, as the ship's boats were launched. The *Elephant* weighed anchor and we began to move. As Richard and I dozed in the stifling fug there was a huge explosion, followed by a scattering of splashing sounds that went on for ten or fifteen seconds.

'Sounds like a magazine went off,' said Richard. I wondered which ship had been blown to pieces, and prayed it was not one of ours.

How long we stayed in the bread room I do not know. No one came with food or water so by the end of the day we were light-headed with hunger and thirst. The lock clicked. The door burst open. A marine sergeant shouted, 'Witchall and Buckley! Present yourselves.'

Out we came. There was a squad of marines, bayonets fixed to their muskets, the blade points threatening in the dim light. This was just like getting pressed. When we tried to ask what was happening, we were abruptly told to shut our mouths. Up we went, through the levels of the ship, out on to the deck. It was dark, so I supposed it was quite late. It was piercingly cold, especially after our hours in the bread room. We were bundled off the ship and into one of the boats. Twenty minutes later the stern of Hyde Parker's flagship HMS *London* loomed above us. Hustled on board with great haste, we were taken to a small store room in the hold.

Waiting for us there was the ship's blacksmith. I was ordered to sit before him and two black iron hoops linked one to the other by a chain were fastened over my ankles. The hoops were held fast by a bolt swiftly hammered into place. No one spoke a word or would even meet my eye. After the door was locked and we were left to ourselves, Richard and I looked at each other, too bewildered to speak.

In the dim lantern light we could see there were two

benches, blankets and a bucket. A small plate with bread and cheese and two mugs of water had been left on the bench. We drank and ate greedily, relieved to finally have some food. 'I can't believe what sort of trouble we're in,' said Richard. He seemed matter of fact, rather than frightened. I had been feeling stunned, and terrified at the prospect of being brought to trial on a false charge of cowardice. I was seething with anger at being duped by Pritchard. Richard's manner gave me courage.

'We just need the chance to explain what's happened,' I said, feeling suddenly hopeful. I laid my head on the bench and tried to sleep, but my change of mood didn't last. Whenever I began to drift off, I could feel the hangman's rope around my neck and woke with a start.

The next few days were measured by the provision of bread and water to us in our cell by surly guards. We tried to ask them what was happening, but they collected and returned our bucket, plates and mugs without a word. We both lost track of the time of day, and even what day it was. I turned fourteen three days after the Battle of Copenhagen, but I couldn't tell you exactly when 5th April actually was. I was too miserable to even mention it to Richard.

This dreary routine was interrupted at last by a visit from Lieutenant Middlewych. He was friendly, concerned and matter of fact.

'It's not looking good, boys. There's to be a court martial. The charge is cowardice and that you're in contravention of Section 12 of the Articles of War.'

It was such a relief to be able to finally talk to someone about what had happened to us. 'This is absurd, sir,' I said. 'Midshipman Pritchard told us to go to the hold. Then he pointed his pistol at us and accused us of scarpering.' I was so livid I wanted to spit and I could feel my face glowing red with anger when I tried to talk about it.

Middlewych maintained a calm neutrality. 'That's precisely your problem, Witchall,' he said patiently. 'It sounds absurd. Can you imagine what the court will make of that?'

I blurted out my story about overhearing Nathaniel Pritchard and John Giddes in drunken conversation. Middlewych shook his head wearily. Then he spoke.

'Oliver Pritchard is an officer of the crown. An officer in training, a very junior one maybe, but no Navy court is going to take the word of two boy sailors over the word of an officer, unless you have witnesses, and especially witnesses who are more senior in rank than Midshipman Pritchard. If you put these extraordinary accusations before the court with no proof to back up your story, they will show you no mercy.'

His tone softened. I could see by the look in his eye that he wanted to do all he could to help us. 'If you plead for forgiveness and we get several of the crew to speak up on your behalf, you may just be looking at a flogging. I will speak for you. I have a very high regard for you both.'

Hearing someone speak well of us moved me. 'Thank you, sir,' I said. 'Do you know when the trial will be?'

'Well, that's some good news at least. Sometimes men wait for months before their court martial, but as the fleet is all assembled, the Vice Admiral has decided to get it over with immediately. You're to be tried tomorrow morning. Think hard about what I've told you. One other thing – don't start blaming each other. I can't imagine you will, but that always looks bad.'

I felt indignant he'd even suggested it, but I suppose he meant well. As he prepared to go I asked him about the battle.

'The Danes are calling for a truce,' said Middlewych briskly. 'We got off very lightly on the *Elephant*. Barely more than twenty men down. All of your gun crew are fine.' He left us with a sorry smile.

Next day began with a bucket of water, brought along with our breakfast. 'Get yourself washed and brushed up boys,' said one of our guards. 'You're up before the court at two bells on the forenoon watch.'

We were ushered up from the hold to the *London*'s great cabin. Inside was all polished oak, plush red furnishings, glistening silver and gold-braided uniforms. Richard and I were sat at a table facing the court, and the proceedings were abruptly explained. Five captains sat before us, assembled to act as a jury. An officer from the *London* was to act as prosecutor, and another officer known as the deputy judge advocate would advise the court on legal matters.

Having spent the previous few days in the hold, the light from the stern windows was blinding, and we felt like dirty urchins before these grandly dressed officers. This ceremony was no doubt supposed to remind us forcefully of the full majesty of the law. It worked. I felt almost too frightened to speak.

The prosecutor began by reading out Section 12 of the Articles of War:

Every person in the fleet, who through cowardice, negligence, or disaffection, shall in time of action withdraw or keep back, or not come into the fight or engagement, or shall not do his utmost to take or destroy every ship which it shall be his duty to engage, and to assist and relieve all and every of His Majesty's ships, or those of his allies, which it shall be his duty to assist and relieve, every such person so offending, and being convicted thereof by the sentence of a court martial, shall suffer death.

When he spoke the word 'death', a horrible chill ran down my spine. We were on trial for our lives.

The prosecutor began to outline the case against us. 'I intend to show that the two defendants deserted their posts at the height of battle, leaving not one, but two carronades on the larboard quarterdeck without powder at a critical moment.'

Oliver Pritchard was called first, and told the court with clear confidence how he had seen us running to the hold. 'The boys had clearly lost their nerve,' he said. 'When I challenged them they clung on to each other like two frightened children. I thought then and there to shoot them, but I supposed justice would be best served by this court.'

The marine, Private Macintosh, was called next. He briefly told what he had seen. Then, much to my distress, I heard the prosecutor call Tom Shepherd to come forward to testify against us.

'Just after the shot hit the quarterdeck and the powder boy from the gun next to us was thrown overboard, they ran off together sir,' said Tom. 'We thought they was goin' for more cartridges, naturally, but that was the last we saw of them.' He must have caught the look of betrayal on my face, because he turned to me unhappily and said, 'I'm sorry Sam, but that's what I saw.'

'The witness will confine his comments to the court only,' barked the deputy judge advocate.

Tom shrugged, and I could see he was upset. 'Please sir,' he said to the judge, 'may I be allowed to speak up for the boys too, as well as against them?'

The man nodded curtly. 'In good time.'

Then the prosecutor called for his final witness. It was John Giddes.

'Tell me exactly what you saw,' said the prosecutor.

'I was assistin' the surgeon in the after cockpit when I was sent to fetch fresh water,' he told the court. 'I saw Witchall and Buckley collect their cartridges from the after powder room. Then there was a loud explosion above us and the ship shook violently. I saw these two look at each other, drop their cartridges just outside the powder room and run for the hold. Just at that moment Midshipman Pritchard and Private Macintosh returned to their station by the powder room and caught the boys. They were both tremblin' with fear. It was a clear case of cowardice.'

The deputy judge advocate spoke up again. 'The witness will confine his comments to the question he is being asked.'

The judge asked us what we had to say for ourselves. This was our big moment, and my heart began to beat hard in my chest. The next few minutes would decide our fate. We had talked about this at length, of course, and had decided that Richard would speak for the two of us. We had reluctantly agreed to follow Middlewych's advice as we could see that there was no point telling the court what had really happened.

Richard was magnificent. Calmly and clearly he told the court of our record in combat and how we had gone out in the boat with Captain Hardy the night before the battle.

'Our records clearly show that neither of us has ever shown cowardice in the face of the enemy,' he went on, 'and that the incident reported by Midshipman Pritchard is a clear misunderstanding of orders in the heat of battle.'

Then Middlewych himself came forward to speak up for us. We knew he could not directly accuse Pritchard of lying, although in his speech he did give our version of events equal weight. Then he said:

'Should the court choose to believe these boys are guilty of cowardice, I would ask them to consider this: just prior to the incident, they had witnessed another powder boy horribly mutilated and thrown over the side whilst still alive. This may have contributed to their alleged actions. Indeed the cartridge box carried by Buckley was covered in the blood of this very boy.'

I stared over at him, horrified. He seemed to be suggesting we were guilty. Middlewych would not catch my eye. Instead, he looked intently at the jury of captains as he continued.

'If the court chooses to believe this incident was a

complete misunderstanding, I would say that both Witchall and Buckley had previously shown commendable courage under fire. Indeed, through their gallant actions they were central to the recapture of their former ship, the frigate *Miranda*, when it fell into Spanish hands in January of this year. In my experience, these boys are not cowards. They are as brave as any man I have served with.'

That was better. I hoped he knew what he was doing.

Then Tom Shepherd came forward again. He spoke briefly about how we were both mess mates he was proud to serve alongside, and how he would trust us both with his life. Then he brought out a petition signed by more than fifty of our comrades on the *Elephant*, begging the court for mercy.

That was it. The deputy judge advocate called a halt to proceedings and announced we were to retire while the jury deliberated. We spent an agonising hour back in our cell waiting for their judgement.

Richard said, 'The problem is that there's no one who can really stick up for us. They can only say what we were like before this happened.'

Silence descended between us. There was nothing more to be said and nothing to do but wait.

The lock was turned back. Out we went, trudging up the companionways with our legs in irons, chains clanking on the steps. We shuffled into the great cabin to see a sea of grim faces. At the nod of the deputy judge advocate, all the officers of the court put their hats on. It was an ominous gesture.

The judge stood up and talked to us directly. 'Richard Buckley and Samuel Witchall, this court finds you guilty of contravening section 12 of the Articles of War. You shall both be hanged by the neck at the yardarm of HMS *Elephant* until you are dead.'

I thought I was going to faint. But I managed to stay on my feet. We were dragged off, a marine at each arm. Before we were taken below, Middlewych came over to us.

'Don't give up hope boys. I shall do my best for you,' he said.

When we returned to our cell, we both broke down and cried like the boys we were. Richard, who had spoken so confidently in court, sobbed, 'Why did I ever let my father talk me into serving in this navy? This could never have happened back home. Now I'll never see my family again.'

I could think of nothing to say that would console him. I could only begin to imagine my parents' grief when they heard the news. I thought with anguish of my sweetheart Rosie, and how I would never see any of them again.

CHAPTER 5

Dead Men

We spent the next few hours on HMS *London*. Richard tried to lift our spirits. 'Middlewych will be pressing for an appeal. And I'll bet Robert Neville will be doing all he can, too.'

But no good news came our way. Late that afternoon a squad of marines came to the cell and we were told our execution would take place the following morning. My legs felt weak and I desperately wanted to sit down, but instead we were dragged off, placed on a boat and rowed through the murky dusk back to the *Elephant*. I looked at the thin pink streaks over the western sky and realised this was the last sunset I would ever see. By the forenoon watch the next morning we'd both be dead.

Back on the *Elephant* a small locker room in the hold had been prepared as a condemned cell. We were given paper and ink so we could write last letters, and this mercifully filled our time.

During the evening, just after the start of the first watch, Robert Neville came down with the ship's cook, who asked us what we would like to eat. I knew at once what I wanted – bacon and eggs, the same meal we'd had the morning after we had survived the wrecking of the *Miranda*. Richard thought this a fine choice and the cook scurried off to prepare our meal.

Robert looked at us with great concern. He was trying hard to keep his composure, but there were tears in his eyes. 'There's nothing more I can do. I've tried to raise the matter with Captain Foley, but he sent me on my way with a flea in my ear. I've written to my father, but I can't imagine he'll get my letter for another two or three weeks. You know I believe you're absolutely innocent, don't you?'

'Will you promise me to watch Oliver Pritchard like a hawk?' I said. 'I don't want him to do this to anyone else.'

Robert took my hand and said solemnly, 'And his father. I swear to you Sam. If I can pay them back for this, I will. One day they'll slip up, and I'll be there to see them hang.' He said it so firmly, I didn't doubt it.

The cook reappeared with two plates of bacon and eggs, and Robert sat with us while we ate. Although none of us could think of anything to say, it was good to have him there. Richard and I gave him our letters, Richard's to his family, mine to my family and Rosie, and Robert promised to make sure they would be delivered. Then it was time for him to go.

'I've got something else for you, too,' he said, fetching a half-bottle of rum from his pocket. 'It's not much but it's the most I could get you. Drink it to help you sleep or share it in the morning. It'll ease the passage of events, and they can hardly flog you for being drunk.'

It seemed like a good idea. We all hugged each other. Then Robert said, 'You've had a tooth out, haven't you Sam, on the *Miranda*? Wasn't that the most painful thing that ever happened to you?' I nodded. 'Well, I'm told being hanged is much less of a trial. It'll be over in an instant.' With that he was gone.

An awkward silence settled between us. I wanted to tell Richard how sorry I was that he had become caught up in this business, and that it was all my fault. But I couldn't think of the right way to say it. Besides, I didn't want him to become angry with me. He was my best friend and an evening of bitter recrimination would be a terrible way to spend our last night on earth.

After a while he spoke, but with no sign of anger. 'You know what the pirates always said,' he smiled. '"A short life but a merry one!" Have you had a merry life Sam?'

I thought about it. 'I've had an interesting life, I suppose. I'm not really old enough to have had a merry one. I do know, though, that I've seen things my father never dreamed of. I can't say I'm sorry to have gone to sea.'

'Me neither,' said Richard. 'Perhaps we should have become pirates. We'd have met the same fate, but had three times as much fun!'

We talked about pirates. Richard had read Captain Charles Johnson's *A General History of the Pyrates* and regaled me with tales of Edward Teach, the Bristol slave trader turned pirate known as Blackbeard. 'Quite a one for the ladies was old Blackbeard,' he laughed. 'Over his life he persuaded fourteen different women to marry him! They realised they'd made a terrible mistake when he insisted on sharing them with the rest of his crew.'

Then Richard grew wistful. 'I always thought this business with girls, you know, kissing and all the rest of it, was soppy. But now I think it would have been nice to have had a girl of my own.'

Later that evening we had another visitor. It was the ship's chaplain, the Reverend Edward Eaves. Neither of us was particularly pleased to see him. His eyes seemed blurry, and his speech slurred. As he leaned close to talk

76

I could smell spirits on his breath. 'I've come to take your confessions, boys, so you may meet your maker with pure hearts.'

Without waiting for a response he went on, 'Do you renounce the devil and all his works, the pomp and vanity of this wicked world, and all the sinful lusts of the flesh?'

We mumbled along with the familiar prayers, and when the ceremony was over I asked the Reverend several questions which had been troubling me. Did God know we are innocent? Did he know we didn't commit the sins for which we were being executed? Would we be given a decent Christian funeral or was this denied to those who are executed?

I hoped Eaves would provide me with words of comfort, as our village parson had done when my two younger brothers had died of the smallpox.

'God knows all things, boys, and is most merciful,' he said. Then his voice faltered. I could see he was struggling to answer. 'The things I've seen this last month aboard this ship. The blood may have washed off my hands, but I'll never forget the smell in the surgeon's cockpit. The screams of the dying. And now this. You two good boys. Heaven knows, you don't deserve to die.'

We seized on his words. Did he know something about Giddes and the Pritchards that could save us? We bombarded him with questions, but he just looked blank. He obviously didn't have a clue what we were talking about. Then he began to cry unashamedly, placing his head on my shoulder. Richard looked on appalled, and then he had an idea. He went to fetch the half-bottle of rum and handed it to him.

'Do you want some of this?' he said.

The Reverend took it without any sign of surprise and much to our amazement drained a quarter of the bottle in a single lengthy swig. Then he collapsed into a mute silence as the powerful spirit coursed around his body.

A few minutes later he began to speak again in a quiet voice. Although he slurred his words still, he sounded lucid and not a little angry. He seemed sunk in despair.

'I've seen more than my share of madness on this ship, but the fact that you boys are facing a desperately unjust fate perplexes me greatly. To tell you frankly, I've increasingly come to believe we live in a rudderless world.'

Then he staggered away, and the guard locked the door behind him.

'Thank you for those words of comfort, Reverend,' said Richard under his breath. 'They were a great help to us both.'

'He's perplexed?' I said. 'Not as much as we are.' The whole exchange had been so odd I started to laugh.

Richard lay his head down and closed his eyes. Soon he was asleep. As for me, I was determined to stay awake all night, alone with my thoughts. I tried to think of my earliest memory, but that part of my life was clouded by the deaths of my younger brothers. So I thought instead of Rosie, and how we had played together as children.

Sometime in the middle of the night I drifted off to sleep. In my dreams I was on the beach at Yarmouth with Rosie, both of us digging furiously with wooden spades in the sand, trying to build a wall strong enough to withstand the assault of the incoming tide. Everything seemed so vivid. The white spume on the waves, the sunlight on the golden sand, the sky a rich blue. The sea made a magical sound tinkling on the pebbles and shells of the beach as it reached further towards us with its foamy tendrils. The smell of the salty water made me feel incredibly alive. As we built our wall, we used the sand to make a mound behind it. Then we retreated to our mound and stood high in the wind, arms around each other, so we wouldn't fall into the approaching water. Then, in my dream, we were no longer children. Rosie was the young woman I had last seen a year ago. We began to caress each other, her skin hot from the sun. She turned her face to mine and we kissed passionately. As the walls we had built dissolved, the sea surrounded our crumbling mound and we fell backwards into the cold water. But even this did not cool her ardour. Rosie kissed me again and I felt so happy I could burst.

There was a brisk commotion outside our door and I woke with a start. Our guards had brought us burgoo and scotch coffee. 'Can't hang a man without a proper breakfast,' said one.

We washed, dressed and waited. We both decided we would not drink the rum. 'I feel sick enough already,' I said. I should have felt more frightened, but our circumstances seemed unreal – almost as if I were still dreaming.

The marine guard arrived. A sergeant bound our hands behind our backs and they took us shuffling out on to the upper deck, irons and chains still round our ankles. Now, in the chilly morning air, everything felt far too real. A yellow flag flew from the mast head, in recognition of the execution to come. I quailed when I saw the two ropes with nooses fashioned at their base. They were run through blocks attached to the foremast yardarm and suspended right above the cathead at the bow of the ship. At the other end of the ropes stood a team of ten men apiece. It would be their job to pull on the rope and hang us. I recognised none of them. They must have been brought on board from another ship.

Over the rails I could see the *Elephant* was surrounded by boats from other ships of the fleet, gathered to bear witness to our fate. The whole of our ship was turned out on deck. 'Who'd have thought we were that important?' said Richard. I took my cue from him. They'd accused us of cowardice. We would show them how wrong they were by dying bravely.

Captain Foley read the Articles of War to the crew, which seemed to take forever. I started to shiver in the dawn, and worried that my shipmates might think I was trembling with fear. I caught the eye of Oliver Pritchard and he smiled a cold-eyed smile. My resolve to be brave began to crumble. The bastard had won. He had framed us and got away with it. A terrible anger rose within me, then a great sadness. I tried to stifle a sob. Richard turned to me. 'Chin up, friend.' He said it so kindly I was consoled.

As Foley droned on, I gazed around. Tom and James were there among the crew. I caught their eyes and gave them a sad smile. It was turning into a beautiful spring morning, much like the one when I had first gone to sea a year before. As we stood there on the deck a strong wind blew in from the west. It was not a cold wind, and I felt invigorated by its presence. I thought of the words from the Bible:

To everything there is a season, and a time to every purpose under the heaven:

A time to be born, and a time to die . . .
Then I noticed Foley had finished reading and was telling the crew why we were to be hanged. We were brought forward to the cathead, and a noose was placed around our necks. The Reverend Eaves was standing close by, looking quite blank. The rope felt coarse and heavy on my skin. My legs began to tremble. 'Stand straight, stand straight,' I told myself. 'Don't let them see you're afraid.'

My eye was drawn to a small gull gliding overhead, its wings bright in the sunlight. It was the last thing I saw before a canvas hood was placed roughly over my head. I reached over to Richard and found his hand. We both held on to each other tight and waited for the Bosun's whistle to pipe 'Hoist away', and the sickening jolt that would hurl us into the air.

CHAPTER 6

The Unspeakable Hulk

I waited and waited, blood pounded in my ears, legs shaking. I feared I would not be able to stand up much longer. Every breath I took, I thought would be the last before the rope tightened mercilessly around my windpipe. Sweet Jesus, get it over with. Why were they taking so long? Then I heard the Bosun pipe 'Stand down'. Hands grabbed me and lifted me off the cathead. The hood and rope were snatched from my head.

I glanced at Richard. He was white as a sheet, looking wildly around. What was happening? Shouldn't we be dead by now?

Captain Foley spoke again, loud and clear, for all the ship's company to hear. 'It is my solemn duty to pronounce that on the authority of the Admiral of the Fleet, the death sentence on Samuel Witchall and Richard Buckley has been commuted. In place of death they will be transported for life.'

The crew gave a cheer. Oliver Pritchard looked flabbergasted. I looked him square in the face. If I get the chance, I thought, I shall kill you one day. Then the world faded from view and I felt a great whirling in my ears.

Pain made me come to my senses. I must have fainted and hit my head on the deck. The next few minutes were a blur. Richard and I were bundled off the *Elephant* and on to a small boat. I must have looked as shocked as he did. He was unable to speak and could barely walk without two marines either side of him.

When it dawned on me that our lives had been spared, I should have felt a great joy. Instead I was indifferent. I kept wondering if I was really dead. If all this was some strange hallucination. But the cold north wind blowing down on us seemed real enough.

We were sculled over to a nearby frigate, the *Aeneas*, and thrown in a storeroom at the bottom of the ship. 'We should be helping to sail her,' I protested. 'We're wasted here, locked in the hold.' I got a sharp rap with a rope for my troubles. Afterwards I felt stupid, but people say silly things when their minds are not working properly.

Richard kept holding his neck and twisting it. He stared straight ahead and refused to speak. When our dinner time ration of bread and water arrived, he ignored it. I wolfed mine down and a feeling of euphoria came over me. I was still breathing, eating, drinking. We were not dead men after all. I would see another sunset. I might even see my mother and father and Rosie again. I spouted this all out to Richard, but he remained in a strange, blank state. Only in the evening did his countenance change. He ate his dreary rations then he became very angry. He picked up his empty mug and threw it hard against the wall. Then he began to shout. 'What a dastardly, low-down, miserable, rotten bastard trick.' He was beside himself.

I was more philosophical. 'I don't know who pulled strings for us – Middlewych? Robert? Maybe even Foley himself?' I suggested. Perhaps those with the power to reprieve us felt we needed to be sufficiently punished before they spared our lives?

He shook his head and muttered, but I could see my words were making sense.

'And what's this about transportation?' he said.

'I've heard about that. They send you off to New South Wales.'

Richard looked puzzled.

'New South Wales. You know, Botany Bay, New Holland,' I said. 'It's called umpteen different things. I don't know much about it other than that it's on the other side of the world, and it's very hot.'

Richard looked close to despair. 'But how will I ever get back to Massachusetts?'

As he said it, it dawned on me that the very great distance would make it difficult for us to escape or even return as free men. If that had been our original sentence, I would have been devastated. But at this moment, anything seemed better than being dead and I was filled with curiosity. Richard returned to his sullen silence.

Later on, one of the ship's hands came to take away our plates and mugs. 'I 'eard they 'ad you up to be 'anged,' he said. 'Then they let you off. I seen that 'appen a few times, but usually you get pardoned. It's rare to get another sentence, like as you 'ave. I've 'eard allsorts about where you're goin'. Some good, some bad. First they'll put you in a prison hulk outside Portsmouth. That's where we're goin'. Should be there in a week. You stay on that 'til there's a ship ready to take you away. If you can survive the hulk, you've got six months at sea to look forward to. Takes that long to get down there. Still, you bein' Navy men, you should be tough enough.'

*　*　*

When after another week or so at sea we were finally brought up from the hold of the *Aeneas*, I saw at once we were back at Portsmouth. We were not taken directly to a prison hulk, but instead spent a couple of weeks in a stinking barracks cell close to the quayside. We slept on a bed of cold straw and talked constantly of our hope for a reprieve.

'They've put us here because they're going to let us go!' I said to Richard.

He shared my hope. 'Maybe they're just playing us along for a bit, like they did when they pretended to hang us. Keep us here for another couple of weeks then let us off?'

When a squad of marines came for us, I couldn't help but ask, 'Have you good news? Are we to be set free?'

The Sergeant commanding didn't even have the heart to hit me for my insolence. 'Shut up, you silly boy,' he said. 'You're off to the hulks.'

'Anything's got to be better than this horrible place,' whispered Richard with a grin.

The Sergeant overheard him. 'You wait and see, lad, you wait and see.' He was beginning to sound impatient. 'Now shut your mouths, the pair of you.'

A small tender ferried us over Portsmouth Sound to our new home. It was a day full of promise for anyone not bound for a prison hulk. On shore, blossoms burst from the trees and the air was filled with fresh scents and sunshine. Despite my fate, my spirits were high. Every day I woke and told myself I was still alive and not slowly turning to corruption at the bottom of the North Sea, with a rope around my broken neck.

Our destination was the *St Louis*, a prison hulk outside Portsmouth harbour, which we were told was a captured French 74. There were ten other prison vessels moored beside the *St Louis*, in the waters leading down to Spithead. I could see them clearly, all moored together in line. What a pitiful sight they made, compared to the proud warship I had seen sailing in line at Copenhagen. The mizzenmast and yardarms had been removed, and just a stump left for the main mast and foremast. No sails or flags billowed proudly from these masts, only a single black pennant. All the ships were the colour of rotten wood, with none of the proud spick and span of a Navy vessel. They looked like a row of loathsome brown toads squatting on the green marble surface of the sea.

Richard and I fell into conversation with an older man on the tender, who had been sent down to Portsmouth from Newgate Prison in London. He had a wrinkled face and mean, ratty eyes, but I thought there must be some good left in his soul as he was keen to give us advice.

'Third time I been sent to one of these,' he told us.

'Didn't you get transported?' I asked him. He shook his head. 'There's plenty on the hulks who never get sent out to Botany Bay. We get sent to the ships because the gaols are full to bursting.

'I expect I'll see a few old mates,' he went on. 'I usually do. Only, as a word of warning to you boys, don't go thinking anyone here is going to be *your* mate. Even me. They're just out to trick you of every possession you have. And if you find the prisoners nasty, you should see the guards. They come from the depths of humankind. Lightermen, rat catchers, slaughtermen, saltpetre men. Most have never held power over another fellow in their life, except on these hulks, and they love to torment the wretches they're charged to mind.'

'So what's the drill?' said Richard, hurriedly trying to change the subject. His cheery optimism of this morning had vanished.

'Every morning, seven o'clock, any man who can stand up is ferried to government works. They work the whole day. Sometimes the work's filthy, sometimes it isn't, but it always wears you to the bone. Then, when it's dusk, we go back to the ship to be locked in the hold 'til six o'clock the next morning.'

'You mean we get to sleep the whole night?' said Richard.

I was impressed too. On some nights in the Navy we were allowed only four hours' rest.

The old man thought we were simpletons. 'You fresh-faced boys won't be getting much sleep. After lockdown the worst of them roam the decks unhindered, tormenting the weaker prisoners. I imagine you'll be getting more than a fair share of their attentions.'

We were used to the rough world of the Navy, but we weren't expecting this.

As the tender grew closer to the *St Louis* my heart sank. On the top deck, ugly wooden huts sprouted like warts on a face. Instead of cannons at the gun ports there were thick iron grills. Instead of colourful pennants or signal flags on the rigging, washing hung out to dry. Then the wind blew in our faces and a choking stench oozed from the ship.

We were shoved up a stairway that stretched from the waterline to the top deck. From a platform at the top, I looked over the deck to see a handful of men, all of them in leg irons, trudging in a circle. Their chains scraped on the planking as they hobbled around.

From below came a strange rattling noise, which I supposed to be the chains of all the other men. Amid the hubbub of voices from within the *St Louis*, I could make out an extraordinary deluge of oaths and execrations new to my ears. Having sailed on a Navy vessel for most of the previous year, I thought I had heard every swear word known to man.

The men were herded below, the more tardy of them suffering blows from the guards' musket butts. When the deck had been cleared we were lined up and addressed by a marine sergeant, who ordered us to strip and wash in the tubs of water provided. Then we were given filthy, ragged clothes and sent over to a black-smith. I sat down before him and once again irons were placed around my ankles. I was swiftly hauled to my feet and staggered over to the hatchway leading below. It was time to meet our fellow prisoners.

I made my way down the ladder to the lower deck, suddenly clumsy with the burden of my leg irons. If I had been descending into hell, I could not have felt more afraid. But there on the crowded deck was a familiar face.

'Well boyos, am I pleased to see you! I heard you were going to be hanged!' It was Vincent Thomas – Vengeful Tattoos himself – our shipmate from the *Elephant* and the *Miranda*.

I had expected to see hollow-eyed men, wandering like the damned, not a cheery Welshman. But the hollow-eyed men were there too – the *St Louis* carried a cargo of human scarecrows.

'What are you doing here?' I was astounded.

Vincent drew me closer, and whispered. 'They said I was getting too friendly with one of the sailmaker's mates. Blew up just after the battle it did. They wanted to hang us too, but couldn't prove anything. So we got packed off here on the double instead. He's been sent to the hulk behind us I think. Bit overcrowded, isn't it?'

'Are they going to transport you?' I asked.

'I shouldn't think so, Sam. I'm hoping they'll just keep us here for a few months and let us go when the fuss dies down. Certainly hope so.'

He seemed remarkably cheerful, considering.

'Well, this is all very nice,' he went on. 'You boys can join our mess. We just had two scoundrels who messed with us taken off and flogged to death. Tried to escape they did. Terrible business. Well you can make up the numbers. Regulations say we need six for a mess. Come and meet your messmates.'

One of them was a boy of seven, a sorry-looking little chap who sucked his thumb and had a bright green blob of snot running down his nose.

'Terrible story it is. You tell it Johnny Onions,' said Vincent.

But the boy remained mute, and hid his face behind Vincent's bulky shoulders.

Vincent smiled at him indulgently. 'Stole some bread, didn't he? Poor lad was hungry. Mother just let him roam the streets of Westminster while she sold lucky heather, and herself too I shouldn't wonder. The judge says to his mother, "You take him home and look after him and the court shall let him go on account of his youthfulness." And what does she do? She says, "You can take him and lock him up for all I cares." Cockney slut. So the boy gets sentenced to transportation, doesn't he? Never you mind, Johnny. We'll look after you, lad.'

Another messmate was even stranger. His name was James Updike. When introduced, he bowed, and spoke with the most affected high-born accent I had ever heard. Although he smiled at us pleasantly, he seemed unwilling to talk. So Vincent told his story too while he looked on with an indulgent smirk.

'Only turned up here with his servant. Course they wouldn't let the lad on with us, so Mr Updike sent him away and had him come back later with his dinner. Fellow sailed up to the bow with a meal in a silver salver. The guards weren't having that either. Told him not to come back. Still, Mr Updike's friend, Lady Farringdon, has made an arrangement with the authorities, ensuring he gets proper food and he in turn has made an arrangement with me, ensuring he gets proper looking after from the more disagreeable sorts in here. We all share his spoils naturally.'

'So what did you do to end up here, Mr Updike?' I asked.

'Never could resist a handsome snuffbox,' he said in a languid drawl. His manners were exquisite, but I thought him the silliest man I had ever met. How anyone with his wealth and connections would be careless enough to land himself in such trouble was beyond me.

The sixth man in our mess was called Joseph Swales. He was a tough-looking salt with blue tattoos all up his arms, and wiry, greying hair. He was happy enough to tell us his story. 'I was transported twelve years ago,' he said. 'Went over in 1790 I did, on the *Neptune*. There were five hundred of us, men and women, packed in like slaves we were. Nearly two hundred of us died on the way, from gaol fever or want of proper nourishment. Then another hundred or so pegged out soon after they landed.'

Swales was a sailor by trade, and had been transported for pilfering supplies. He had made an extraordinary escape. 'Caught me a Yankee merchantman in Port Jackson, didn't I?' he boasted. 'Stowed away in the hold. When they found out I was a sailor they let me work my passage to Jamaica. Spent a good few years there, then worked a ship back to London. Thought I'd be able to settle down there. All them people, it's easy to blend in, get lost in the crowd. But first thing I sees is me bleedin' old ship's first lieutenant down on the Strand. He had me arrested at once and sent back to the hulks. Lucky I wasn't hanged. My old mate Will Moulder, who pulled the same trick, got strung up at Newgate he did.'

Swales told us some of the transport ships were run by cruel captains and crews recruited direct from the slave ships. 'I knew some of them. I worked those slave ships myself before I joined the Navy. They keep their cargo double-ironed for the whole journey. They're frightened of a mutiny. One man who tried to stir things up, he got snitched on. They gave him three hundred lashes then rested him for the night and brought him out to give him five hundred more the next day. Poor bastard died halfway through. I heard some fellows nearly got away with it once. When most of the crew were up in the rigging and the officers were having their dinner, they rushed the guards by the quarterdeck and tried to break into the ship's armoury. Right bloody mess it was. Fifteen of them killed before they gave up, then the ring leaders were hanged, them that were still alive.

'Some of the transport ships, the women and men were packed in together. Only let them on deck for a few minutes a day. Even in the tropics, when the ship was becalmed they had to stay below and swelter. They called them hell ships, those. They reckon the Devil came to have a look at them to get a better idea of how to torment the damned.'

Swales struck me as someone who had fallen foul of the law through a moment's temptation and ill luck. He wasn't a dyed-in-the-wool villain. I was pleased to have him as part of our mess. His stories had frightened me, though.

'And these ships, Mr Swales. Are they still like that now?'

'Shouldn't think they've changed much. We'll find out soon enough.'

We ate our supper, then it was time to prepare for bed. A large wooden board that had acted as a partition during the day was laid flat against the wall, and a hay-filled mattress placed on top.

Vincent addressed us. 'Now I'll tell you exactly how we're going to sleep. Joseph on the outside, then me, then Mr Updike, then Johnny, then you and Richard.'

'Why's that?' I asked.

'No one's going to stick a knife in Joseph because they know I'd kill them. If I'm on the end, they could get me while I'm asleep. You boys can stay well on the other side of us because that's where you'll be safest. It'll all make sense come bedtime.'

We did as Vincent said. There were lice in the blankets and rats scurried around our bodies. I jumped up the first few times I heard one, then I learned not to.

'You can worry about them if they bite you,' said Vincent.

As night fell the sound of hatches being locked echoed around the interior. After a short while the guard and ship's officers retired to their cabins on the quarterdeck. Although barriers were placed on the stairways between the decks, the decks themselves were open, and the gangs began to roam. We saw very little, but heard screaming, whimpering and begging from the younger inmates. It was a terrifying place and I lay awake long into the night haunted by the thought of what would happen to us if Vincent was not here to look after us.

The next morning we were taken from the ship and sent to work. Our shackles weighed heavy on our ankles as we spent the day clearing earth from the embankment by the harbour. The overseers stood by with drawn cutlasses, and beat with a stick any man they thought was slacking. Although the work on the embankment was hard, it was not exhausting, as everyone seemed to go at the pace of the most emaciated and weary convicts. There was no talking, and certainly no singing. I missed the rhythm of the sailor songs we used to sing to help us with our work on the *Elephant*. I realised how much they had assisted us in hauling up anchors and sails, and scrubbing wooden decks.

I was amazed to see a crowd of well-dressed men and women peering over the railings by the quayside to stare and point at us. 'Worthless scum,' whispered one convict to me. 'You'd think they'd have something better to do with their money. They can't go an' gawp at lunatics anymore, they put a stop to that, so they pay to come and gloat at us instead.'

Back on the hulk at the end of the day I asked Vincent how often people tried to escape.

'Well, not much,' he said. 'You get hung for it, see. Or flogged to death. Or put down in the hold in a dark room for months on end. Or you get double-ironed for life. So, it's a bit of a risk.

'There's enough to worry about already,' he went on, 'so I'm sitting tight. That James Updike, he's got friends in high places. He's told me that if I look after him, he'll try and get me out of here. You won't be here long, Sam. You'll be off to New South Wales any day, so you don't go worrying yourself. But I hope Mr Updike gets me and him away before there's an outbreak of something. I don't want to waste away with typhus or dysentery in this stinking hell hole . . .' he tailed off. It wasn't like Vincent to admit to his worries.

I expected trouble from the inmates and it came soon enough. One ratty-looking thug cornered me with a knife soon after I arrived. 'I know you got valuables, boy. Everyone has when they come aboard. Are you going to give them to me, or do I have to slice your guts open to get them?'

Vincent came up quietly behind him. Seizing his shirt he lifted him clean off the ground so that the man choked on his collar. The rotten fabric ripped within seconds and Vincent threw him to the deck in a heap. 'This lad's a friend of mine,' he said quietly. 'And you're making me angry.' That was enough. Word went round the worst of the prisoners and Richard and I were spared their bullying.

After a few days, we realised that if we kept our heads down and did as we were told, the guards were no worse than the Navy bosuns. What was worse than the Navy, though, was the food. If the inmates had not been starving, I doubt any man on board would have been able to eat it. The bread was always mouldy. On a ship at sea for several months this was unavoidable, but on a vessel moored offshore and visited daily by boats from the harbour it seemed a deliberate part of our cruel punishment.

'Most of what we get here,' said Vincent, 'is old bulls or cows that have died of age or famine.' One of our most frequent meals was something the men called 'smiggins', a thin soup of water thickened with barley, in which beef was boiled. If it wasn't for Mr Updike's food deliveries, which were shared between the six of us messmates, we would have become weak from hunger and prey to disease.

What disgusted me most about the *St Louis* was how little the guards or convicts cared about the cleanliness of the ship. The stench near the 'necessary', as the men called it, was enough to make your eyes water. 'Surely they could put us lot to work cleaning the place to make it more bearable to live in,' I said to Vincent. 'You're thinking like a sailor, Sam,' he said to me. 'They're not concerned with our welfare. In fact if we die, it just means they don't have to cough up to feed us.'

Ever since Vincent had mentioned it, I worried constantly about disease sweeping us away. For even without epidemics, people died often on the *St Louis*. Usually it was the men who had been there for years. With no fever or other disorders upon them, they seemed to die merely from lowness of spirit. The doctor who worked the ship had an arrangement with the officer in charge. When his patients gave up the ghost, they were taken away. All of us believed they were destined for the dissection table at the local hospital. They certainly weren't going for a Christian burial in a leafy churchyard.

The weeks merged into one another. The threat of disease, murder or molestation hung over us like a shadow. I held my fear at bay by hoping every day would bring a reprieve. Vincent was our salvation. He could not have protected us better if we were his family. Everyone, it seemed, had a healthy respect for Vincent Thomas. His sheer size, and those vengeful tattoos, were enough to warn both the guards and inmates that anyone who crossed him, and his pals, was in trouble.

One Sunday morning, towards the end of May, I was washing my clothes up on the deck when the Bosun called over, 'Oi Witchall, you got visitors.'

My spirits lifted at once. This must be the reprieve I had hoped for.

I was taken to a cabin on the quarterdeck with bare wooden benches. 'Wait there,' said the Bosun, and the door was locked. I wondered with mounting excitement who was coming to see me. For the first time aboard the hulk I let myself believe it might be Lieutenant Middlewych or Robert Neville, come to tell me the villainy of the Pritchards had been revealed, and Richard and I were now free men. A minute later, there was a kerfuffle at the door and in came my father, mother and Rosie.

We hugged and cried and shrieked with delight. My father looked older – he was grey round the temples and his hands were shaking. My mother looked drawn. Rosie stood back from them, feeling out of place.

Then, after that first flurry of excitement, I felt a twinge of disappointment. Middlewych and Neville had let me down. As we settled I blurted out, 'Do you have news of my reprieve?'

'No son,' said my father softly. 'We've come to say goodbye.'

'What do you mean?' I said, suddenly alarmed.

'Our news is that you're to be sent to New South Wales when the convoy sails in June.'

Tears of desperation streamed down my face. 'But we didn't do it. Surely they would have found that out by now? We've been double-crossed. You know that, don't you? Please tell me you don't think we're cowards.' The whole story came tumbling out – the overheard conversation, the business with Pritchard in the hold, the mock execution . . .

My father shook his head. 'Of course I believe you, son. But even if you had hidden from the battle, no decent soul would blame you. It's a cruel world we live in, where boys as young as you are sent out to be killed for their country.'

'It's like seeing a ghost, Sam,' said my mother. 'We all got the letters you wrote before they were going to hang you. I felt too sad to cry. Then another letter arrived about a week after that, to say you'd had your sentence commuted. It's a right mess you've got yourself into, Samuel. You and your going away to sea. Why didn't you stay in the village? Now there's only Thomas left. Three children I've had taken from me. And what's this about New South Wales? They might as well be sending you to the Moon. We'll never see you again.' She started to sob.

Seeing them after so long, and after so much had happened, was strange. I had been their little boy when I went to sea. I still was, I suppose, but I didn't feel like it.

My father spoke. 'Look, we've got this for you. Where you're going, you'll need influence. We don't know anyone of influence so you'll have to make do with valuables. Here's ten pounds. I'm sorry I can't give you more, but it will be of some use.'

Then my mother slipped off a ring my father had given her before they were married. It had been the most valuable thing his family possessed. 'I can't take that,' I said, although I knew the sapphires and emeralds set in gold were worth a pretty penny.

'It's all right,' she said. 'Your father and I, we've discussed this. You need looking after, Sam. We're not here to look after you, and we won't be able to help you on the other side of the world. Wear it on a cord around your neck.' She fished out a thin silk ribbon. 'If you don't have to trade it, then let it be a reminder of me and your father, and how much we love you.'

'We're going to go for a breath of fresh air,' my father said, ushering my mother to the door. 'Leave you two alone for a minute.' They banged on the door, waited for it to be unlocked, then went out on to the deck.

I turned to Rosie. I hadn't really looked at her until now, so taken up was I with my parents. She wasn't exactly as I had pictured her. Not quite the willowy, dark-haired beauty of my memory. She was now an inch or so taller than me, even though I had grown over the last year. Her hair was longer, and hung black and straight down past her shoulders, making her look even skinnier. Then she smiled, and I remembered at once why I had fallen for her. She was pretty when she smiled, and I felt so protective of her. This was my Rosie, who I had thought of every day at sea.

I suppose this was meant to be a great romantic moment. But it didn't feel right in this shabby little cabin. On the *St Louis* we had to wash in stagnant water and dry ourselves with a filthy towel. I felt like a dirty urchin in my prison clothes, irons on my ankles. I wanted Rosie to see me at my best – freshly scrubbed, with new clothes and money in my pocket.

'There was talk of a midshipman post,' I said. 'Before all this –'

She wasn't interested in that.

'I haven't got a ring to give you, Sam,' she said, 'haven't really got anything.' She seemed awkward, and her eyes would not meet mine. This wasn't how I'd imagined our meeting again.

'I cried for a week when I heard they were going to hang you. They say you're a coward. I suppose I wanted you to be a hero. People have been saying such horrible things. And now you're telling us it's all lies. Well, I'm sorry I ever doubted you.'

I flushed red with anger. She could see, and quickly began to talk of something else.

'I've thought of you so much since you went away. I read your letters so often I could tell you every word. You write a good letter, Sam.'

She was in tears now, and we hugged each other tight. She was so slight and frail. I could feel the bones of her back hard against my finger tips. My anger faded. She held my face in her warm hands and kissed me softly on the lips.

Shy once again, she moved away.

'Well look at you now, Sam.' She stood back, holding my left hand. 'Even growing a little moustache, I see.' She giggled. 'Doesn't really suit you.'

I blushed with embarrassment. I had not seen my reflection in a looking glass for many months. 'They don't let us have razors,' I said. 'I'll have to ask the barber to shave me when he visits.'

'I like your hair though.' Like many tars, I had grown it long and wore it tied back.

At that moment I wished more than anything to be alone with her in the empty fields at Wroxham. Just us and a picnic on a warm summer day. Nestling miles from anyone else, in the dappled light of the riverbank trees.

'You know I'll wait for you, Sam,' she said. 'You're my sweetheart. I don't want anyone else.'

Before we could say anything more, the door opened with a rattle of the lock and my parents returned.

'Bosun says we've got to go, Sam,' said my father, his voice stiff with regret.

It was a terrible farewell. 'You may as well be dead, Sam,' my mother sobbed. 'People say no one ever comes back from New South Wales. And you with your life sentence –'

I felt a rush of defiance. 'I swear I'll be back. Even if I have to escape. I shall see you all again. I know it in my bones. I'll write to you as often as I can. If the letters stop, you'll know I'm coming home.'

But I didn't really believe what I was saying. As I watched them go, I thought I would never see them again.

I wrote to Rosie that afternoon. I told her how pleased I had been to see her, and how, over the last year, the thought of her had made me smile on the dreariest of days. I told her I would always remember her as a dear friend, but that she should not wait for me to return to England. I cried when I wrote that letter, but I didn't tell her. I wanted her to forget about me. It was only right she should not waste the rest of her youth waiting for me to return.

One early morning a few days later, the *St Louis*'s Bosun came round the lower deck calling out names. 'Richard Buckley,' I heard quite clearly. We all knew what this meant. Those selected for transportation were to be ferried to the ship that would take them to New South Wales. I was gripped with anxiety. What if they took Richard and left me here? What if they took Vincent and left me here? I strained hard to hear. Soon enough my name was called, and I breathed easier. Johnny Onions was coming, and Joseph Swales. Shortly after, the Bosun stopped calling out names. Mr Updike was staying. Perhaps his friends in high places had helped him out. Vincent was staying too. I said a little prayer, asking God to forgive them and send them off the hulk soon.

We gathered our few belongings and said our goodbyes. Vincent gave me a bear hug. 'Thank you for looking after us, Mr Thomas,' I said. 'We'll miss you.'

Those of us who had been called were lined up on the upper deck. A blacksmith was present and we were ordered forward to be double-ironed with heavier chains.

'When will these come off?' I asked, only to be struck around the head with a switch.

The chains weighed heavy on my ankles, and put paid to any idea of jumping overboard and swimming to freedom. After a few hours they began to chafe and rub my skin raw. We were about to take the first steps on a journey to the other side of the world. If Joseph Swales' stories were still true, we'd be lucky to get halfway there.

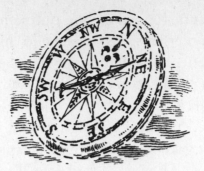

CHAPTER 7

Over the Dark Blue Ocean

A small boat ferried us towards a three-mast cargo ship. Above the gilded windows of the stern we saw her name, *Euphrates*. Her quarterdeck ran level with the upper deck, like a frigate, although she was not so sleek. I thought she looked a small vessel for so great a journey, but Joseph Swales assured me Captain Bligh had sailed to the South Seas on such a ship, the *Bounty*. The *Euphrates* had been well prepared for our arrival. The hold had recently been fumigated. As soon as I came aboard, the smell of tar, brimstone and vinegar caught in my throat.

Under the watchful eye of a squad of marines we were lined up and told to strip naked. This order was made comical by the fact that our leg irons prevented the removal of our trousers. A marine came down the line with a bayonet, and cut the garments from our legs. The clothes were gathered up and bundled overboard, considered too louse-ridden or diseased to be worth washing and re-issuing.

As we stood shivering in the sharp wind blowing down the Solent, they called us forward one by one to be doused in several buckets of seawater. A swift examination followed, conducted by a piggy-eyed man I took to be the ship's surgeon. In his manner he might well have been examining a sheep at market.

We were given new clothes – two pairs of trousers and two shirts. Each was marked with a large A or B. The trousers were buttoned on either side of the leg, to allow them to be removed over leg irons. I said a silent prayer, entreating God to spare us from being double-ironed for the whole voyage.

'You will wear items A on the first week, and items B on the second week,' barked the Bosun, 'and wash these clothes with care and regularity.'

Then came the bedding. I was disappointed to discover we would be sleeping in bunks. I had got used to a hammock and the way it rolled with the waves. Bunks wouldn't be as comfortable. Each bed roll had a large black number painted on it, as did the three threadbare blankets we were given. Finally, each of us was issued with a worn, wooden pillow, also marked with a black number.

'They're spoiling us,' whispered Richard. 'These clothes look too thin to keep anyone warm. We'll need to wear both shirts at once when the North Wind blows.'

We tramped downstairs. Despite Swales' warnings I didn't feel the same trepidation as when I had entered the hulk. There was something about the look and feel of this ship that told me it was going to be well run. Besides, I was glad to be away from the *St Louis*. It was such a threatening, dangerous place, I knew our luck would not have held for ever.

On the lower deck a corridor with cells either side stretched almost the whole length of the ship. Richard, Johnny and I were pointed to a small cell with four bunks, next to the stairway. There was already one occupant in it, a tall young man with spectacles and a bright, inquiring face. 'Dr Daniel Sadler,' he said with a pleasant smile, and stood up to shake our hands. What was a man like this doing in here?

When I saw some of the other prisoners file past, I was glad not to be sharing with them. There was another small cell on the deck, but the rest held ten or more men. I guessed there must have been a hundred or so convicts on board, men and boys of all shapes and sizes. We certainly had some villains among us.

The *Euphrates* sailed later that morning. As we were confined to our cells for the first week of that voyage, I couldn't see Portsmouth and the coast of England slowly slip away from us. Perhaps it was a good thing. It would have been too distressing. I tried not to reflect on everything I was leaving behind, but I couldn't help myself.

It was not just the thought of leaving loved ones I would never see again, it was everything I had ever seen and done and known. One late August day, at the end of my last summer at Wroxham, I stood on the pebbly banks of the River Bure just where a small tributary flows into it. There I watched the water babble through the shallows and the cross currents push against each other. Three cows came to see me, staring in their benevolent way and the river bank was still full of flowers. Now I would never stand there again.

My mood lifted when our shackles were removed. As the ship passed the last of England we were allowed to walk in the fresh air on the deck. I saw at once we were sailing in convoy. There were three convict ships, of which we were the smallest, with two Navy sloops for escort. I longed to be on one of the warships as part of the crew. It felt wrong being on a ship and doing nothing useful.

* * *

The Captain of the *Euphrates* was a stern Liverpudlian named Casewell. He paced the quarterdeck with a quiet authority. Looking at his weather-beaten face and wiry frame, I guessed he had been at sea from a very young age. Although he was courteous to everyone, crew and convicts alike, there was something in his manner that suggested it would be very unwise to disregard what he was saying. The First Lieutenant, in contrast, was a haughty toff called Holkham. I could see at once it was an uneasy partnership.

Casewell's crew were a scruffy bunch. I thought they could do with our help. Also aboard were a platoon of marines, some of whom had brought their wives and children. It was pleasant to see women on board, and to hear young children playing and reciting skipping rhymes. It made our ship seem less sinister and more part of an everyday, ordinary world.

Among the passengers I noticed a beautiful young woman. Doctor Dan told me her name was Lizzie Borrow. She was the daughter of one of the Governor's officials, and was travelling out to be reunited with her father. Casewell must have felt confident in the security of his ship to carry such a passenger. Clearly, Joseph Swales' dire predictions for the voyage were proving to be wrong.

Most of the time Lizzie remained in her quarters close

to the Captain's cabin, but occasionally she would take the air on deck. Richard noticed her too and was smitten. She was sixteen, only slightly older than him. He often tried to catch her eye, in the hope of winning a smile.

We could not have hoped for a better cell mate in Doctor Daniel and I swiftly began to think of him as a friend. He told us he had been a ship's surgeon aboard the frigate HMS *Esmeralda*. There had been a rebellion among the crew, occasioned by the behaviour of a brutal officer. The Doctor had mediated between crew and captain. He had argued so fiercely in favour of the crew, the captain had him court-martialled. Doctor Daniel was duly sentenced to transportation for seven years. He seemed to take his fate remarkably lightly. 'Probably short of medical men down in New South Wales,' he said with a bitter laugh. Captain Casewell had taken a shine to him as soon as he came on board, which was why he had been given a small cabin with us boys for company. He was asked to assist the bumbling ship's surgeon Nicholas Privett. In return he was provided with extra food.

Dan and Privett would often clash over what to do with a patient, and he enjoyed telling us about it. 'Privett just believes in bleeding,' he said. 'Anything wrong that can't be remedied by opening a vein and extracting a pint of blood, and he's stuck for an answer. George Randall has an ulcer on his leg from an ill-fitting iron that was left on too long. When I suggested powdered Peruvian bark and citric acid, Privett looked at me as if I were reciting a spell. "Do we need some bat's blood and snake skin too, Doctor Sadler?" he said. He can't bear the fact that one of the convicts knows more about medicine than him.

'Bloody fool even wanted to bleed an eight-month-old baby. Sergeant Tomlins' little girl has awful colic. Been with her since she cut her first tooth. She needs mercury and chalk with a little powdered rhubarb root. Privett has got all this stuff in his medicine cabinet, I think he's just forgotten how to use it. He let that poor little girl suffer for another week with his thrice-weekly bleeding, until she was at death's door. Then he asked me to make up the medicine I'd suggested. The child is getting better, but she still looks sickly.'

As soon as we had won his trust, Doctor Dan told Captain Casewell that he had two skilled seamen among his cargo of villains. We were put to work caulking the deck and repairing sails and rigging. We were given extra rations as our reward, and we shared our good fortune with Johnny Onions.

Despite our kindness, Johnny proved to be a surly, difficult cell mate. He would mimic our accents and manners, and even steal food from our plates. He often just stared at us with baleful hostility. He couldn't help himself. 'He wasn't like this on the *St Louis*,' I said to Daniel. 'Vincent was such a terrifying-looking fellow, I suppose he was too frightened to misbehave. I think he thinks we're soft.'

We tried to show him how to read and write, but he had no patience with us. I didn't know if he was dull or just not interested, but he never remembered a thing we taught him.

Doctor Daniel saw him as a project – a boy to be reformed. 'I've never met a more abandoned wretch in my life. When I was younger I just accepted that corporal punishment was the only way to impart a sense of common decency in such people. But now I know from first-hand experience this merely makes them worse. Punishing a man or boy with a thumbscrew or clapping him in iron fetters for a month isn't going to make him want to sip tea with a dainty little finger, or talk to the vicar about the flower arrangement in the nave. He'll still swear worse than a Billingsgate fishmonger and his soul will be even more corrupted.'

Being at sea was second nature to Richard and me, but for most of our fellow convicts it was a bewildering experience. Many of them had never been away from their town or village before they fell foul of the law. They were astonished by the sights they saw. The vast, circling albatross that sometimes shadowed our ship frightened them. I heard several say that these were birds who attacked a drowning man, pecking at his head with their vicious beaks as he struggled to stay above the surface.

The men would gather in the forecastle, when our routine permitted, to gawp at the porpoises that darted to and fro in the turbulence of our bow. Flying fish leaping from the waves amazed them, and dolphins they often took for mermaids or mermen.

The weather got warmer as we headed south. Having spent some of December the previous year around Gibraltar this was no great surprise. The further south we sailed, the more muggy and sticky it became.

There was only one stop on our journey, the island of Tenerife, where we picked up fresh water. We were all shackled again and confined below deck for the two days we spent moored at harbourside. Casewell was determined no one was going to escape.

As we journeyed south, we got to know the other convicts. Men separated from wives and children were especially devastated by their fate. They had as much chance of seeing their loved ones again as if they were dead and buried. But many of the younger men, especially those with no families of their own, were excited. Stories had filtered back to England making New South Wales sound just the place to make a fresh start. True, there were unsettling elements to these stories: the strange, savage inhabitants; the unforgiving nature of the land, which was covered in thick bush; the fiery heat of the day; the brutal iron gangs for the second offenders, chained together for years at a time. But if a man kept himself out of trouble, it seemed life promised to be quite bearable.

Much to my relief, the fearful atmosphere of the hulks was lacking aboard the *Euphrates*. Because of the marines and the fact that the men were under constant guard both night and day, the worst of them could not form into gangs to terrorise their weaker fellows. Ill-discipline was dealt with abruptly by Captain Casewell. Men who were insolent or violent were flogged without hesitation. Soon after Tenerite, the convoy halted to witness a public execution aboard the Navy escort HMS *Adelphi*. These escorts carried a small cargo of convicts and three of them had been stirring up mutiny. We were all herded on deck to witness the spectacle. Seeing these hooded figures kicking their legs in their death throes as they swung from the yardarm had a suitably aweing effect on the assembled prisoners. It was an ugly reminder of the fate we had so narrowly missed and I turned away as I couldn't bear to watch.

Occasionally a ship would be sighted on the horizon, but none came close enough to threaten us. No doubt our Navy escort kept them away. I had heard that some pirate ships off the North African coast hunted for slaves to man their galleys. The life of a galley slave, chained to an oar and worked to death, filled my sleep with nightmares until I knew in my bones we were far south enough to be well out of their clutches.

During the long nights locked in the cells, gambling mania gripped the convicts. We would hear the arguments and wails of despair from other cells as men lost their shirts or rations. They would bet anything they had. One man even lost his wedding ring.

Richard and I would have been tempted, if we had been in more disreputable company. We could see the attraction in this illicit activity. But Dan would not hear of it. We still got dragged into the craze, though. Little things in our cabin started to go missing. A quill Doctor Dan used to write his journal, my belt, the laces on Richard's shoes. There could only be one culprit, Johnny Onions. Dan sat him down and gave him a stern talking to. He confessed. Johnny had been trading these bits and bobs with the more determined gamblers in return for extra food. Even though he promised to stop I never trusted him again. If he had stolen my mother's ring, I would have cheerfully strangled him.

'We could have had far worse,' said Richard, looking over the forecastle to two lads the same age as us named Eddie Clark and Ben Sommers. London boys they were, and pickpockets. They strutted around like Cockney lords. Quick to take offence and quick to throw their weight around, they looked down on the mere thieves among them.

'Any fool can steal a waistcoat from a shop or a pound of cheese from a market stall,' scoffed Ben. 'It takes years of practice to pick a pocket.'

'Didn't do you any good in the end though, did it?' said Richard.

As the voyage wore on, the Captain frequently invited Doctor Daniel to dine with him. Dan was impressed with Casewell's good judgement.

'He can't abide Privett, and no wonder, the man's a bloody idiot. And the Lieutenant, Holkham, is a thug despite his fancy manners. He came straight from a slave trader, so that tells you exactly what manner of man he is. But the Captain's determined to keep the ship clean and his 'cargo' healthy. He wants to keep us all well exercised, despite the protests of the Lieutenant. If he had his way, we'd all be marched round the deck twice a day, and double-ironed for the whole voyage.'

I hoped the Captain stayed well. If he died, then Holkham would take command. We were a heartbeat away from reliving Swales' previous journey to Australia. As things stood, some days aboard the *Euphrates* were surprisingly pleasant. When the sun shone and the sea was calm we would gather on the weather deck and pass the time with charades or mock trials. Sometimes we would fish with hook and line. I was always thrilled when the line grew tight in my hand. Everyone cheered when one of us managed to reel in a catch.

Sitting on the deck in the sunshine it was easy to forget I was on my way to exile on the far side of the world. Still, the voyage was not without its troubles. As we sailed on, the ship began to show its age. Water seeped steadily through the strakes and we were constantly employed in caulking the planking. The hold was frequently awash with water after stormy weather, and a rota was set up for the convicts to man the pumps. Most of the men seemed to relish the idea of doing hard exercise. 'You need to be fit and strong where we're going,' Joseph Swales told us.

Despite our attempts to keep the ship clean it still stank, and after a spell of bad weather the smell of vomit seemed to permeate its very fibre. This problem became worse when the *Euphrates* entered the tropical latitudes and we were becalmed north of the Equator. Rats and insects thrived in the enervating heat and even Privett became concerned that some outbreak of contagious disease was inevitable. Windsails were rigged to direct air below decks, and gunpowder mixed with oil of tar and lime was exploded to sweeten the air.

After those dull, listless days sailing across the Equator, we began to pick up fresher winds as we reached the Southern Ocean. These waters were unknown to me and Swales told us to expect the worst. When the storms came, the *Euphrates* was dwarfed by massive green waves. I had never felt so small and insignificant a speck on the surface of our planet. During a storm even the most villainous of our fellows would get down on his knees and pray for God to deliver him.

The weeks went by. The sails billowed, the rigging creaked and the bow ploughed through the waves, but we seemed forever in the same place sailing towards the same unchanging horizon. It was as if the world was turning too fast for us to catch up with it.

I became desperately bored. In the Navy I had got used to living a life where every day could be my last, and on the hulk I had to be constantly wary of dangerous men. Casewell's ship was so well managed death had become an outside possibility rather than a daily threat. There were few books aboard to while away the hours. Instead, the ship was well supplied with religious tracts such as *Two Hundred Exercises Against Lying*, *Dissuasions from Stealing* and *Caution to Swearers*. I avidly read *Exhortation to Chastity* and discovered that it was not just men who were tempted by the sins of the flesh.

As we sailed through the Southern Ocean several of

us decided to fill our time by putting on a play. After a fortnight's rehearsals we performed *The Beggar's Opera*, with screeching accompaniment from the ship's makeshift band. Richard and I took the parts of Betty Doxy and Polly Peachum.

At the end of the play Lizzie Borrow came up to us and said, 'Well done boys, a most convincing performance,' before she was hurriedly escorted away. The Captain, it appeared, was not so impressed. Dan later told us Casewell had thought the tale of the highwayman Macheath and his escape from the gallows was too subversive, and had decided at once that there would be no more plays.

Lizzie's compliments left us feeling as high as kites. And after that our interest in her blossomed. We would watch her walking the deck when we were up in the yards or working on the bowsprit. Several times up in the rigging we both avoided certain death by a hairsbreadth, because we were not paying proper attention to our work. She walked alone, or with her maid or one of the ship's officers. Sometimes she looked earnest when she talked, other times she giggled and seemed playful. I longed to talk with her and discover what she was really like.

She was a tall girl, as tall as Richard at least, and had a mane of thick curly hair. Her face was a source of constant wonder. She had quite a prominent nose. Not trim and petite, but strong. Strong but well shaped. Great big eyes and a sulky, pouting mouth. 'She not sulky, she's just bored,' said Richard who would not hear a thing said against her. 'She just needs the company of a young man her own age, like me!' One time, when Richard and I were in the forecastle, she walked away from us along the deck with the sun behind her. We could see right through her thin cotton dress. Neither of us breathed or blinked until she disappeared down the companionway back to her quarters.

The voyage dragged on. Captain Casewell made great attempts to keep up the morale of his crew and cargo. Classes were held in reading and writing, and Richard and I helped our fellow convicts write letters home. Doctor Dan gave interesting talks on the behaviour of animals, Richard told us all about life in Boston. He talked perfectly well until he noticed Lizzie had joined the audience right at the back, with Captain Casewell. Then he began to stumble, and there were long pauses between his sentences. He would have dried up altogether had not Doctor Dan and I kept asking him questions to keep him going.

Daily inspections were introduced to keep the ship as clean as possible, and in the long summer evenings prisoners were allowed to stay on deck till ten o'clock at night. There was singing and even dancing, and some of the convicts were so wild I wondered fearfully what they would be like when they had a drink inside them. It was extraordinary how the character of a captain could affect the whole ship. Casewell believed in reward rather than punishment, and the better the convicts behaved, the more freedom they were given. The worst of them had realised their best hope of survival lay in keeping out of mischief. In the last two months of the voyage only two men were flogged, and then given the minimum punishment of twelve lashes.

Almost no voyage of this length passes without fatalities. The wife of one of the marines died in childbirth together with her baby. The whole crew was badly affected for a week after. The poor husband was left with two young boys to raise alone. Three of the convicts died of a wasting disease, and one of the crew fell from the rigging. But no contagious diseases swept our ranks. Luck was with us on this ship and I began to fear the moment when we would make landfall in the strange new world that was our destination.

CHAPTER 8

The Far Distant Land

After what seemed an endless journey through the Southern Ocean, we sighted land at last in early November. For weeks we sailed close to the shore around the southern coast and I started to gain some understanding of exactly how big this country was. Staring out at the dense green land we could see nothing but forest or bush. There was sometimes smoke from bush fires, but no sign of life. I thought at least we would see small villages along the coast, or perhaps a party of natives would row out to throw spears or sell us food. But nothing of this sort happened.

It was early December when we rounded the most easterly point of the land, and our little fleet turned north. Christmas was three weeks away but it was hotter than any August day I had ever known. The brilliant sunshine and endless, uninhabited green coast unsettled me. On a globe I knew that New South Wales was down there at the bottom. Summer and winter were the wrong way round here and the stars back to front in the sky. This was a world turned upside down.

We were sorting oakum on deck during a hot afternoon when a lookout called, 'Smoke ahoy!' We rushed to the forecastle. There in the distance were several thin trails of smoke rising into the still summer air. These were from chimneys or small open fires, rather than smoke from blazing bush. Then our lookout spotted the sails of a ship heading towards us.

By early evening the ship had met with us, and sent out a boat with several marines and officials. At once all prisoners were sent below deck and we listened intently to hear what was going on.

'Are any of your crew or prisoners suffering from contagious disease?' shouted an unfamiliar voice.

'No sir, they are not,' replied the Captain confidently.

I realised our voyage was almost over. All at once I was both fearful and excited. Feelings I had kept hidden during the journey began to well up. Who would we meet in this new world? What would it feel like to live here? Would there be good people among the bad? After so long aboard the *Euphrates* it would be wonderful to walk on dry land and eat fresh food. But I felt resentment too, being so far from home. Richard felt exactly the same way.

'This could be a great adventure, Sam, or it could be a terrible nightmare.'

The ship that came to meet us left a pilot on board who was to guide us into Sydney. Although most of the prisoners were confined to their cells, Richard and I were called upon to help sail the ship into the harbour. It was a beautiful evening and we arrived just as the sun was setting.

For months we had seen nothing but the sea or silent coast. But for our own little convoy and the occasional passing vessel we could have believed we were the last people left on earth. Now, for the first time on this immense continent, I saw evidence of a human hand on the landscape. Standing next to each other, high in the sails, Richard and I had a splendid view of the settlement. As we turned into a substantial inlet, a tall clock tower and the roofs of some buildings on higher ground could be seen. Then, the spindly sails of a couple of windmills, followed by the whole spread of the town, which was small but densely packed along the shoreline of a bay. Having noted how thickly the forest grew along the coast, I was awed to see how much had been cleared to make this settlement. In front of us were carefully laid out streets and houses, and grand government buildings. On the western side of the inlet were more humble abodes, all higgledy-piggledy on the rocks. Here, at the furthest reach, a coal-fire beacon flickered in the sea breeze, and a battery of long guns pointed menacingly out over the harbour entrance.

On the other side of the bay I noticed scores of little lights floating on the water. This looked magical. Next to us in the rigging was a leathery sea dog called Isaac who had been here several times already. A telescope hung at his waist and I borrowed it to peer through the gloom. There were several small canoes, and the lights seemed to be fires burning in the centre of each vessel. Aboard, two to a boat, were lithe black men – one piloting with some skill, the other casting a line into the water. Isaac took a look too. He told me the men cooked the fish right there in their canoes.

'Clever buggers,' he said with some admiration. 'They make those canoes from tree bark and place a slab of mud down in the middle and build a fire on it. It's not easy lighting and keeping a fire on a small boat. And look at him, standing up to do his fishing. It's a wonder the boat don't capsize.'

We watched in silence then Isaac spoke again. 'There's been trouble with them natives ever since we first got here. Some say they're no better than vermin, and shoot them if they can. Some of the natives kill any of our men they catch alone. I'd keep well away from them.'

He seemed torn in his reaction to these dark-skinned men. 'I've been all over the world on my travels,' he told us. 'Everywhere I've been – from Zanzibar to Timor to Bombay – the natives have made the land their own. They've built cities and farmed the soil, and have nabobs or shahs or sultans to rule them. They speak a common tongue and have a common God. They have armies and laws and rules. But not the natives here, boys. They talk all right, in a funny grunty language, but this lot here will speak a different tongue from another lot just a day's walk away. They don't seem to like each other much either. Most of the time they laze around, doing nothing all day. But now and then they get angry about something and start attacking another bunch.'

We were both fascinated and begged him to tell us more.

His brow furrowed. 'What else can I tell you? They live on the land like animals, grazing on fruit and berries, hunting or fishing when they need flesh in their bellies. They have no buildings. When they need shelter they take bark from the trees and make a little haven. No one can tell what manner of god they worship. Just when you begin to wonder if they're some kind of cunning, hairless monkey they'll take out a spear and hurl it with a sling, fast and true, and with a reach much greater than any of us could throw. And they have these curved wooden throwing sticks which they use to bring down birds and land animals. The thing spins in the air, and if it misses it spins back to the man who threw it. I never seen a monkey do that.'

His ruminations were interrupted by the ship's master, calling on us to shorten our sails. The ship anchored. Our work done, Richard and I were escorted back to our cell to await the morning. I drifted off to sleep full of curiosity for this strange new land.

We woke in sharp sunlight to the cries of unfamiliar voices.

'Who has come?'

'Who brings letters?'

'Who hails from Somerset?'

The names of any one of twenty other towns or counties were called out. The *Euphrates* was surrounded by little boats, each with two or three occupants. After six months passed among the same faces it was strange to see so many new ones. Casewell leaned over the side of the ship, accompanied by marines.

'Be off with you all, before I order my men to open fire.'

Bright and early the *Euphrates* was boarded by a Naval officer and surgeon. They marched past our cell, inspecting the ship and its passengers for any sign of disease. Much to my surprise, it was announced that the Governor of the colony, His Excellency Philip Gidley King, was to come aboard.

A tall, noble-looking man, with the hint of a Cornish accent, he talked to us with genuine concern. He was obviously a decent fellow, if a little worn down with the cares of the world. He seemed interested to know if our journey had been a good one, and whether any of us prisoners had any complaint against the men and officers of the ship.

As we prepared to go ashore, Captain Casewell came over to Richard and me. He quietly gave us each a small bag of coins. 'I couldn't let your efforts go without reward boys,' he said. 'It's not much, but it'll start you off.' We had some money, of course, carefully hoarded throughout the voyage, but this was a welcome addition.

We were taken by boat to a supply ship over the bay. As we left the *Euphrates* I noticed goods from England piled up on the deck ready for unloading. There were boxes of nails, perhaps hundreds of thousands of them, axes piled in bundles, women's petticoats, leather shoes and even a printing press. We were importing our civilisation to this untamed land, lock, stock and barrel.

Once aboard the supply ship we washed ourselves and were given new clothes. Then we were taken to the shore. Milling around on the quayside was a large crowd of men, women and children curious to see who would be joining them. I expected to see a collection of sickly, ragged scarecrows, but I was wrong. They were a brown and weather-beaten lot for landlubbers, but they seemed to be in good health and looked well fed. Their clothes were no better or worse than those you would see in any English town.

As we grew nearer, the cries began again.

'Who is from London?'

'Who is from Lancaster?'

'Does any man have news of William Sharrock?'

Most often of all: 'Who has letters?'

This was what exile did. Left you desperate for news of home. Now, all of a sudden, I felt desolate and very far from Norfolk.

Our boat pulled up to the quay and we were hustled ashore, placing our feet on dry land for the first time in maybe seven months. It was a peculiar experience, especially for those among us who had never been to sea before. Some of them staggered around as if drunk, and could not stop themselves swaying. Some were so befuddled by the change they began to vomit.

As we assembled on the quay, a strange ritual was being enacted on the other side of the harbour, where women from one of the other convict ships were disembarking. They were lined up along the waterside, and hundreds of men flocked to see them. The bolder among them would approach a girl and then drop a handkerchief at her feet. If she picked it up, he would take her off with him.

'That's what passes for courtship round here,' said Joseph Swales, who had come to the quay with Daniel, Richard and I. 'The finest women have already been picked up by the officers and officials on board. They'll have taken them as housekeepers and nurses for their children, but it's always the prettiest that get chosen rather than the sturdiest and soberest. Then six months later, half of them are with child and get cast out into the street to fend for themselves.'

If it was true, then Sydney was a place where those who held power could be just as wicked as the villains they were charged to mind.

Those of us from the *Euphrates* were marched up a small hill. We assembled in a courtyard in front of the Governor's office and were surrounded by ranks of marines. Away from the cooling breeze of the bay the sun burned fiercely on our heads. Governor King appeared with another official who proceeded to give us a well-rehearsed sermon.

'Many of you here will be feeling a deep sense of melancholy as you contemplate your exile from family and friends in your homeland. But, although it may not seem like it at the moment, your first day here in the colony is the start of a considerable opportunity. Sydney is not a prison, it is a town. You may come and go within its boundaries, conditional upon your duties, and with some degree of freedom. Instead of walls and bars you have the forest and ocean to keep you here. Sharks patrol the seas around you and any man foolish enough to venture into the bush that surrounds our enclave will soon die of thirst and hunger. The natives are out there waiting with their spears to kill and eat you.'

I heard Swales snort to himself. 'Now that's a pretty tale,' he said quietly. 'I never heard of no native eatin' one of us.'

I strained to hear the rest of the speech. 'Any man who can call himself a craftsman or has skills that constitute a trade may step forward now and declare himself.'

This was the moment we had been waiting for. Captain Casewell had spoken of it to Doctor Dan, and we were well prepared for what would happen next. Dan, Richard and I stood forward. So did several other men from the *Euphrates* who had been carpenters, blacksmiths, wainwrights and the like. We were ushered into a side room in the barracks by the house.

As we walked away I heard the speaker continue, 'Some of you here will be assigned to work on the farms of officers, government officials and free settlers. They will provide you with shelter and sustenance. Some of you will also work for your new masters as servants.'

I felt a surge of pity for the men we were leaving behind. Swales had told me how some masters were kind but most were heartless, treating their men and women as little better than slaves. He knew of one fellow from his time before here, who served out his seven-year sentence on a farm. The man was from Somerset and well used to agricultural work, unlike many of the other convicts, most of whom were townies from London or Lancashire. As this man's sentence came to an end he was told he would be given his own plot of land to farm. The master didn't want to lose this man so he accused him of theft, almost on his last day. He was flogged and sentenced to a further seven years' labour on the farm. The story took an even darker turn when the man murdered his master and went on the run. By the time they caught him he had killed two of his pursuers.

'Hung he was,' said Swales, 'on the edge of town, overlooking the fields he should have been farming for himself. You keep out of any assignments with farmers, boys. They'll feed you gruel and work you to death.'

My thoughts were interrupted by a marine calling me into a small room with a desk on which was placed a large leather-bound ledger. Behind it sat a slight, bespectacled young man two or three years older than me. He had about him a raffish air and seemed faintly amused by the whole proceedings. His hands were so soft he had obviously never done a day's hard work in his life. We were left alone. He nodded at me to sit and gave a friendly smile.

'So, my friend, what's your line of business?'

I recognised that accent at once. Ordinarily, I would not be so forward with officials but this fellow invited an easy intimacy. 'You're from Norwich, aren't you,' I said with a grin.

'I certainly am, sir,' he laughed. 'James Lyons at your service. And whereabouts in Norfolk might you be from?'

I was taken aback. I had expected a stern officer accompanied by an even sterner marine, ready to enter me into a muster book with scant ceremony. Certainly not this good-natured fellow.

We went through the usual questions, date and place of birth, previous occupation. James was most interested in the fact that I could read and write.

'Now I need to ask you the date of your trial, the nature of your offence and the length of your sentence.'

I told him. 'April of this year. Cowardice. Death commuted to a life sentence of transportation.' I thought to myself, 'What a story.'

Rather than writing this all down, James pulled his seat forward and leaned closer. 'Did you know the *Euphrates* arrived with no record of the crimes and sentences of its convicts?'

I was astounded. Then I felt despair sweep over me

for giving so much away.

James could tell what I was thinking. 'Let's ask these questions again, shall we? But before we proceed, I have to tell you there'll be an administrative fee for the processing of the records.' He was still smiling, but his manner had turned more weaselly. Perhaps he was not quite as nice as I had thought.

'Er . . . What sort of fee would we be looking at?' I said, searching his face for any clue.

His mouth turned down, revealing his teeth as he sucked in air sharply. 'Hmmm. From life to seven years. Can't do you any less than that, but you'll have prospects when you're done. Especially as you've a trade in your sailing skills, and you can read and write. What's that worth, Sam?'

I resented his familiar manner, but he was offering me an extraordinary opportunity. My mind raced with fear and excitement. Could I trust him? What if I said the wrong thing and he changed his mind about helping me? What if he was found out? But then, when would I have another opportunity like this? I reached for my mother's ring on the ribbon around my neck and placed it on the table.

'Oh, no,' he said in an oddly patient way, and shook his head. 'That's quite inappropriate.'

I began to panic. Was it not enough? It was the most valuable thing I owned.

'I'm just looking for a few shillings, you dolt. You could almost buy a house for that round here.'

I couldn't believe my luck. This James wasn't so bad after all.

I took the ten shillings Captain Casewell had given me and placed that down on the table. James counted out seven coins and gave me back three.

'You can buy me a beer with some of that down at the Sailor's Arms. I'm sure to see you in there one night soon enough. It's down by the Rocks. That's where all of us government men live.'

'Government men?' I was puzzled.

'No one likes to be called a convict round here, Sam,' he said. 'Best learn that right from the start.'

I was taken aback. 'You're a convict?' I had expected the clerks to be marines or officials of some sort.

'Government man. I am, yes. Now let's see,' he began to write in the record book. 'Seven years, for – What d'you fancy? Banditry? Coining? Treasonable conduct? Being overfamiliar with a sheep?' I looked horrified. He laughed. 'Had all that lot in from one of the other boats just now. They came with their records, more's the pity for them.' After a brief pause he said, 'Let's go for theft. Most of them are here for theft, so that won't stand out as anything unusual. Now, your next stop is the Navy office. They're particularly keen to see fellows like you.' He gave me directions and our meeting was over.

Richard joined me out in the sunshine. I could hardly keep the grin from my face. He seemed in good spirits too. As soon as we could talk I told him what had happened.

'Me too, me too!' he laughed, no longer needing to conceal his delight. 'Thank heavens. I couldn't have borne it if they'd not done this for you too.'

I told him about James Lyons. 'Mine was called Randall,' said Richard. 'Older man than yours. Big stout fellow. Obviously keen on his spirits.'

'How much did you have to give him?'

Richard paused. 'He took a guinea. I told him it was all I had. The fool!'

He wasn't so pleased when I told him James had only taken seven shillings from me. But he soon cheered up.

'I think I'm going to like this place,' he said as we neared the Navy office.

CHAPTER 9

On the Rocks

Richard and I were greeted warmly in the Navy office, and immediately set to work repairing and maintaining the colony's vessels.

'You won't be doing any sailing, boys,' said an officer tartly. 'We don't want you sailing off over the horizon on your own.'

As convicts, we were expected to work from daylight until three o'clock in the afternoon, Monday to Friday. Six hours on a Saturday. Sunday off. In return we were given a ration of food, clothes and paid a small sum of money. After our day's work we could make more money hiring ourselves out to free settler and emancipists, as the ex-convicts were called.

With our wages we were to find lodgings. Before we were separated, Doctor Daniel suggested we three find a place together.

'What's happened to Johnny Onions?' I asked, when we met up later that afternoon.

'Saw him being marched off by a parson and his wife,' said Dan. 'Let's hope they have better luck with him than we did.'

I felt relieved of a burden. I didn't like Johnny, but would not have wanted to abandon him here. I hoped the parson was a good man and that he would not beat the boy too severely when his household goods started to go missing.

We went down to the Rocks, a ramshackle part of town facing over the bay, and made enquiries in the Sailor's Arms. The landlady introduced us to one of her customers who swiftly agreed to rent us a two-room house with a small garden close to the hospital where Dan was to work. It was a humble dwelling, with a thatched roof and walls of hardened clay. But it would be enough to keep the weather out and provide us with more space and privacy than we ever had on a Navy ship. Doctor Daniel had one room, Richard and I the other. Up the road from us was a windmill. That night the sound of its flapping sails reminded me of life aboard a ship.

The paths in this part of town were too narrow for a horse and cart, and the buildings stood among dead and dying tree stumps, hastily cleared when the Rocks were first settled. The houses snaked along rock ledges and into any nook or cranny where there was a flat surface large enough to place down posts and build walls and a roof.

Along with the pub there was a bakery and other shops. There was also a ramshackle prison, recently built on the same spot as a prison which had been burned to the ground. Some of the locals had turned their own houses into little shops or drinking dens. Close to the bay were market stalls selling fruit and vegetables. The Rocks was full of people trying to make a living, honest or otherwise.

Further down from the Rocks at the southern end of the bay were government stores and houses. Here flags fluttered over barracks, a school and a church. A small shipyard nestled at the water's edge, the skeleton of a hull propped up on the slipway, waiting for its strakes to be hammered in. Here too were the grander houses and gardens of senior officers and government officials. The Governor's house sat at the top of a hill, looking down on the town. Further to the south, towards the outskirts of Sydney, were neatly laid out houses for soldiers with families.

It took twenty minutes to walk from the northern tip

of the Rocks to the edge of town, where there were farms and fields of cultivated land. Thick green forest lurked beyond. Here also was a road leading to Parramatta, another settlement further west.

We may have been free to walk around but the threat of retribution hung heavy in the air. Floggings were frequent and our overseers were the marines and an army division called the New South Wales Corps. By the side of the Parramatta road were two sets of gallows, often with bodies left to twist in the wind. Further away from town, I heard, fear of rebellion led masters to punish the convicts who worked for them more harshly. Any answering back or neglect of duty would result in twenty-five or fifty lashes with the cat. The cats here were crueller instruments than those used in the Navy. 'Six foot long with nine knots in each tail,' one convict told us. 'Each one tipped with wax. Horrible things. You can hear a man being whipped half a mile away. Stand nearby on a windy day and flesh and blood'll fly in your face.'

But along with the daily threat of punishment, there was also some hope for a better life. Those who behaved well, and showed themselves to be reformed, could prosper. All our fellow residents on the Rocks were convicts or ex-convicts, and many of them owned the house they had built there and the little patch of land that went with it.

'It's a funny business here, isn't it?' mused Richard, after we'd been in our new home a couple of days. 'We could just choose a patch here and put up a hut. No one to buy land off. We'd just build and have it. Imagine that – from condemned men to men of property in less than a year. Not quite the punishment the Navy had in mind.'

Being able to build your own hut was not all Sydney had to offer. We heard stories of men on the earliest fleets who had come over as convicts and now had their own thriving farms.

On our first Sunday off Richard and I set off to explore our new domain. Close to the western edge of town we spied the most extraordinary creature I had ever seen bounding through the fields. It had a face quite like a dog, but with large, pointed ears. Its trunk had two short limbs, like arms, and it stood upright on two huge and powerful hind legs. These it used with fantastic effect to bounce, rather than run, at great speed. As it leaped forward it used its long thick tail as a kind of balance to the upper part of its body.

'Look, it's got a head half way down its body,' I shouted. It did too. A smaller head poked out of its belly.

'What on earth is it?' said Richard. It was easily the same height as the two of us, although its small mouth suggested it would not be dangerous to man. It saw us and backed away, so we moved under cover to watch it some more.

'It's just had a baby!' yelled Richard. Sure enough, as we watched, a miniature version of the creature tumbled out of its mother's stomach and bounded around.

'That doesn't look like any new-born I've ever seen,' I said.

We watched with open-mouthed fascination. As the infant bounced around, the mother lay flat on the ground, resting her head on one of her front paws. Shortly after, a stray dog from the town approached and began to threaten the baby. At once it bounced back to its mother and got back in the same way it had come out.

The mother turned aggressively towards the dog and advanced. The mutt growled angrily and would not back down. As it crouched to leap forward, the mother spun its heavy tail round and delivered an almighty blow to the dog, which fell at once to the ground. The creature bound off, and it was several minutes before the dog regained strength enough to limp away.

'That, my dear boys, is a kangaroo,' said Doctor Dan, when we told him about it. 'What you saw coming out of it was a kangaroo cub. She carries it around in a sort of pouch. It's not new born at all. Might have been six months old. Aren't they marvellous?'

These wonders did not cease. The skies and trees were filled with birds of amazingly bright plumage. These, as a sort, were called parrots, and individually, according to Doctor Dan, there were lories, cockatoos and parakeets. Despite their beauty, the cockatoos were particularly hated by the farmers, because they would descend as a flock on a ripe crop of wheat and destroy it.

These were far from being the strangest birds on the territory. One, called an emu, was comical in appearance. Lacking the grace of the other creatures we had seen, it had a huge body of shaggy, dirty feathers shaped like a mound of earth, and long skinny legs. Its head protruded from a scrawny neck and was covered in bright blue feathers. Its wings were tiny and seemed of no use. It made up for its flightless state by running at great speed. Richard had heard the meat tasted like beef.

Some of the new animals looked as lovable as kittens or puppies. There was one kind of bear-like creature called a koala. It was no bigger than a small dog, though much rounder and grey in colour. These animals squatted silently in trees with their babies on their backs.

Not all the animals around here were so appealing. Our sleep was often interrupted by the cries of birds or other tree dwellers. Some, called possums, kept us awake with their strange laughter, which sounded like a consumptive old man clearing his throat. They seemed to be calling to each other, for when one started, another would reply from some distance away.

Insects plagued us. Flies descended every time we

brought out food to eat. Every night we would search our hut to drive out mosquitoes before we could settle down to sleep. Almost always we missed one, and I would wake to hear the detestable creature buzzing near my ear.

The hours we had been given to work seemed long, but we soon discovered we were rarely expected to keep to them. We'd be given daily tasks – decks to be caulked, sails repaired, rigging tarred. If we worked hard, we could be finished by late morning. We usually ended up having our dinner in the Sailor's Arms. James Lyons was often there and after we'd bought each other several drinks I couldn't help but ask him, 'Why did you only take seven shillings from me? I would have given you that ring.'

'I know, but you would have soon found out how much less other men paid and then you would have been my enemy for life. It's a small place is Sydney. You're shorter than me now, but you won't be forever. I'm a scribe Sam, and not much of a fighter. It doesn't do to tussle with fellows who spend their life hauling up sails or anchors, or heaving timber. Most of us government clerks have never lifted anything heavier than a goose-feather quill. We have an easy life, so why ruin it by making enemies? Besides, thieves' honour and all that. We're all in the same boat.'

James had a logic about him that intrigued me. He had a sharp mind and was forever on the lookout for some way to fleece his masters. But he was clever enough to know how far he should go. It was a lesson he had learned the hard way.

'I was apprenticed as a clerk to my uncle, who was a lawyer in Norwich. We used to siphon off a few guineas from old ladies who leave their estates to the church. One day we got greedy. My uncle danced on the end of a rope. I was sent here. Silly, weren't we?' He looked wistful. 'Still, it's an easy life. Just keep your nose clean, keep your tongue still when you're shouted at by soldiers or government officers, and for heaven's sake don't hit one of them. Do that and you'll find yourself lashed on the triangle then packed off to the country to work in an iron gang.'

I didn't know what he meant.

'They clap you in irons, eight men all linked together. Then you spend your days clearing bush or chopping down trees. Everyone off the boats gets a chance to prove they're decent sorts, but if you do something that upsets them, then the authorities come down on you like a ton of hot bricks.

'You and your pal Richard are bright boys,' he went on. 'You could get a job with the clerks if you asked. It's an easy life and we're always short of them that can read and write.'

I said I'd think about it. But I liked my work in the Navy office and I felt uneasy with the little fiddles of the clerks. They were likeable rogues, but I wanted to do an honest job.

We went to the Sailor's Arms almost every day to meet with James and soon got to know his friends there. They were not the sort of people my father would have approved of. James liked his company rough, and would often buy drinks for the most dangerous-looking men in the pub.

'Pays to be on the right side of the worst ones,' he whispered.

One night we got to talking with some of them about Captain Bligh and the *Bounty* mutiny. They thought the crew should have killed Bligh rather than set him adrift in an open boat. 'That Fletcher Christian was a bleedin' nancy,' said Edward Bean, who was one of my close neighbours. 'If they'd slit the throats of all the men that didn't side with 'em, they'd have stood a better chance of getting away with it.'

Bean was a frightening fellow at the best of times. I was amazed at his ability to hold such hatred for someone he had never met. 'That bastard Bligh, I know his type. If he ever comes my way, I'll run him through soon as look at him.'

Among James's friends were several girls around his age and I was particularly fascinated by one called

Orlagh Killett. Orlagh I immediately assumed to be Irish, so I was surprised to hear her speak with a Liverpudlian accent. Her parents had come over from Ireland before she was born, she explained. She was a skinny, striking girl with a mane of glorious red hair, and had two children by a man who had left her for another girl when the second child was three days old. Orlagh's mother-in-law would sometimes turn up at the pub, demanding she return home to mind the children. The mother-in-law was a terrifying-looking woman, painfully thin, with straggly grey hair. The skin on her face was mottled and sallow but tight too, so it looked like a skeletal mask with darting, angry eyes. She and Orlagh quarrelled incessantly and would often start shouting abuse as soon as they saw each other.

Orlagh was utterly beyond what I had been brought up to believe was 'respectable', but I liked her. She told a good story. The first day we had a drink together she recounted the tale of her two neighbours, the Cluttons.

'Met each other over here soon as they came off the transport ship. Anyway the old man got ill, and one of the missionaries here lent him some money for food and the like. Any road, he called in to ask the Cluttons for his money back. So old man Clutton attacks him with a knife. Then his missus smashes him on the head with an axe. That's nice, isn't it. Blood all over the place. Anyway, they wait until it's dark and drag him out to dump the body in some bushes. Did a rotten job. Next morning some woman's walking by and sees this foot sticking out. She screams and then there's people all over the place. Soon after that, the Magistrate arrives with a squad of marines. Stupid thing was, there was a trail of blood leading from the bushes straight to the house. The Cluttons started arguing and screaming at each other, each blaming the other for the murder. They made it up by the time they got sent to the gallows. Hung 'em side by side, and they were holding hands. I like a nice ending to a story.'

We were all roaring drunk when we heard the tale and thought it hysterically funny. But when I recounted it to Doctor Dan the next day he looked quite blank. 'What a terrible story. You boys ought to watch who you're mixing with. You don't want to get yourself into any more trouble.'

But I found myself constantly drawn to Orlagh. She was afraid of nothing and swore like a trooper. She was funny and slow to judge anyone. When I drunkenly admitted in the pub that we had originally been sent here for cowardice, some of James's friends started to cluck like chickens. She turned on them and gave them a tongue-lashing. 'You lot'd cack your pants as soon as you saw a spider. You boys were mad lettin' yerself get mixed up with the Navy in the first place. *I* wouldn't blame you if you had hidden in the hold.' They stopped clucking. Everyone was frightened of Orlagh.

She treated Richard and me like her younger brothers. 'They'd be around your age, if they're still alive,' she said. Hers was a shocking story. When she was ten she and a friend had stolen a bonnet from a younger girl as she headed home from market and pawned it for a few pennies. To them it had been a childish prank, but they were arrested by the city constables. Charged with felonious assault and putting a child in fear of her life, they were both sentenced to hang. 'I cried m'self to sleep every night, in that condemned cell, in all the stink and filth and rats scurrying round me feet. Me mate Molly, who was sentenced with me, she died of gaol fever. Then they let me off and sent me here. After all that you're afraid of nothing.'

Orlagh was a survivor and I admired her greatly. She provided for her children any way she could, stealing vegetables from allotments and sometimes, it was whispered, going with men for money. She seemed to have some sort of loose relationship with James, but they would both leave the pub arm in arm with other people.

The drinkers in the Sailor's Arms were sometimes violent and unpredictable, but they were feisty and generous and took people as they found them. They liked to gamble, and they swore and they stole. I could tell by his pained expression when we talked about them that Doctor Dan didn't approve of our new friends, but I wasn't going to turn my nose up at them.

*   *   *

Our house had little furniture, but we had iron pots and a stove to cook with. There was a small piece of garden around the hut too, which we planted with vegetables. Doctor Dan advised potatoes, as they could provide two crops a year. This we did, and also peas and cabbage. We jealously guarded our vegetables, but our precious crops were frequently stolen in the night, often before they were ready to eat. I sometimes wondered if Orlagh had taken any. I would have gladly given her some.

The Rocks was a noisy, restless place most hours of the day. In daylight babies howled, children screeched and tumbled, and the women who lived there called out across gardens and streets to their friends in nearby houses. By night, when people drank, there was singing and fighting, and arguments, always arguments. Dogs barked day and night, and pigs snuffled underfoot, in and out of any garden they could get into. Broken glass was everywhere, not least because children would throw bottles at each other for sport. People here lived by their wits and fists.

Across the street from us lived Edward Bean, who we often saw in the Sailor's Arms. His wife had died the previous year and he'd had her buried just outside his front door. Some nights he would sit alone drinking rum from the bottle, talking to her as if she was still alive. Occasionally he would pour a portion over the grave, saying, 'I know you like a drop. A bit more won't hurt you.'

It was not just the convicts who lived their life free from the reason and regimentation of England. On the other side of the Rocks was a former marine who deserted soon after arriving here. He was sentenced to death. On the day of his execution it was raining cats and dogs. The hanging was postponed for a week and he endured another wait alone in his cell. When the day came he was taken out again to the gallows by the Parramatta road. But it was still raining torrents and again the execution was postponed. This time, when he returned to his cell, he was told the Governor had commuted his sentence. He was now a convict and found lodgings on the Rocks. Everyone was convinced the execution had been postponed because the officers called out to witness it did not want to get wet.

Doctor Dan was kept busy in the hospital. 'Most of my patients are convicts or their families,' he told us. 'I rarely see any of the "keepers", unless it's soldiers with a dose of the pox. Doctor Reynolds at the hospital has been here almost since the beginning. He told me there used to be an epidemic every time a new fleet came in from England. Smallpox, dysentery, some unnamed fevers. Always affected the natives the worse. I don't think there are any diseases here that are new to Europeans. We've brought these plagues with us – it's very much a one-way trade. Poor savages, we cultivate their land, we bring them the gospels, we teach them shame so they want to wear clothes, we bring the marvellous sciences of navigation and shipbuilding and metal working. But they seem to have managed well enough without, before we arrived.'

'But they just roam around like animals, living off the land,' I said.

'Why settle down in one spot if the earth provides you with food wherever you wander?' Daniel replied.

We had taken several tips from the natives to add to our diet, not least their habit of foraging for seafood – fishing and gathering shellfish. I rarely saw them though, they kept away from our town. I was horrified to see how they were treated by the British settlers. One evening we saw two native men, who had obviously been drinking, having a vicious fight near to the edge of town. A whole gang of soldiers gathered around to cheer, as if they were watching two dogs fighting. I was shocked to see there was even an officer with them.

When I described the incident to Daniel he shook his head in disgust. 'The New South Wales Corps, those men are on the side of the devil. The Governor's always trying to curb their behaviour, but they are the ones with the real power here.'

For all its advantages, Sydney was a peculiar, unsettling place.

CHAPTER 10

Friends and Enemies

One bright afternoon in the early autumn, Richard noticed a familiar face down at the market. 'What the hell is *he* doing here?' he said. 'I thought we'd seen the last of him when the Spanish hauled him off.'

I peered through the crowd. My stomach turned. It was Lewis Tuck, the bullying bosun's mate from the *Miranda*. His towering size and his curly fair hair made him easy enough to spot.

We slipped away without being seen. But a day later, while we were walking home from the Navy office, he came up to us in the street. 'Well I never,' he jeered. 'What are you pair doing here?'

We told him a little of what had happened. He laughed. 'All those books never did you any good after all, Witchall,' he said. Tuck had always mocked my ability to read and write. I suppose he had an almighty chip on his shoulder because he could do neither.

'So what are *you* doing here?' said Richard.

I winced instinctively. On the *Miranda* such a question would have been considered impertinent and earned a sharp blow with a rope. But Tuck carried on talking to us as if our time together on the *Miranda* had been a jovial adventure.

'Those of us they took prisoner, they only held for a couple of months. There was an exchange of prisoners and we were paid off. I went to Tenerife to pick up a ship back to England, but decided to try my luck in New South Wales instead. There's plenty of work for men like me, and plenty of prospects, from what I've heard.'

I was staggered by his manner. Here was a man who had taunted and hounded me mercilessly on the *Miranda.* He had beaten me at every opportunity and would have had me flogged if we had not been captured by that Spanish frigate. Now he was talking to us like we were old shipmates. Perhaps he thought behaving as he had done was just part of his job, and the men who suffered his bullying would understand that?

'Keep out of mischief,' he smirked and sauntered off, leaving me seething and staring daggers.

It was a funny day for meeting old faces. Walking back to the hut later that morning, my eye was drawn to a young woman walking with a soldier in his bright red jacket. As I came nearer I saw it was Lizzie Borrow. She held the arm of a handsome young lieutenant.

Before I could say hello there was a terrible commotion behind us. We all ran over to a small group of children who were staring fearfully down a well, their eyes wide with horror, hands held up to their mouths. Like many wells around the Rocks, it was uncovered and a danger to anyone, drunk or sober.

A little girl rushed up. 'Joshua falled in,' she said. I looked at once to the Lieutenant, expecting him to take command of the situation, but he seemed aloof, as if it were none of his affair. I knew we had to act immediately. I peered down the well and could see the surface catching in the light about seven feet down. Whoever had fallen in was under the water. I looked around frantically for any stick, plank or rope I could use to try to get this child out. There was nothing. I had a horrible decision to make. If I waited any longer the child would surely drown. If I jumped into the narrow hole, I could drown down there myself, and even kill the child as I hit the water.

There was no time to think. I turned to Lizzie and the

Lieutenant and shouted, 'Get a rope or a ladder!' then I climbed over the lip of the well. Looking for footholds along the sides I lowered my body down until I was hanging on to the edge by my finger tips. I launched myself into the void, falling three or four feet into chilly black water. On the way down I banged my elbow hard on the side of the well, but made no contact with the child in the water. I surfaced, spluttering and shuddering with the cold, reeling with a sharp shooting pain in my arm. The water was deep, for despite my fall I did not touch the bottom. There was barely space to pull my arms up through the water to launch myself down again, and my fingers caught the side of the well as I forced air from my lungs to let myself sink below. This time my foot brushed against a solid object. I let myself sink deeper into the black water, feeling the pressure grow in my ears. Moving my hands before me I touched solid flesh and bone and sodden clothing. I grabbed his shirt and kicked my legs hard, but the child was heavier than I imagined.

My lungs felt painfully tight and my head buzzed fit to burst, so desperate was I for breath. I kicked again and broke surface, treading water with the weight of the child pulling me down. Before I had got my breath I yelled 'HELP' at the top of my voice, and we immediately sank again, as my lungs emptied of air.

I kicked hard to regain the surface, and felt around in the gloom for some hole or projection to hold on to. If there were none, I would surely drown. I held on to the child with one hand as the other searched the walls. There was nothing. My legs were tired and I was beginning to panic. Just then, the child began to splutter and cough, spewing out a lungful of water and gasping in air.

'Hold tight, little bundle,' I said quickly. 'We'll be out of here in no time.'

I felt the weight of the child lessen in the water, as he filled his lungs. For the moment at least the task of keeping him afloat became easier. But the water was very cold and I knew I could not keep this up much longer.

What on earth was that bloody lieutenant doing, I thought.

I shouted again and much to my relief a face poked over the edge of the bright circle of light at the top of the well. 'You hold on, young man,' said a woman, 'and I'll run to get a rope and bucket.'

A minute later, someone threw down the bucket on a rope. It landed with a huge splash just as I pulled myself and the boy towards the side of the well to avoid it.

I bit my tongue, wanting to curse whoever had thrown it so carelessly. 'Put the child in the bucket,' shouted down a male voice. I raised Joshua up with my failing strength and told him to hold tight.

It took an age to raise Joshua up to the surface, and when they did I could hear a great wailing – part horror part relief. That must be his mother. Then I heard her scold the child, and several other voices joined in, agreeing with her or telling her to be thankful the child had been rescued.

I lost patience. 'Hey, what about me?' I yelled up. By now the cold was piercing me to the bone, and my elbow was throbbing sharply.

This time a rope snaked down through the darkness, and landed hard on my head.

'Hang on while we tie this to a tree,' someone shouted down. Then, a minute later: 'Come on then, let's have you up.'

They pulled the rope. I hung on for dear life with my frozen fingers, pushing up with my legs whenever I could.

I emerged from the well, blinking into sharp sunlight to be confronted with a large crowd. They cheered and several ran to help me to my feet. Of Lizzie and the officer there was no sign. The dripping, sodden child was being cradled by its mother who in turn was being fussed over by a tall, kindly-looking man wearing a clerical collar.

He came over and shook my hand. 'My name is the Reverend Graham. Thank you for saving the life of my child. Can we take you home to dry your clothes and offer you some dinner?' He had a round face, made even rounder as he was almost completely bald. He seemed like a nice man, so I accepted his offer.

Dinner with the Grahams was an unexpected pleasure. I hadn't eaten a more delicious joint of pork since I lived at home. Reverend Graham let it be known that he was a personal friend of the Governor. 'If I can do you any favour in return,' he told me, 'I can assure you I have His Excellency's ear.'

I smiled to myself. I knew enough about the ways of the world to realise I had just made a very useful friend.

Two days later I was walking home from work with Richard when we saw Lizzie Borrow close to the quayside. She was out walking with her maid, a pretty dark-haired girl a couple of years younger. The light from the sun formed a halo around Lizzie's mane of hair, making her look luminously beautiful.

She greeted us with a smile. 'You're the boy who rescued the child! And –' she looked puzzled as if trying to place us both. 'And in fact, you're the boys from the boat! And from the play! Let me see, it's . . . Richard? And Samuel?' She seemed quite excited to see us. I was pleased she had taken the trouble to discover our names. Looking around she lowered her voice and said to me, 'I'm glad there was someone at the well who didn't mind getting his clothes wet.'

There was a telling pause in the conversation. Then Lizzie said, 'So boys, how are you faring?'

We tumbled over each other to tell her how well we were doing. We had a fine house down by the Rocks, we were highly regarded down at the Navy office, everything was absolutely marvellous and we had every hope of an early pardon.

'And how are you Miss Borrow?' I said. 'Is Sydney to your liking?'

'Terribly hot,' she said. 'So enervating. And very little in the way of entertaining company.'

Richard spoke boldly. 'Well Miss, we'd be delighted to accompany you on a stroll around the bay.'

I admired his pluck.

Lizzie's maid giggled. She had a lovely smile. Lizzie made a sorry face.

'I'd love to boys, but my fiancé would probably have something to say about it.'

Richard bowed gracefully. 'And who is the lucky fellow?' he asked.

'Lieutenant John Gray,' she said briskly. 'New South Wales Corps. Well, I suppose we ought to be off.'

Out of earshot I laughed. 'You didn't really think she'd come for a walk with us did you?' I said. 'Daughter of a high official talking with a couple of convicts. That's enough to get tongues wagging already.'

'You English,' said Richard. 'You're such stick-in-the-muds. "Fortune favours the bold," that's what my old dad always says.'

Richard and I enjoyed our free time and I came to think of the Sailor's Arms as my second home. The pub did a fine trade in hearty dinners. We would spend a couple of hours in blistering January sunshine drinking ale and munching our way through a mutton pie and mulberry and quince tart, usually in the company of James and Orlagh. Many of the pubs in Sydney were run by women and the Sailor's Arms was no exception. The landlady was known as Mad Bet. She was small and wiry, with skin as nut-brown and weather-beaten as any tar. Clay pipe clenched between blackened teeth, she had the sharpest tongue in Sydney and would have made a fine bosun's mate.

When we'd drunk our wages and filled our stomachs we would wander back to the hut and sleep the rest of the afternoon. After our tightly regulated life of the Navy, and our confinement on the hulk and convict transport, having this much freedom was heady stuff.

We didn't often visit the pub in the evening, partly because we couldn't afford to, but also because it was a violent place at night. Instead we would sit in front of our hut sipping black tea or peach cider, talking with Doctor Dan and the neighbours. They were a mixed bunch, but usually good company. Most of them couldn't read so Dan or I would read out books to our fellows. I rarely felt happier in Sydney than when we were sitting around in a group on a warm night, smoking pipes, sipping our drinks and reading by candlelight.

One late afternoon, Dan came back from the hospital to

find Richard and me still asleep after our visit to the pub. As he busied himself frying some fish he said, 'You know, you two could make something of yourselves in Sydney. I'm not going to be here to look after you for ever. If you didn't drink your wages, you could work afternoons and make even more money. Think about it.'

As a shot across the bow, it could not have been gentler, but we got the message loud and clear. When work finished we still went to the Sailor's Arms to eat, but we'd only have a single drink and by two o'clock we'd be out earning money. There was plenty of work to be had on nearby farms clearing timber, planting corn and the like. But it was back-breaking and we soon started thinking up schemes that were less exhausting. One of our neighbours had taught us how to repair the clay walls of our house with soil, cow dung and grass. 'Whitewash that with lime, apple tree ash and sour milk,' he said, 'and it's as good as new.' We went from door to door with our stinking mixture, offering to patch up holes in walls. It was hard work. Sometimes we would walk for miles and find very few customers.

One evening Richard had a brilliant idea. 'Fishing! Let's go fishing. There's plenty of fish in the bay. We could sell them door to door.'

That very afternoon we went to a general store in the middle of the town and bought ourselves fish hooks and line. We made a pair of rods from some useful-looking branches, whittling them into shape that very evening. Our first afternoon fishing off the northern tip of the Rocks was not a success.

'You need a boat, friend,' said a passing stranger. 'And I know just the man to rent you one.'

'Who's that?' I said.

'Me.'

His name was Henry Coates and he offered us a good deal. Three shillings an afternoon, or half our catch. We settled for half the catch. 'If we don't catch much, then we haven't lost much either,' reasoned Richard.

Next day we ventured out in the small rowing boat into the choppy waters and sat for a long afternoon in the middle of the bay. We caught mullet, mackerel and rock cod by the bucketful. It was barely any work at all. That evening we sold our share of the fish all around the Rocks and made the best part of five shillings.

The scheme worked well for a week, but there was a catch, and it turned out we were it.

One Friday afternoon in early February we set off into the bay. By four o'clock that afternoon we were landing fish after fish, filling our wooden bucket very nicely.

I was just fixing a bloody bit of bait from our tray of chopped up fish pieces when Richard got up to pee over the side of the boat. Whenever one of us did this the other would move to the other side to balance the vessel.

'Another hour and that bucket will be full, I reckon,' he said.

Just then something nudged the keel, making the boat wobble violently. Richard lost his balance and pitched into the sea. I fell off my seat, setting the bait tin into the water. I looked over to see a bloody cloud of cut up pieces slowly sinking from view.

At that instant, in that same spot, a huge demonic face loomed from the depths and lurched out of the water. Its pointy snout almost touched my nose. Jagged white teeth bared in lethal rows, a cold black eye looking straight through me. I thought I could taste its foul fishy breath but that may have been my own terror. Without thinking I brought a clenched fist down on the tip of its nose. A fierce pain shot through my flesh. The shark's hide was so rough it was like smashing my hand down on a barnacle-covered rock.

The blow enraged the beast and it lurched up even higher. This time it reached over the side of the strakes. I could see its eye covered by a white flap of skin. Its top jaw seemed to have swung forward in its mouth, making it look even more ugly and vicious.

'Quick! Help!' shouted Richard, who was by now hanging onto the side of the boat. 'It's a bloody great shark,' I yelled, rather unnecessarily.

I stumbled over to heave him in, and had just grabbed his soaking shirtsleeve when I saw the shark coming back straight for him, its triangular fin skimming through the water at speed.

The boat rocked dangerously, taking in water, and he scrabbled to get his legs in as I heaved him over the strakes. The shark made a lunge for him, and just at that moment one of his shoes fell off and into the creature's jaws.

'Back to shore, quick as we can,' I said. 'Take an oar and row like hell.'

'Batter the bastard with them if he comes back,' said Richard.

'Better not,' I said. 'What if the thing eats one. Then we'll be really lost.'

We rowed together, side by side, heading for the shallows a quarter of a mile away.

There was one other weapon aboard – a wooden boat hook with a metal tip that lay under our feet.

'If he comes back, I'll row and you hit him with that,' said Richard, 'but don't drop your oar.' Despite my fear, I felt quite calm. We had not escaped the noose to end up as shark supper.

The boat lurched in the water. We kept rowing. This monster was circling us again.

'Look, he's over there on the larboard side,' shouted Richard, 'coming back for another go.'

We could see a long, dark shape, maybe seven foot in length, slipping through the water. Then it disappeared.

After a while our fear began to subside – enough for me to notice the hot afternoon sun on the back of my neck. 'I need a stiff drink,' said Richard.

'D'you think he's gone?' I said. I began to feel sick with the thought of what had just happened, and my bleeding hand was throbbing with pain.

We carried on rowing as fast as our trembling hands would let us, and the shore grew nearer. I heaved a sigh of relief, closed my eyes and made a silent prayer of thanks.

At once I was conscious of the bow of the boat rising in the water. I opened my eyes to see the shark halfway out of the sea, its fins resting on the stern which was now level with the surface and taking in water. Its thrashing upper body seemed to be wriggling its way towards us, teeth chomping furiously at our feet.

We both screamed in terror. This was more horrifying than any battle I had been in. My hands reached for the boat hook and my oar fell into the water.

I brought the hook down on the shark's pointy head with all my strength, splitting the wood in two. The monster flipped its body up over the stern and disappeared again.

Richard was furious. 'You idiot,' he screamed at me. 'We're dead men now.'

I started to sob. 'I'm sorry, I'm sorry,' I said, feeling utterly wretched, and buried my head in my hands.

Seeing me so upset calmed him. 'I'm sorry Sam.' He

reached over and put an arm around me. 'Come on, let's try to get that oar.'

It had drifted twenty or so yards away from us, further out to sea.

'We can always put a rowlock on the stern and row with just one,' I said.

'Not likely,' said Richard. 'Not after seeing how that thing came up on the stern. If we lose the other oar, we wouldn't stand a chance. Here, I'll try to edge us over while you bail.'

We had taken in a lot of water after the last attack, and our ankles were now awash.

After ten minutes of patient sculling, we edged nearer our oar. But to my dismay, we had drifted further out to sea.

There was the oar. I began to dread plunging my bleeding hand into the water, fearing this would be the moment our shark would hurl itself out and snap my arm off. Richard read my mind. 'Take my oar, I'll get it.'

Before I could protest he reached over the side to grab the oar.

Nothing happened.

We sat there another minute, getting our nerve and our strength back.

We rowed again in silence. After twenty minutes we both began to tire. 'Nearly there,' I said.

Then a fin drifted past the starboard side of the boat.

'Oh Jesus,' said Richard. 'He's back.'

An idea flashed into my head. I passed my oar over to Richard. 'You row.'

I moved carefully to the stern and scanned the surface. The shark was there ten yards off, biding its time. I picked up a snapper from the catch of fish in our bucket and heaved it over. The cruel mouth cut through the water and devoured the fish in an instant.

'Keep going.'

Whenever he drew dangerously near I threw in another fish.

We both found the whole thing almost funny. 'Not so much as a thank you,' said Richard. 'What an ill-mannered shark.'

By the time we reached the quay there were only three fish left. I threw them all out, to give us enough time to clamber out of the boat.

We sat down on dry land and both began to laugh hysterically. The good fortune we felt at our escape was marred only by Henry Coates who insisted on charging us for his broken boat hook.

'That'll be a pound,' he said.

'Come off it, Henry,' said Richard. 'You can buy them for ten shillings in the store down town.'

'Mine was a pound,' he said.

We paid up. He knew, and we knew, that we would not be going fishing again.

CHAPTER 11

Folly and Ruination

As we sat sipping beer with James and Orlagh in the Sailor's Arms one Sunday afternoon, our thoughts turned to Lewis Tuck. 'He's working in the prison, I've heard,' Richard told me. 'One week in three he works overnight. I think we ought to pay his house a visit. See if we can play a little prank on him.'

'You know where he lives?' I asked.

'Just on the edge of town. He's bought himself a nice little cottage near the timber yard.'

We told our friends about what a bullying thug he'd been. Orlagh, in particular, was greatly amused by the idea of us carrying out some sort of revenge on the man. 'I like to see a bully get a dose of his own medicine.'

We had another tankard of ale then all four of us walked over to the western side of Sydney to take a look. From a safe distance behind a high hedge we could see a pretty cottage surrounded by tall gum trees. Tuck had chosen his spot well. There was little else around the house other than lush meadows and a freshwater stream.

'Are you sure it's his?' I said.

'Yeah. I think so anyway. Rylett at the Navy office told me,' replied Richard.

A wicked plan came to me in a flash of diabolical inspiration. 'If we find out when he's working the night watch we could sneak out here and see if we can cut one of those trees to fall right down on the roof!' I thought it would impress Orlagh, and sure enough, in our drunken state, the idea seemed so wonderful we all laughed until our stomachs ached.

Just as we began to walk back home, Tuck came out of his front door and started to bustle around his small garden. We lay still by the hedge careful not to be seen. It was his house for sure. Seeing him strutting around, Orlagh said, 'He *does* look like he needs bringing down a peg.'

Even when we had slept off our lunchtime drinking it still seemed like a good idea. 'Not a word to Doctor Daniel, though,' I said to Richard. 'I doubt he'd approve.'

Our friend Rylett in the Navy office had a drinking partner who was one of the guards at the prison. We found out he worked the same watch as Tuck. When we saw him in the Sailor's Arms, we always asked him how things were with the prison. One evening, when the moon was waning, he let slip he would not be in the pub all the next week because he was working the night watch. Our chance had come.

The night of Tuesday 16th May was pleasantly cool with a warm east wind blowing in across the town. Autumn had arrived in Sydney, but here it was like a lovely spring day back home in Norfolk. It rained a bit more, but it was still mild and rarely cold. We had thought our plan through carefully. Richard and me set off with Orlagh, who had begged us to take her along. We left at nine o'clock in the evening. If we were out too late, we might raise suspicions with the soldiers who patrolled the streets. We carried a heavy saw wrapped in a canvas bag, newly purchased from Simeon Lord's Commission Warehouse. As we headed over to Tuck's we double-checked our story.

'We've been having a drink in the Sailor's Arms with Harry Stokes. He's a carpenter by trade and he's just left his saw behind, so we're returning it to him. Got that?' said Richard.

'Where does Harry live again?' I asked.

'Close by the windmill and government bakery. That's right on the western end of the town. Once we're past there, all we need to do is keep off the roads and head for Tuck's.'

Sure enough, we were stopped a couple of times by the patrols. They were not unfriendly and merely asked us what we were doing. Our explanation seemed quite reasonable. This all seemed like a great adventure.

We reached Tuck's around half past nine, and peered through the darkness at his cottage. Not a single light could be seen. 'He's out, let's go!'

We selected a tall tree behind the house. It was a splendid choice. Thin trunk, but wide, spreading boughs and high enough to fall with some force by the time it hit Tuck's roof.

Richard and I sawed together, slightly alarmed that the noise our blade made gnawing into the wood would travel through the night air. Orlagh kept watch for us but we still stopped at regular intervals to listen, trying to pick up any sound other than the frequent gusts of wind. She whispered for us to stop only once, when two people passed close by with a noisy dog.

Two minutes later we were sawing again, and within ten minutes the trunk was almost sawed through. Richard had a bright idea. 'Let's leave it like this. Next time there's a really fierce wind, it'll blow right over. And we'll be gone with a bit of luck.'

'Yes, but will it blow the right way?' I said.

'But we've cut it so it can only fall forward!' He was beginning to sound impatient.

My conscience was bothering me. Now we were so near to completing our prank, I had begun to feel guilty about going through with it. But I didn't want to look spineless in front of Orlagh.

She could see we were faltering. 'Do it now,' she said. 'No one's in. If it falls later, it might kill him, and anyone else who might be in the house. Then you'd be up for murder, if they caught you.'

It was practical advice, I suppose. Then I thought of Tuck beating me in front of the crew of the *Miranda* because I had accidentally spilt tar on the deck.

Richard and I both nodded, stood up and leaned on the trunk. There was barely a half inch left uncut close to the roots and this quickly splintered as the tree began its passage to the ground. It hit the house with a mighty wallop and splintering of roof and walls that must have been heard all over the western side of Sydney.

We all ran like blazes before any of Tuck's neighbours could get over to investigate.

'What did you do with the saw?' said Richard when we stopped in some bushes to get our breath back.

'What did *I* do with it?' I said. 'I thought *you* had it.'

Richard looked angry. Orlagh cut him short. 'Look, he's hardly going to believe the ants ate the tree trunk is he? He'll see it's been cut down with a saw, so it doesn't really matter whether he finds the one you left.'

We ran off into the dark. The fun had gone out of our escapade. Whenever we heard or spotted patrols in front of us, we hid till they were gone. I felt fear now, rather than excitement. If we were caught and linked to the destruction of Tuck's house, we would be flogged at the very least, maybe even hanged. By half past eleven we had reached the safety of the Rocks. As ever, the streets were still full of people, and the pub was doing a roaring trade. We slunk quietly back home, trying our best not to wake Doctor Dan.

A few days later I was cooking supper at home for the three of us. Richard and Doctor Dan were sitting outside in the garden, catching the last of the late afternoon sun. I heard Richard say in a low voice, 'Look out Sam, that bastard Tuck's coming to see us.'

I came out into the garden to see Lewis Tuck marching purposefully up to our house. He had a face like thunder and was clutching the saw in his right hand.

As he came to our garden path Doctor Dan looked up. 'Can we help you, sir?'

Tuck ignored him. Richard and I were standing by the door and he came right up to us and snarled in our faces. 'I know it was you. My neighbour Henry Rickards said he saw two boys and a girl running away as soon as the tree fell. Couldn't see who in the dark, but *I'm* sure the two boys were you. And I've just been to see the warehouse manager. He says he sold you this saw last Thursday.' He waved it in our faces. 'It's in his ledger.'

'We had our saw stolen last Saturday,' said Richard, with brazen ingenuity. 'We were cutting wood for a picket fence around the garden and I foolishly left it out overnight. Vanished in the morning. That looks exactly like the one we had, so if it's not yours perhaps you could let us have it back.'

Tuck was seething with rage. I feared at any moment he would grab one of us by the throat.

Doctor Dan intervened. 'What is the problem here, sir?'

Tuck always did kowtow to his betters, and even though he knew Daniel was a convict he spoke to him as he would an officer.

'These boys, sir, on Tuesday evening, have maliciously sawed down a tree on my property so that it fell on my house, almost demolishing it.'

'I'm very sorry to hear about your misfortune, sir. But I can assure you neither Sam nor Richard could have done something so stupid. Both of them spent the entire Tuesday evening here in the house with me.'

Tuck knew he was going to get no further.

Turning to Richard and me he said in a low, mean voice, 'I'll see you little buggers swing for this if it's the last thing I do.'

He stomped off down the street.

Richard and I had a fit of sniggering as soon as he disappeared from view. Doctor Dan said nothing. When he spoke he was really angry. 'You bloody idiots. What the hell did you think you were doing?'

His voice was shaking and we had never seen him in such a fury. We were both shocked into silence.

Doctor Dan carried on in a voice that was cold with disgust. 'And who was it with you? One of your ne'er-do-well friends from the pub, I'll bet. Was she impressed with your prank? You have both been extraordinarily stupid. If he can prove it was you, you'll be hanged if you're lucky, and sent to one of the country iron gangs if you're not. How does that strike you? Seven years chained together, with six other thugs. That'll wipe the smiles off your stupid faces. And if he does get a court to convict you, I'll be flogged too, for lying to protect you. How do you feel about that?'

Our mirth had dissolved. My chest felt tight and it was all I could do not to cry.

Daniel went on, 'And if he can't get a court to convict you, he'll just murder you in your beds, or on the way back from the pub, or when you're taking a Sunday stroll around the bay. How d'you like the sound of that?'

His anger spent, he started to sound more concerned.

'You didn't think this through, did you?'

'It'll blow over,' said Richard, but his bravado was not convincing.

We barely spoke for the rest of the evening and I went to bed with a heavy heart.

Walking back from work alone, on a chilly Thursday afternoon, I was wrapped up in my troubles. We had seen Tuck around town several times since his visit. He greeted us both with an icy politeness, and his eyes brimmed with malice. I kept thinking of Doctor Dan's warning: 'He'll just murder you in your beds.'

It was now a week since the incident. No soldiers or marines had come to drag us from our home. Whatever clues we left were clearly not enough to convince the authorities. All the more reason for Tuck to take matters into his own hands.

Richard had said, 'He's up to something, all right. From now on, I'm sleeping with a knife under my pillow. You too, Sam, if you've any sense.'

But I didn't think Tuck would come for us in our own hut. He'd have to kill Dan too, and then, if he were caught, he'd be hanged. On the *Miranda* he was known to be a first-class shot with a musket, and I thought he might try to shoot us both from a distance, when there were few people around – perhaps when we took a walk around the town on a Sunday or on our way home from work. I had become tense and nervous, and jumped at any sudden sound. My sleep had become fitful and in my dreams Tuck would loom out of the darkness, like the shark had loomed up from the deep, his teeth sharp and gleaming, a cold, dead look in his eyes.

I could not believe my own stupidity. What was it James Lyons had said about not making enemies? Richard and I had only talked a little about what we had done since. Although we had yet to start blaming the other for the idea, we were sullen and distant with each other, which hurt me. Orlagh, too, had not been back to the pub since we had seen her that night. Perhaps she felt guilty about encouraging us to do something so stupid? In truth, I was glad not to see her. I was afraid she'd start drunkenly boasting about our escapade, and soon the whole town would know what we'd done.

When I walked over the quayside towards the Rocks in the afternoon I looked up to see Lizzie Borrow. I had only glimpsed her from a distance since the day we had met her before. Seeing her now I was struck again by how beautiful she was. Today she wore a plain white cotton dress with a short brown jacket that drew attention to the curve of her back and slight swell of her hips. She looked magnificently sullen, waiting outside a harbour-front shop that sold boating and fishing material.

I didn't want to talk to her. I needed to feel strong and

confident to talk to Lizzie Borrow. Today was not a good day. I put my head down and walked close to the waterside so as to place a distance between us.

'Oh Sam!' she called over.

Her bright blue eyes peered from under a bright red bonnet. 'The Lieutenant is attending to his nautical requirements,' she said in a delightfully mocking manner, 'and I'm wishing I'd stayed at home with a good book.' She looked out of place in this rough world. 'And Sam, I hear you're living with Doctor Sadler, as well as that American fellow.' She had remembered my name and forgotten Richard's!

Our backs to the shop, shading our eyes from the sun, we fell into easy conversation. I forgot my troubles and could have chatted with Lizzie for hours. I heard the bell of the shop door ping and a rough hand pushed me to one side so hard I fell to the floor.

'Is this urchin bothering you, Miss Borrow?' It could only be Lieutenant John Gray.

I caught the expression on Lizzie's face. She was looking at Gray with utter bewilderment. I was so angry at being humiliated I rushed back on my feet, determined to punch him. He sidestepped my clumsy attack and drew his sword, holding the blade under my chin so hard it broke the skin. I wondered whether he was going to cut my throat then and there. His eyes were full of dull contempt. I could smell spirits on his breath and he seemed unsteady on his feet.

'Threatening an officer of the Crown –' he got no further. Richard had been following close behind trying to catch me up, and had seen the whole incident. He grabbed a walking stick from a pile laid out in front of the shop next door, and deftly knocked the sword from Gray's hand. It clattered to the ground and in the terrible silence that followed, everyone at the quayside turned to look.

How the incident would have played itself out if a squad of soldiers had not been passing by, I do not know. Perhaps Gray would have drawn his dagger or picked up his sword and slain Richard on the spot. Instead, looking to rescue himself from embarrassment, he snarled, 'Sergeant, arrest these two ragamuffins at once.'

A second later, Richard and I were both staring down the barrels of six muskets. 'You're looking at a flogging, if you're lucky,' said Gray. We were marched to the guardhouse up the hill from the quay and left to stew in a small cell for the rest of the day. We both felt sick in the pit of our stomach at the thought of a flogging. I wondered how many lashes they'd give two boys and whether we'd be able to stand up to the punishment? I remembered the steward, Hartley, aboard the *Miranda*, and how he had died after a mere thirty-six lashes. We both knew the cat o' nine tails here were larger and more wicked implements than the Navy ones.

Doctor Dan came to see us that evening, carrying a couple of pork pies and a flagon of ale. As we ate and drank, he talked to us softly and quickly. He'd obviously been busy. 'I heard what happened,' he said, cutting off our attempts to explain. 'Now I think I can get you off a flogging, but this will mean a sentence to an outlying farm. You're probably looking at seven years –'

'But he attacked me!' I said, trying to hold back my tears. 'He was going to kill me.'

Dan shook his head. 'The New South Wales Corps have an inordinate amount of influence here, Sam. Lieutenant Gray is prominent among them. Even the Governor is wary of the Corps, and lives in fear of an army revolt. However, I know the Magistrate – I looked after his wife when she nearly died in childbirth – so he owes me a favour. And if we get your friend the Reverend Graham to put in a good word for you too, I think we can get you off a flogging. But I can't get you off a further sentence.'

Richard spoke. 'I'd rather have a flogging than a seven-year sentence.'

Dan shook his head. 'It's usually a flogging *and* a seven-year sentence. And a hundred lashes strapped to a triangle could cripple a couple of lads like you for life.'

An awkward silence descended. What else could we say?

Dan left us with a promise. 'I'll see what I can do, but I'm still a convict myself. Let's look on the bright side. The Navy office can say you're exemplary workers. Maybe, if the right things get said to the right people, we'll be able to reduce your sentence by a few years.'

That night we could find few words to say to each other. 'You didn't have to get involved Richard,' I said to him sorrowfully.

'I wasn't going to see him stick a sword in your throat,' he said.

The ale and food had made me drowsy and I was soon asleep. But I woke in the middle of the night. Ahead of us were seven years of hard labour – cutting down trees, hauling ploughs as human beasts of burden, clearing bushland. And we would probably have to work side by side with the most villainous men in the colony.

Richard could tell from my breathing I was awake. 'I can't sleep either,' he said in a matter of fact way. 'We've been in worse scrapes before. Whatever's in front of us can't be any worse than going into battle or being brought out to be hanged. We'll be all right Sam, as long as we stick together.'

We were brought before the court in little more than a week. Our fate was quickly decided. We were to be sent to the farm of a Benjamin Perrion, at Green Hills on the Hawkesbury River, forty miles north of Sydney.

Doctor Dan had done his work. The Magistrate told us we were very lucky to escape a flogging, but due to our youth he would forgo this punishment for attacking an officer of the crown.

Soon after dawn the next day we were shackled with chains on our ankles and placed on a small horse-drawn cart. Two soldiers, unsmiling and silent, sat next to us with bayonets fixed to their muskets.

We headed west away from Sydney and I felt a great pang of helplessness as the town receded with every clop of the horse's hooves. We were leaving behind our home, our friends, and the good life we were beginning to enjoy, and most of all, the protection of Doctor Dan.

The dirt road was poor and made for a rough ride, but at least there was a road. After midday one of the soldiers stood up and shouted, 'Savages!', and fired off a shot into the bush that surrounded us. 'They'll eat your liver for breakfast boys, if they ever catch you,' he said as he swabbed out his musket and loaded another cartridge and shot.

We travelled on with barely a break, and reached the Hawkesbury River at dusk. It was a strangely comforting sight seeing the settlement after an entire day surrounded by a wild landscape. On the slopes running down to the far side of the river was a cluster of buildings with lamps burning in the windows. Some were brick, others mere huts, similar to the one we had lived in on the Rocks. We passed a group of natives huddled around a fire. They seemed hardly aware of us even being there.

As far as I could see in the fading light, the land around the settlement was all cleared and some of the fields were under cultivation. Then I remembered what we had been sent here to do. It would be us doing the clearing – hauling away timber and breaking up the ground. I shuddered again at our misfortune. There would be seven years of this before we would be allowed to return to Sydney.

The cart stopped, we clambered off in our chains, and boarded a small ferry. Quickly transported across the river, we were marched up the steep river bank and taken to a small hut. I thought we were going to be fed, but I was wrong.

We were left with our thoughts. I lay awake seething at my own stupidity and wondering what manner of man Benjamin Perrion would be.

CHAPTER 12

Exile in Exile

We were roused at dawn by our escort and taken in our chains to a farm further down the river from the main settlement at Green Hills. My empty stomach gurgled and groaned, and I felt light-headed from hunger. Shuffling along the dusty road in the chill early morning, it was cold enough to see our breath. Bright sunshine cast long shadows over the dewy fields and I noticed how beautiful the countryside was. There were young apple, apricot and peach trees, all brought from England, sitting side by side with the most handsome native shrubs. This was a land of plenty, and I could see at once why settlers had come to this spot to farm. All around, tilled fields lay prepared for the coming winter, close to granaries filled with sacks of grain.

How wonderful it would have been to have come here as free men rather than Perrion's slaves. I tried not to dwell too much on the terrible reversal in our fortunes. Perhaps I was not meant for an easy life?

We walked down a dried mud path to an impressive brick building surrounded by several smaller stores and huts. 'There you are boys, Charlotte Farm. Make the most of it,' said one of the soldiers. A small dog came bounding up the path to greet us, barking excitedly and wagging its tail as if possessed. Richard was confident with dogs and offered a hand for it to sniff. The dog licked it, and jumped up to be petted.

'Some guard dog this is,' said Richard.

Bustling around the veranda of a single-storey brick house was a stout ruddy-faced man. Curly white hair sprouted from the side of his balding head, and I judged him to be fifty or so. He seemed to be bursting with mithering impatience. 'Tinker, come back here at once, you wretched animal,' he roared.

He turned to look at us, then shouted into the house. 'They've sent us two boys. I asked for some good solid brutes and I get boys. Marvellous, marvellous.'

This must be Benjamin Perrion.

He turned to greet us. 'Good morning boys. Have you had breakfast?' His manner was pleasant enough, as though we were not meant to have heard his previous remarks. 'Charlotte! Tell Heaton to bring bread and scotch coffee.'

The house looked luxurious compared with our spartan hut in Sydney, and I glimpsed inside with envy. There was a tiled floor, wallpaper, soft furnishings. I hadn't seen furniture like this since leaving England.

A moment later a large, thickset man walked round from the other side of the house. Perrion said, 'This is William O'Brian, my farm manager.'

O'Brian spoke with a slow, country drawl. Beneath his floppy, dark hair, his eyes seemed kind, even sensitive. In his manner too, he was oddly diffident for someone whose job it was to instil fear in his charges.

'You boys behave yourself and you'll be treated right. Mess me around and we'll have to beat you.' He didn't sound convincing.

Richard asked, 'Do we work with our chains on? We'd get a lot more done with them off.'

O'Brian let him finish before he rapped him on the back with a switch he kept in his boot. 'You'll talk when you're spoken to,' he said. But the blow was barely more than a tap. It was almost as if O'Brian had been told that was how he should treat his convict labourers, but didn't have the heart to do so. 'If I feel I can trust you, the chains will come off. We'll have to see, won't we?'

'You get fed by the job here, boys,' Perrion said. 'Clear me an acre of timber in a week, or break up an acre of ground and that's your full rations guaranteed. You'll sleep in the hut next to the granary. You can chop your own wood for the fire. O'Brian will give you blankets. See him when the clothes fall off your backs. If you work well, we'll keep you. If you're troublesome or lazy, we'll send you to the iron gangs. Think on. I'm not a sentimental man so don't let me down. Now have some breakfast and then you can start felling those rubber trees over there.'

An old woman in a filthy overall came out with a couple of mugs of scotch coffee and a hunk of bread and cheese, and we were left alone to eat. 'Rum bunch, these settlers. They seem too soft to be out here with the re-offenders,' commented Richard. 'Wonder who else works here? Half the people we know down in the Rocks would eat these two alive.'

As we ate, a woman in her thirties with lank, wispy hair came out of the house and nodded to us. Although her clothes were well cared for and she was obviously the mistress of the house, she had a blank, defeated look about her. This must be Charlotte. She had once been attractive, I could see that, but something about her life here had ground her down. Two young girls peeped

191

round her skirt and stared at us mournfully.

O'Brian arrived with a couple of axes. We shuffled after him into the nearby field, where we could see two other men dragging a fallen tree down to the river. 'Mr Perrion's just bought these riverside fields, and you'll be clearing them for pasture,' he said.

'Please sir,' I asked, wondering if he would hit me like he had hit Richard, 'if we have to wear chains, could you give us some cloth to wrap around them, so as not to rub our ankles raw, sir?' Mine were already hurting, and the weight was draining the strength from my legs.

O'Brian looked penitent. 'I'd have them off you today, lad, but the master insists. I'll bring you cloth when I bring you dinner.'

As we walked he gave us brief instructions on felling cuts, direction of fall and so on. He was concerned that we should do our work safely. 'Felling trees is dangerous work, lads,' he said. Didn't we know it.

He also warned us about the creatures that lurked in the undergrowth around the farm. 'Keep your eyes peeled for the tiger snake – big brown thing with yellow stripes, likes to lurk in piles of timber. If that bites you, you're as good as dead. Leave him alone and he'll leave you alone, so don't be too worried about him. Watch out for spiders too. Especially if you see anything that looks like a nest. Some of them have a bite that'll kill you too.'

O'Brian introduced us to our fellow labourers, John Barrie and William Bell. They both nodded indifferently, and carried on hauling their tree, shuffling awkwardly in their chains. O'Brian pointed to three trees and said he expected us to cut them down and haul them to the river by dinner time, then he left us to it.

No sooner had he gone than Barrie and Bell stopped working and lit up their pipes. We went over to talk to them. 'Savages work like dogs,' said Barrie in a Cockney drawl. 'And then only when you stand over them with a whip. Me and Mr Bell, we like to take things easy, don't we Mr Bell? You boys ain't keen are you? Better not be!' He gave a mirthless chuckle.

'O'Brian's not cut out for this job,' said Bell. 'You might've noticed.' I could tell by his accent that he was a Londoner too.

Barrie squinted at us. 'How much did he ask you to do this mornin'?' We told him about the three trees. 'Just do two. Then he'll ask you less in future. He used to be one of us, y'know. Ticket of leave man, he is. Came 'ere to work for the little fat man. Three years into his sentence, Perrion liked him so much he took him on as farm manager. Don't think they'll be doing that with us, Mr Bell.'

'Don't think they will, Mr Barrie.'

They had this slow, lazy way of talking, like they were some sort of theatrical act, but without the jokes.

When we were alone, Richard said, 'Barrie's right I suppose, or is it Bell? If we work hard, they'll expect more from us.' It was difficult, even a year or so later, to get out of the Navy habit of doing everything properly and as quickly as possible. I could see how that would work against us in a place like this.

'Barrie's the smaller one, right?' said Richard. 'Bell's the tall one.'

'I keep getting them mixed up too,' I said. 'Bell tower – that's tall. That'll help.'

As we toiled away, at our slower pace, I kept glancing over to Barrie and Bell. Barrie was a swarthy, stocky man. He had great mutton-chop whiskers either side of his broad face, and lank, thinning hair tied back in a ponytail. There was an almost permanent smile on his lips, as if he was enjoying a sly joke at someone else's expense. He moved with a deliberate slowness, and usually had his hands in his pockets. Bell was tall and thin, with a gaunt, pointy face. His lower jaw jutted out, giving him an obstinate air. Although he moved with Barrie's surly slowness, his eyes were forever darting to and fro. Something about them just spelt trouble. So when Barrie asked us to come over to their hut that evening we were both apprehensive.

Barrie poured us both a tot of rum from a bottle he kept in the corner. The hut they shared was similar to ours.

There was just a single room inside. The place was well maintained and they had built themselves a bed apiece and lived in some comfort. The conversation started awkwardly.

'Do Perrion or O'Brian ever let you out of your chains?' said Richard.

They both swore horribly. 'He did once,' said Bell. 'But I nipped into his kitchen and borrowed a bit o' tea. Had me flogged for that, the bastard. Chains went back on the both of us too, and we can't get him to take 'em off.' His tone of voice suggested he thought this was monstrously unfair.

Barrie gave a little chuckle. 'Before we came out here from Sydney, Mr Bell had been flogged so often it was no skin off his back – 'cept it was, of course.'

'You can laugh, ye smug git,' said Bell. 'You didn't like it much when they nailed your ears to the pillory.' I could still see the scars.

For an awful moment I thought they were going to have a fight. 'So what did you get sent out here for?' I said, eager to move the conversation on.

Barrie was happy to tell us. 'I'm a forger, me. Best ten pound note you'll ever see in your life. Wills, marriage certificates, letters. Sentenced to death in 1794, sent over 'ere a year on. Made a good living as a clerk until some nosy bugger noticed I was victualling a chain gang out in Richmond Hill – one that wasn't there. I was making a few quid a week from that one. I know who it was shopped me, too. When I get back to Sydney, they'll be having a little accident.'

Bell was not proud of his own downfall, so it was left to Barrie to tell us. 'Only went and stole some lead off a roof in Whitechapel, didn't he. Nothing wrong with that, but it was snowing at the time, and they just followed the footprints back to his house a couple of streets away. Then, after he got sent over here, he got caught by the constables stealing vegetables from some officer's garden. So he was packed off here with me.'

We told the pair of them why we had been sent to the farm. I embroidered the story about Gray. 'Told him to keep his nose out of it,' I laughed, trying to make myself look game. 'Officers need taking down a peg, cocky bastards.'

I felt foolish, trying to sound tough and rebellious for these London crooks, and their expressions suggested they didn't believe half of what I was saying. But we were stuck with them for the next few years, so I thought we ought to try to get on with them.

'We got packed off to an iron gang,' said Bell, 'when we was first sent out 'ere. Six month, chained together eight at a time, clearing the roads out to Richmond. Gets a bit old after a week, that does. When the sun goes down they put you in a big wooden box on wheels that's pulled out there by a couple o' horses. If you need to piss in the night, you have to get all the rest of the gang to come with you. It's so small you can't sit down nor stand up proper. Only time the chains came off was when someone died. Fellow next to me coughed himself to death during the night. We had to pick him up either side – stone cold he was – and take him out the box. Buried him then and there at the side of the road, they did.'

This was what Perrion had threatened us with, if we ruffled his feathers. Here we were, one step away. It was like standing on the edge of a sheer cliff and peering over.

Out of the blue Barrie asked us, 'You boys planning on running away? You got seven years o' this in front of you.'

I shook my head. 'We're in enough trouble already.'

Richard chimed in. 'I think we're going to sit this out until we can go back to Sydney. What about you?'

Barrie gave one of his little half-smiles. 'Might be, might not be. If you fancy it, let us know.'

It was a grim life on Charlotte Farm, but no worse in its discomfort and cruelty than the one we had lived in the Navy. At first we kept a constant look out for snakes and spiders. I saw the yellow-banded snakes from time to time, but after a couple of weeks I decided they were more frightened of me than I was of them, and that put my fear of being bitten to the back of my mind.

Our real punishment was the monotony of our work and the lack of companionship that had made being at sea more bearable. Barrie and Bell were happy to leave Richard and me to do the lion's share of the work. I kept hoping we'd wake up one morning and find they'd run away, or that they would irritate Perrion so much he would send them somewhere else. But they knew exactly how little they could get away with and still escape the wrath of their master.

Although I was never allowed in the farmhouse, I could glimpse through its windows to see its luxurious interior. There was a mahogany piano, of an upright design, and Perrion would play morning and evening as the fancy took him. I often wondered how something as fragile and heavy as a piano had managed to make such a journey from England. O'Brian told me Perrion had bought it at auction in Sydney for three hundred guineas. I could barely imagine making so much money in my life.

Perrion was a man of conflicting moods. How he was feeling was often reflected in the music he played on that piano. When his music was wild and agitated, we knew he would be out to curse and beat us as we worked. If it was soft and melancholy, he would be polite and even concerned with our wellbeing.

His wife played the piano as well. From her we heard

only hymns. She seemed gripped by a quiet desperation. The two daughters were podgy, graceless girls who looked like their father. At first I hoped they would befriend us – we needed friends out here with only Barrie and Bell for company. But they kept a haughty distance and I soon grew irritated by their sullen, unsmiling faces staring at us from out of the window.

O'Brian continued to direct us in our labour. He knew we worked hard, and in return he would bring us extra rations – bread, biscuits or a couple of apples, which he would give us surreptitiously when he was sure no one could see him. One morning a month or so after we had arrived, he told us, 'You and Richard are good lads. I know you work a lot harder than that pair of useless clods. When I think it's the right moment I'll ask the master about taking your chains off. I'm sure you can be trusted. You won't let me down now will you?'

A week passed, and O'Brian said nothing more. Then, out of the blue, he told us he was riding on horseback to Sydney with Perrion that morning and he would ask him about our shackles on the journey. 'The master's pleased with the way the field's shaping up,' he said with a smile. 'This'll be a good time to ask.'

All day we waited, then the next. The following morning we saw Perrion returning alone. He looked quite despondent.

'So where the hell is O'Brian?' Richard said to me. Something was up.

'Maybe he's gone to another farm? Got a better offer?' I said. 'Don't suppose he felt he could mention it to us.' I felt cheated and angry with O'Brian for raising our hopes and then deserting us.

Perrion came to our hut later in the day. He was grave and sober, like a parson at a funeral.

'I have some sad news for you boys. Mr O'Brian fell from his horse on the way to Sydney. He broke his neck.'

'Will he be all right? Will he recover?' I asked. This was terrible news. For him and for us.

Perrion looked irritated. 'He's dead, you stupid boy. Tell Barrie and Bell for me, will you. Right now I can't bear the thought of their smirking, stupid faces.'

I decided not to ask him about the shackles. As O'Brian had said, there was a right moment to ask.

Perrion oversaw us every day after that. His moods were as unpredictable as ever, but without O'Brian around to protect him he was less inclined to hit us as we worked. One day he spoke to us as we took a break from chopping wood.

'I've appointed a new farm manager,' he told us. 'He's coming up here in a week or two. He's a Navy man, like you two boys. Used to be a bosun's mate.'

My heart sank.

'Could I ask you his name, sir?' I said.

'Lewis Tuck. Fine figure of a man. Don't imagine he'll stand for any slacking.'

'He won't believe his luck when he finds it's us he's looking after,' said Richard. 'He'll work us to death, and Bell and Barrie.'

I could imagine exactly what Tuck would make of Bell and Barrie. He would see them as a challenge, and I suspected Tuck was a man who liked a challenge. Years of back-breaking labour, sadistic beatings and floggings stretched ahead. Before O'Brian had died I had begun to tell myself that we were going to survive this farm. Now I was convinced we would die here.

We told our companions about Tuck and what they could expect. Out of the blue Barrie made an announcement. 'Well that's it. We're going. Me and Mr Bell have been hatching a plot to get away for several months now. You coming with us?'

We had never thought of escaping. 'Where are you going to go?' I said. 'Come and see us tonight,' said Barrie. 'We'll have ourselves a little chat.'

'Is this wise?' said Richard as soon as we were alone. 'I wouldn't trust Bell and Barrie as far as I could throw them, never mind run away with them.'

'Neither would I,' I said. 'But I want to get away from here before Tuck arrives. I wouldn't know where to start plotting an escape, so let's see what they've got to say.'

That evening we sat around a fire they made in their hut. We all had a tot of rum and started to plan our escape.

'We can't get away with these chains,' I said. 'How are we going to get them off?'

'We need some help,' said Barrie. 'I know someone who might be persuaded. These shackles are no great shakes to get off. You need a hammer and chisel and a steady hand, that's all. Me and Mr Bell we know one of Perrion's neighbours, Charlie Palmer. Comes to see us to sell us rum. It'll cost us though. Quite a bit. We ain't got enough, have you?'

Perhaps it was the first heady rush of rum, but I was feeling reckless. I fished the ring my mother had given me from round my neck. 'What will this get us?'

Bell and Barrie's eyes lit up. 'Quite a lot, son. Quite a lot.'

Barrie said, 'You give me that and I'll see if I can get Charlie to get us out of these chains and give us a pistol or two. Just a warning though, taking these chains off is worth at least a hundred lashes, so if we're going, we better make sure we really go.'

I handed over the ring, regretting my generosity at once. But what else could I do?

Where should we go? Barrie and Bell were full of wild rumours and strange stories about places we could head for. Bell, I thought, he'd believe anything. But I was surprised a clever man like Barric had swallowed the stories he was spouting.

'We should go to China,' he said, nursing his third tot of rum. 'I've seen it on plates. Beautiful blue bridges and buildings, lovely ladies in kimonos, lots of weeping willow trees. I likes the look of China.'

Richard and I had both seen maps of the world. We knew where New South Wales was and we knew where China was. We also knew how long it would take to get there.

'China is too far to the north,' said Richard. 'It would take months to sail there, and years to walk – even if you could walk all the way, which you can't.'

'I've heard it's only a month or so,' said Bell. 'I'm up for it.'

Barrie had taken in what we had said. 'These boys know their onions, Mr Bell. I think we should listen to them. But I've heard there's a place maybe three, four hundred miles north up the coast from 'ere – another colony. White people, French, Dutch, I can't remember, but they welcome the likes of us with open arms. We could walk that in a few weeks. They need white people working there, not like these lazy savages.'

I had to suppress a smile. Bell and Barrie were the two laziest people I'd ever met in my life.

'What about the natives?' I said. 'Don't they eat the

white people they catch?'

Barrie shook his head. 'That's all stories to stop us running away, Sam. The only time those savages get violent is when one of our lot does them a mischief.'

We started to argue. Richard and I had never heard of this colony. Bell was growing impatient. 'So what else is there? You come up with a better idea, and I'll go along with you. I still say we oughta go to China. There's another place on the west coast here, I've heard. Another colony. We could try for that.'

Richard sounded impatient. 'Come on now. You're not thinking straight. It took our ship a month to sail along the south coast. It'll take, what, a year to walk it? Then what if we get there and find nobody's there?'

'What about New Zealand, then?' I said. I knew it was several weeks at sea, but we seemed to be running out of options.

'New Zealand?' snapped Bell. 'Where've you been? Now that's a place where they *do* eat people. I'm not going there.'

I realised like never before what a good place New South Wales was to build a convict colony. Where the hell were we going to go?

'We don't have a great deal of choice,' said Richard. 'So, I suggest we go north and see if we can find this mythical colony of yours. If we stay here, we're all dead men. Tuck will flog you two to death,' he nodded at

Barrie and Bell, 'and he'll string our guts up to dry on the nearest tree.'

'We're not too far from the coast. It'll be east of here,' I said. 'If we follow the sun and the stars to get there, we can go north along the shoreline.' They all nodded, warming to this idea. My confidence grew. 'And the beach will be easier to walk along than the forest, and we'll have a greater chance of finding food on our way. The natives eat mussels and oysters along the coastal rocks. We should do the same.'

'North,' we all said, raising our glasses in a toast. Then Richard and I slunk away to bed.

He was uneasy about our plan. 'After all that excitement, I don't think there is a colony in the north,' he said. 'Do you?'

'There's only the flimsiest hope that this colony in the north actually exists,' I said. 'But that's better than no hope at all, isn't it?' I was trying hard to convince myself we weren't doing something stupid.

Richard shook his head and said nothing. Then, as we lay in the dark, he voiced his worries.

'Perhaps we should sneak back to Sydney and try to stow away aboard an outbound ship? There are French and American ships that stop off to reprovision or trade. Perhaps one of them will take runaways? I've heard there are American whalers too, whose captains were happy to take skilled seamen.'

'They'd take us,' I said. 'But they'd take one look at Bell and Barrie and know they'd be useless *and* trouble.'

Richard gave a mirthless laugh. 'They'd never agree to that, so it's not even worth raising it. I wish we weren't a package. You and me. Bell and Barrie.'

'We need them to escape from here, don't we?' I said. 'I like the idea of trying to get on a ship in Sydney, but it may be weeks or months before one comes in. We can't bet on staying in hiding that long. And even if we did manage to get aboard, the captain might refuse to take us. We'll just have to take our chances with those two.'

Richard let out a long weary sigh and said no more.

I felt unhappy lying down to sleep without my mother's ring around my neck. I was used to having it there, warm against my skin. I had long thought of it as a good luck charm to keep me safe, like Rosie's letters had been on the *Miranda*, and I had hoped to always be able to keep it. It was my one solid link with my family and home.

As I drifted off, a stray thought kept nagging away at the back of my mind. I had heard people talking about this colony of white men somewhere outside Sydney. It came up in conversations I had overheard in the Sailor's Arms. Only I could swear that the place they all talked about was somewhere south of Sydney, not north.

CHAPTER 13

Fugitives

Although I was anxious about trusting him with the ring, Barrie was as good as his word. Charlie Palmer agreed to help, and provided us with weapons and food to see us through the first few days of our escape. Every day we wondered when to go. 'We need a good moonshiney night,' said Barrie. 'No good going on a new moon. We might as well put on blind-folds and run away.'

Charlie was to remove our shackles as soon as we were left alone in the evening. We knew that Perrion often stayed awake until midnight playing his piano.

Any disturbance after that would be sure to be detected, especially by Tinker the dog.

On the day of our escape we went to Barrie and Bell's hut an hour after dark. They were both cagey. 'What if Palmer don't turn up?' Bell kept saying.

The thought of failure in our escape hung over me like a sullen phantom. What could I expect? Flogging, hanging. Even if we got away from the farm we faced starvation, exhaustion, a grisly death at the hands of the natives. No one could be bothered to make small talk. We just sat and listened. Insects chirped. Possums cackled. Fear gripped my insides.

There was a rustle in the grass outside the hut, and we heard Tinker bark in the distance. A round-faced man poked his head through the door. He looked flushed and anxious. He was out of breath and, despite the coolness of the night, sweat dripped down his forehead. Barrie spoke curtly.

'You took yer time, Charlie.'

'What a palaver,' he said. 'I'm not used to this lurking around. There's enough in this bag to get me hung three times over.'

There was too. Hammer, chisel, a pistol, shot and powder, an axe, hunting knives, fish hook and twine, bread, cheese, meat. Charlie Palmer had done his best for us.

Barrie spoke. 'We'll do the boys first. Mr Bell will sort

you out. He's done this before.'

Charlie handed over his tools. I lay down, face to the ground, the smell of earth sharp in my nostrils. This was the point of no return. Once the shackles were off, I had to escape.

Bell brought the hammer down hard. A sharp pain shot through my ankle and a loud CLANG disturbed the evening quiet.

The shackle fell away. 'That hurt,' I said, rubbing my bruised ankle. 'Shut your face,' said Bell, 'I'm more worried about the bloody noise we're making.'

I had no right to whinge; the blow hadn't even broken the skin. 'Quick,' said Barrie, 'let's do the other one and be done with it.'

I lay down again and Bell took the hammer to the other shackle. I winced with pain as the blow came down on the iron cuff round my ankle. Then the shackles were off. I staggered to my feet, feeling as light-footed as a gambolling lamb. I wanted to dash out of the hut and run and run until my chest was bursting. To be able to move without those chains was a joy. But the pleasure was short-lived.

'This is going to make an awful racket,' said Bell, 'doing all four of us.'

'Keep this up and we'll have Perrion down 'ere in no time,' said Barrie.

I listened with mounting anxiety. 'So what are you

saying? You're not going to take off the other shackles?'

No one said anything. I began to wonder what I was going to say to Perrion in the morning.

Then Barrie's face lit up. 'What happens about this time every evening?'

We all looked blank.

'The ducks and geese come over, making one hell of a commotion. That's the time to strike off the shackles.'

We listened intently, eager for the first distant sounds of flapping and honking. The minutes dragged until, at last, we heard them coming and I started to breathe a little easier.

In the midst of this unholy racket, Richard's shackles came off, then Barrie's. Finally, and in some haste, Barrie took the hammer and chisel and began to hack at Bell's ankles before the noise subsided. He made a bad job of it. Bell shot up in agony, as the chisel missed its bolt and the iron bit into his flesh. 'Hold still, you arse,' said Barrie, and quickly finished the job before the last of the fowl landed in the river.

'You bleedin' idiot,' said Bell, holding on to his left ankle. Blood was seeping out of a nasty gash.

'Shut up with yer moaning,' said Barrie. 'Bone's not broken, is it.'

When they weren't being courteous to each other they bickered like a couple who had been married forty years and hated the sight of each other.

Bell got up. He hobbled with the pain, but he didn't seem too distressed. 'Not had these off me for three years,' he said. 'I could run a mile without a pause for breath.'

'Right,' said Barrie. 'Job done. Thank you Charlie. Now wish us luck. The next time you see us we might be dangling from a gallows.'

Charlie Palmer crept away. Later in the evening, the piano playing started. First the hymns – that must be Mrs Perrion – then a succession of slow and beautiful melodies. Perrion played from the soul, and the notes floated into the still night air and over the fields and bush that surrounded Green Hills. If they were out there, I wondered what the natives made of such music. Theirs had its own beguiling rhythm and a low throb which seemed to come from the very core of the earth. Would this elegant succession of notes sound as foreign to them as their own music did to me?

The music stopped. We waited until complete stillness descended, then crept out. Richard and me hurried over to our own hut to pick up a few more clothes, a little food we had managed to hoard, a blanket apiece and a mess tin each to cook with. We hoped there would be plenty of fresh water in the streams that would cross our path.

Then we stole away, slowly at first, nervous of any

snapping twig or clumsy stumble. But even Tinker did not stir to signal our escape, and the sound of our feet swishing through the long grass went undetected. The further we got from the farm the faster we ran.

It was past dawn when we stopped to rest. So far, the journey had taken us through lush meadow, and past outlying farms. Pausing to wolf down a slice of bread and a couple of plums, we scanned the horizon behind us for any sign that we were being followed. Ahead lay thicker bush.

'Once we get to that, they'll never find us,' said Barrie between hurried mouthfuls.

We scurried through enveloping ferns, tangled roots and fallen branches that now marked our every step away from Green Hills. Trees crowded around our heads, their branches blocking the light and heat from the sun.

Every distant noise made me start, and I wondered if we would be able to outrun the search party that would be sent after us. On that first day of our escape we were gripped by a constant anxiety that men and dogs would appear as distant dots behind us, but they never did. Perhaps they had set out looking for us in another direction?

'Maybe they think we wouldn't be stupid enough to head for that colony in the north?' I said, and immediately wished I hadn't. Almost as soon as we had left I had started to believe we were on a hiding to nowhere.

'We agreed this is the best way,' said Barrie angrily, 'so we're not changing our route now.'

'Yeah,' said Bell. 'And don't go thinking you're heading off different from us. I'm not having you two squealing on us when you get caught, or giving up and going back to the farm. I'll snap your necks like a couple of chickens before you do.'

Richard tried to make the peace. 'Once we get to the coast we'll be sure of something to eat, so let's not waste our time arguing.'

Barrie held up a hand to hush him. 'What's that ahead?'

There in a clearing we could make out a mouldy old boot, lying flat on the ground. When the wind blew strong in our direction the smell hit us – sickly sweet and cloying. The sound of buzzing flies reached our ears. As we approached the corpse, three sullen crows fluttered away.

I forced myself to look at the body. Half rotted, half pecked to pieces, two wooden spears through the chest pinned it to the ground. 'This one fell foul of the savages,' said Bell. 'We'd best make sure we don't give the buggers the chance to do the same to us.'

We moved on quickly. For now, the landscape varied between bush and lush grassland. Ahead, on the hills that loomed over the plain, was dense bush, as far as the eye could see. We would be there in a day or so and the journey would become more difficult.

That first day we saw two other bodies, now just dirty, off-white skeletons. There was something sinister about the grinning skulls, but unlike the corpse we had encountered earlier they had no smell about them. I stared with fascination, and wondered what had happened to them.

Towards evening Richard held up a hand to stop us. We peered through the grass. In the distance, a party of natives were walking slowly west along the plain before us. They all carried long spears. 'Let's stay 'ere for now,' said Barrie. 'You never know with this lot whether they'll be friend or foe.'

We reached dense bushland as night fell. When the clear blue sky turned icy pale, the cold began to pierce our bones. Constant movement and the excitement of our escape had prevented me from noticing how chilly it was. We gathered brushwood and, as Barrie and Bell set about lighting a campfire, Richard and I scoured the surrounding forest for familiar-looking fruit. We found none. On our return we were cursed roundly for our failure. 'Yer useless gits,' said Bell. 'These rations aren't going to last us more than a couple of days.'

'You go out there and have a look then,' said Richard angrily.

Bell grabbed him by the shirt. 'Less of your lip, Yankee boy.'

Barrie put a hand on his shoulder. 'Easy now, Mr Bell. I'm sure the boys did the best they could,' he growled.

We sat around the fire, them on one side, us on the other, and ate our salted beef and bread in silence. Looking at Bell and Barrie through the curling flames I began to imagine we had created a hell of our own, and our two disagreeable companions would only make our difficulties worse. When we finished eating the only noises we heard were gusts of wind in the trees and the squawk and flutter of the night birds. We gathered fallen branches to cover our bodies and stoked the fire high to warm ourselves. The forest enveloped us. Outside the circle of light around our fire was a sinister world of murderous savages and poisonous snakes. The trees looked down, branches nodding in the wind – cold, unthinking, indifferent to our plight.

I woke shivering. The fire was still smouldering but not aflame, and a chilling dew had settled on us. Over in the east the sky was getting light. I had slept deeply, and felt refreshed and ready for another day's march. Then drops of rain fell on my face. It was not a good start to the day.

The others began to stir as the rain fell more heavily. Bell and Barrie rivalled themselves in the foulness of their cursing. Richard, as ever, had the best idea. 'Let's get up and go. We'll only freeze to death here.'

We breakfasted from our dwindling supply of meat and bread, and stumbled through the dawn. First we needed to establish our direction. The sun was coming up in the east, and that was where the nearest coast was, so we headed towards the brimming sky. Bell fell badly on a tangled vine and bruised his head on a rock. Then he began to complain about his ankle. We stopped when it got properly light and took a look. The gash Barrie had made while hacking off Bell's shackles had turned an ugly green and yellow. 'I've seen worse, Mr Bell,' said Barrie. 'You'll just have to keep going and ignore it. It'll get better on its own.'

The rain stopped and the sky cleared to a fresh blue. We climbed up to the top of the valley and made our way along a ridge that followed the curve of a river.

'We need to find a shallow place to cross,' said Bell.

'Now if we could make ourselves a boat, we could float our way to the sea,' suggested Barrie.

Bell disagreed. 'Four scarecrows in a boat in the middle of a river. Now wouldn't that make it easy for us to be spotted? We need to stick to the forest.'

'We'd need to find a boat,' I agreed with Barrie. 'I've seen the ones the natives make from bark. They just cut away a whole side of a tree. But then we'd need twine and a needle to sew up the ends for the bow and the stern.'

'Boat sounds good to me,' said Richard.

I said, 'If we had a boat, we could travel along the river at night, and rest during the day. That way they'd be less likely to spot us.'

Bell and Barrie ignored our comments. We were clearly irritating them with our ideas. Then Barrie muttered, 'Mr Bell can't swim. Anyway, boats make me nervous.'

'But it was your idea in the first place.' I thought it but I didn't say it. I walked off shaking my head. Sooner or later we would have to cross the rivers that lay between us and our journey east.

Once we reached the ridge we had a clear view over the plain we had left behind and the territory that stretched out in front of us. We were still close enough to Green Hills to be able to see smoke rising from settlement fires. But if we made good progress today, we could be confident of escaping the clutches of any search party from Charlotte Farm.

Although the sun was out, a sharp wind pierced our damp clothing. 'Let's get down from the top of this hill, and get out of the wind,' said Barrie.

We argued about this. It was easier going on the ridge, with less vegetation to snag our feet. And we could see where we were going. But Barrie was insistent. I was alarmed to notice Bell beginning to walk with a limp. His wound was slowing him down.

Away from the wind the sun warmed our bodies and

we began to feel more cheerful. At noon we stopped to rest and eat on a rocky outcrop. We spread our blankets on the rock to dry them and sat looking over the lush forest below. Tall evergreens swayed in the breeze. Sandstone rocks gleamed in the bright sunshine along the dizzying drop to the valley bottom. Among the curves of the land we could see patches of the bright blue river below, and hear the screeching of river fowl. A haze lay over the forest like a light smoke, floating among the tree tops.

'This is a beautiful country,' I said to Richard. 'I wish we were here as explorers rather than fugitives.'

'I wish we knew how to find food like the natives,' said Richard wistfully.

We ate our bread and cheese, and shared an apple. There was a little left for supper. After that we would have to find our food out in the forest. So far we had seen nothing we could safely eat, nor come across any animal we could spear or shoot.

We followed the ridge down. A cluster of rock formed around the dark hole of a cave. In the dim light around the entrance I could see a wall of handprints. Barrie followed me in. 'D'you know how they do that?' he said. 'Fill their mouth full of paint and blow around their hand. I seen 'em do it.

'I suppose this means there's scores of the buggers round here, then,' he continued. 'Let's hope this pistol scares them off if they ever decide they want us for dinner.'

The afternoon was heavy going, up and down hill, and more exhausting than the previous day's walking. But the sun felt hot on our faces and the wind blew warm. We stopped at the bottom of the valley, close to the river. We were all thirsty now, and needed to drink. Barrie had cheered up, pleased by the day's progress. But Bell had barely spoken a word, and he was making an effort to be pleasant. It was not hard to see why. He was worried his ankle would slow him down and had realised he needed all the help and sympathy he could get. 'Too late for that,' snapped Richard, when we talked as we gathered firewood.

That evening we ate our final rations – a sliver of dried pork, a carrot and a pear. From the next day we would have to find our own food. Nothing, so far, had reassured me that we would be able to. As I shuffled restlessly beneath my blanket, trying to get comfortable enough to sleep, I began to fret over the folly of escaping with these two villains. But what else could we have done? They knew someone who would help us escape. We didn't. I was certain Tuck would have worked us to death, or flogged the life out of us. Staying behind was no choice at all.

I began to think of other escapes I had heard about back in Sydney, and counted my blessings. At least we hadn't tried to flee to Ireland heading south, assuming that as Ireland was colder than New South Wales, it must be in the same direction the cold wind came from. And we hadn't used a compass drawn on a piece of paper to guide us. Both these stories were doing the rounds when I arrived in the colony. At first I didn't believe them, thinking nobody could be so stupid. I mentioned this to Doctor Dan one night. 'I've met some of the men who tried to do this,' he told me. 'They're not stupid. They're just simple country people.'

As I drifted off to sleep, I was tormented by the bad luck that had landed Richard and me in this awful situation. If only I had laid there in the dust, and let that despicable John Gray laugh at me, instead of launching myself at him. Wouldn't life have turned out differently then?

We walked east the next morning. We had no breakfast so instead we drank as much as we could from the river. We stuck to the river bank too, but this was a mistake. Here the vegetation was thicker and there were many inlets and coves to navigate. To traverse them we had much climbing up and down steep sandstone rocks, and by mid-morning I was exhausted. My toes throbbed, my heart beat hard in my chest, and I was soon drenched with sweat. As we staggered along, the four of us grew more separate. Barrie leading, Richard following, me next and Bell straggling behind. We headed up the valley and the day dragged on. I was too exhausted to feel hungry. Just one step in front of another. I gave myself little goals. Get to the rock by the far tree, and then you can have a rest. Get to the bush by the sandstone outcrop, then you can stop.

I kept thinking of Oliver Pritchard. His words at our trial came back to taunt me. 'The boys had clearly lost their nerve . . . They clung on to each other like two frightened children . . . I thought then and there to shoot them . . .' The hatred I felt for him drove me on. He was not going to beat me. I was determined to survive.

Soon after midday I realised I had lost the others. I sat down to get my breath, and when my chest stopped aching I shouted at the top of my voice:

'RICHARD!'

The word echoed around the still forest.

RICHARD!

Richard!

Richard!

I climbed the side of the valley, hoping to catch sight of the others. In my exhausted state the forest began to take on a peculiar aspect. Trees looked as if they were made of stone. White rocks, cracked into small cauliflower-like ridges, resembled the human brains I had seen in battle. The silence of the forest seemed deeper than ever, broken only by my own laboured breathing.

CHAPTER 14

Friends Reunited

As I edged up the smooth sandstone rock I was afraid of falling. I could break my ankle or leg, or crack my head and knock myself unconscious, and be lost here for ever. I sat down and fought back my tears. Then I became angry. Come on Sam, act like a man. I forced my aching legs on, staggering through the green tendrils that grasped my feet.

The sun reached its highest point, and despite the cool wind, it felt uncomfortably hot. My tongue was thick in my mouth, which was as dry and foul-tasting as baked mud. I stopped for a few minutes to rest, and my stomach began to rumble. When I felt the strength returning to my legs I blundered off again. A while later, I found a stream and drank until I could drink no more.

By mid-afternoon the shadows were growing longer and my fear returned. If I didn't find the others soon, I would have to spend the night alone. Barrie had our only sparking kit and without that I couldn't make a fire.

The moon rose in a clear blue sky and the air grew colder. I looked around the forest, wondering how I could make myself warm enough to sleep. A rocky outcrop had a small opening that was almost a cave. It was damp, but it offered some shelter. I dragged in a collection of branches and laid them down on the ground to make a barrier between myself and the cold stone. Wrapped in my blanket I tried to rest, but sleep would not come. I turned this way and that, trying to find a comfy position for my weary body. After several hours the rocks seemed to be closing in around me, so I stood up to look at the night sky.

I climbed up the rock above the cave and looked down the valley. There, miracle of miracles, some way below, I could see the glow of a fire. It must be Richard, Barrie and Bell. I gathered up my blanket and ran as fast as I could towards them. But what if it wasn't them? It could be natives. It could be soldiers.

I fought my way through the forest, often losing direction and having to climb higher to see if I could still find the fire. I knew I was nearly there when the smell of roast meat reached my nostrils. My stomach lurched and began to gurgle loudly. I hoped it was them, and I hoped there was still some food left to eat.

Now I could see the fire ahead of me and silhouettes of people around it. It was them all right. As I approached my foot snapped a branch and Barrie grabbed his pistol and fired into the darkness. The shot hit a tree trunk above my head, showering me with splinters.

'It's me, you idiot,' I shouted.

Richard cried out, 'Sam!' I could hear the relief in his voice. He ran up and hugged me. 'We thought we'd lost you. Come and have some duck.' He handed me a leg of roast meat. As I crunched into the fatty blackened skin, juice ran down the side of my mouth. It was the most delicious thing I'd ever tasted.

'I called for you all afternoon, Sam,' said Richard. 'I heard you shouting once or twice, but I could never make out where your voice was coming from. I'm amazed you didn't hear me.'

As I ate I realised neither Barrie nor Bell had said anything. 'Well good evening to you too,' I said with some irritation. 'Who else did you think it could be, out here in the middle of nowhere?'

Barrie leered at me through the flickering light of the fire. 'Thought we'd lost you for good, Samuel. Mr Bell and me were looking forward to your portion of duck.

But young Buckley 'ere's been guarding it jealously. If you'd come ten minutes later, you'd have been too late.'

Richard spoke up. 'Caught the thing late this afternoon. Whole party of them came into land on the river and sailed right up to us. Mr Barrie waded in but they all started to peck him. I leapt in and grabbed one by the neck while it was distracted. You make fine duck bait, Mr Barrie!'

Barrie gave a sardonic little smile. Bell tried to be friendly. No doubt he was still worried that his injured ankle would be holding us up. 'I called out for you too, Sam,' he said. 'But we heard nothing back.' Richard looked at him is disbelief. 'I'll bet you did,' I thought.

In the morning light I noticed how filthy we were. Our clothes and shoes in tatters, our bodies caked in dirt. As we set off, hunger returned. 'Sooner we reach the coast, the better,' said Richard. 'Then we can have clams and oysters for breakfast, and a nice fat fish for tea.'

That morning the wind picked up, and clouds began to form in the blue sky. Soon a gale was howling through the trees, and we had to hang our blankets around our shoulders as we walked. Bell was limping badly, and I could tell his injured ankle was causing him pain. When we stopped for a rest he lifted his trouser leg to look at it. The yellow and green bruising around the wound had spread and the gash made by the shackle was livid and weeping.

It began to rain soon after noon. Great sheets hammered down, soaking us and our blankets. The rest of the day brought only misery. Progress was slow and we argued bitterly about whether or not to take shelter. Barrie was finally persuaded that it would be better to conserve our dwindling strength than press on until dark. We found another cave and tried to light a fire. But everything in the forest was now so wet it would not catch alight. It was a wretched, miserable night. Sleep was impossible and the morning brought only more rain. One look at the sky told us it was set to stay like this for the day.

We walked on, chilled to the marrow, too miserable to speak. Only Barrie's voice could be heard, cursing at Bell to keep up with us. He was getting slower every day. After a while, a numb indifference to the world seemed to come over me, and the hunger and the cold receded. It was not until the afternoon that the rain stopped, but the clouds stayed and the sun did not appear to dry the woods around us.

That night there was no cave and we were too tired to walk further to look for one. We rested in the low boughs of trees as we could not bring ourselves to lie on the wet ground. But as sleep claimed us, one by one, we would fall from our perches, and wake with a painful jolt. Barrie's temper grew worse and all three of us tried not to speak to him so as to avoid a tongue-lashing. We could only wrap our arms around ourselves and shiver.

I did sleep that night, in fits and starts, but only because my bones were so weary I could have slept through a battle. We were all awake to watch the dawn and set off as soon as it was light enough to see the ground before us. Richard and me led the way, Barrie and Bell trailed behind.

'I thought he was trying to kill me, when he fired the other night,' I said. 'Yes,' said Richard. 'They didn't seem worried about you. "Less mouths to feed," Barrie kept saying to himself.'

'The sooner we find something to eat, the sooner we'll feel better,' said Richard. Talk of food made my stomach contract into a little ball. Finding some red berries, I picked one to taste.

'Careful now,' said Richard. 'Crush it in your hand and smell it first.' I did, on the tip of my finger and thumb. The berry was not moist, and broke down to a paste. I placed the tip of my tongue on the mush and recoiled with disgust. The taste was so bitter it burned my tongue and lodged in the back of my throat. Barrie and Bell caught up with us to see me retching, hands on knees. Barrie grabbed the berries at once. 'You can't fool me with your antics,' he said, and stuffed them in his mouth. The berries came out as quickly as they had gone in.

'What the hell did you do that for?' said Richard, aghast.

'Thought you were playin' a game,' said Barrie, between sputters, 'to keep me and Mr Bell away from food.'

The taste of that single berry stayed in my mouth for the rest of the morning, until we found a muddy stream swollen with the recent rain, and I drank down the cloudy water. I kept thinking what Barrie's mouth must have tasted like, and tried not to smile.

By noon our hunger was so intense we could think of nothing but food. The sun came out, and in the early afternoon we stopped by a large rock to spread our blankets to dry. As Richard and I lay there in the sunshine soaking up the warmth, Barrie came over to us. 'I'm going looking for food, and Mr Bell is gathering wood for a fire. You two can make yerselves useful an' all. Meet back here and see what we've got.'

We drifted aimlessly. There was nothing here except ferns, trees and cones. 'We could try boiling up some of the ferns,' I suggested.

'Let's see if Bell has the strength to gather and light a fire. You'd think there'd be some sort of fruit or vegetable for us to eat,' said Richard.

After another hour's wandering we returned with a handful of ferns for want of anything better to eat. Bell had done well. A fire blazed under the overhang of a rocky outcrop and we boiled water from a nearby stream in a billy can. Barrie had found nothing. 'Where are all the bloody kangaroos?' he said. 'We saw them every day on the farm, and not a single one out here. I could eat a whole kangaroo right now.'

We boiled up the ferns and I volunteered to eat them. 'If we boil them long enough, that should take the poison out of them,' I told myself.

So when they were just a soggy mess and the water in the billy can had gone bright green, I lifted some stalks out with a clean twig. 'Wish me luck,' I said to them all, as they gathered round to watch. The smell of the ferns gave nothing away. They smelt slightly sharp, like tomatoes.

I blew to cool them, while Bell and Barrie urged me on. When I placed the soggy mess in my mouth, I could see them drooling, they were so hungry. The ferns were too woody, I chewed and chewed and still they did not seem ready to swallow. The taste, too, was bitter.

At last I swallowed, then tried another mouthful. But as I chewed I was seized by a violent desire to be sick. Out came the fern, and I knelt and retched for ten minutes. Afterwards, I felt weak and dizzy, and lay down away from the campfire to rest. Bright light seemed to make me worse. I couldn't bear to look at the fire glinting on the brass buttons on Barrie's jacket. Still, eating the ferns had cured me of my hunger for the moment. I slept well until daylight, when the raging hunger returned.

That next morning we all looked dreadful. It was now

the seventh day of our escape, and the fourth since we had eaten. We talked about what to do. 'Keep going east I suppose,' said Richard. 'Sooner we get to the coast the better.'

'No sense in that,' said Bell. 'We'd just be wearing ourselves out, and getting nowhere. If we could find something to eat, we'd all have the strength to walk faster and maybe this blasted leg would begin to heal.'

His ankle looked even more swollen and he hobbled everywhere.

'Let's walk on until we find a cave that can do as our base,' I said. 'Somewhere we can shelter if it rains and we can store dry wood and build a fire that can't be seen by soldiers or natives. Then we can go out hunting and meet back there.'

'Right,' said Barrie. 'But you're coming with me, Witchall. I don't trust you two to share anything you find with us.'

Richard was indignant. 'We'd trust you. You've got no reason to say that.'

'All right then,' he said. 'But if I find out you've been eating food and not sharing it, I'll have you for supper myself.'

Richard and I went to the river with the fish hook and twine Charlie Palmer had brought us. Barrie and Bell scoured the forest for edible plants. 'Those two wouldn't know an edible plant if it bit them in the ass,' said Richard. 'They've spent their whole lives in London or prison. Not much opportunity for foraging there. They probably wouldn't even recognise a raspberry.'

The day was mild enough for us to wash our filthy clothes and bodies in the river. Sitting by the waterside in the winter sun, waiting for a fish to take the bait, I did feel a sense of contentment. It was midwinter here, and as mild as a late spring day in England. The valley was lush and beautiful. If we could find food, we'd be in paradise.

Morning came and went with no success, although our clothes had dried by noon. It felt good to wear something not caked in mud and that didn't stink of stale sweat. The fish were not interested in the frond we used for bait. There were ducks around, and cormorants, although I couldn't imagine their scraggy black bodies making a tasty meal. Unfortunately, the birds kept their distance.

By late afternoon we'd caught nothing. On the weary trek back to our base I began to dread the tongue-lashing we'd get from Barrie. We returned to find a fire lit, and Barrie and Bell looking expectantly up at us, desperate hope burning in their faces. We shook our heads. Barrie and Bell uttered the foulest curses. 'We're all going to waste away to nothing here,' wailed Bell. We passed the evening eyeing each other warily on either side of the camp fire.

*　　*　　*

On our fourth day without food, I wondered how much longer we could go on. 'Let's spend the morning by the river and the afternoon combing the wood,' I suggested. 'Better still,' said Richard, 'let's take it in turns to do one or the other.'

It was a good idea. We were so weak and dizzy with hunger, sitting by the river with a fishing line was about all we were up to. I found drinking a great deal of water helped, but it could not extinguish this overwhelming desire to eat. 'It's all I can think about,' I told Richard.

'Me too, but don't start talking about it.'

He volunteered to go into the forest first. I sat on a rock by the river, and daydreamed about moist roast chicken, and steaming potatoes and carrots dripping with melted butter, and bread and butter pudding with a dollop of cream, and beef and horseradish sandwiches. By the time Richard returned I felt so hollow I was sure I had a hole in my middle.

'Sam!' he seemed excited. 'I found a couple of kangaroo apples. I've seen these in the market at Sydney. I searched around the spot for more. But something's eaten the rest.'

'Do you think we should save one for Bell and Barrie?' I asked.

Richard looked at me doubtfully. 'Do you think for a second they'd share such a meagre haul with us? If I'd found a whole sackful, I'd bring some back.'

He was right. We ate the fruit as slowly as we could bear to. It tasted like unripe tomato. Then we both washed our faces and hands several times in the river. 'If they smell anything on us, they'll kill us,' said Richard.

That afternoon I foraged, Richard fished. I was surprised how much better I felt with even a morsel of food inside me. By late afternoon my exhaustion had returned. Every step seemed a chore and I had to fight an overwhelming desire to curl up on the ground and go to sleep. I returned to the river to find Richard lying on the bank, dozing. He'd wrapped his fishing line around his hand.

'We better get back,' said Richard wearily, when I woke him.

'If we can walk that far,' I said.

We headed up the side of the valley but I couldn't keep up. 'Wait for me, Richard,' I shouted angrily.

'Hurry up then, you lummox,' shouted Richard.

'You've just spent the afternoon sitting on your arse and dozing,' I shouted, 'while I hunted around this bloody forest. Have some patience.'

'And *you* didn't find a bloody thing, did you?' said Richard.

'Shut up you idiot,' I hissed in his face. I was close to tears. 'Bell and Barrie might hear you. They'll kill us if they find out we've eaten something we didn't share with them.'

We walked on in sullen silence. 'We've got to stick

together,' I kept thinking. We couldn't be falling out with each other like this. But I was too angry with Richard to say it.

It took an age to return to the cave. Barrie was there on his own and didn't notice us return. He had lit a fire and was staring into it in a morose way, wrapped up in his own world. He had a livid bruise on the right side of his temple.

'Where's Mr Bell?' I said. He jumped out of his skin, and a look of horror came over his face.

'He's been killed by the savages,' he said.

The hair on the back of my neck stood up. In an instant I wondered whether they were stalking us even now.

I kept expecting Barrie to tell us more, but he stayed silent. I had to prompt him. 'What happened?'

Barrie carried on staring into the fire, moving his head slightly from side to side. He seemed to be collecting his thoughts.

'We were walking over the ridge at the top of the valley,' he finally said. 'Then Mr Bell just stopped dead in his tracks and fell forward. I look around and he's got a spear through him. Straight out of the blue. I ran off as fast as I could, didn't I. No point staying to help someone with a spear straight through him.'

'What happened to your face, then?' said Richard.

Barrie looked him hard in the eye. His mood was

changing from morose to angry. 'Ran straight into a tree I did, as I tried to get away.'

'And where's Bell now?' I asked, feeling increasingly perplexed by this turn of events.

'How the bleedin' 'ell should I know,' said Barrie. 'Savages must've carried him off to eat him.'

We sat there as the forest grew dark around us. My anger with Richard faded. I needed to talk to him. Barrie was being too shifty. He didn't look like a man who had just survived a near-fatal encounter with the natives. Neither did he seem upset about the death of his friend.

We stoked up the fire. No one said a word. The brass buttons on Barrie's jacket glinted in the firelight. One of them was missing.

We slept fitfully that night. I woke often, with hunger burrowing at my innards. They say that when a man is starving the body begins to eat itself – how else would starving men begin to resemble the skeletons they may soon become? I couldn't help but think about my body gnawing away at my vital organs.

Dawn brought the promise of another bright day. That cheered us a little. I couldn't have faced a day of cold and driving rain.

Barrie was especially listless that morning, and didn't stir when Richard and I roused ourselves. We set off together to look for food, glad to have the opportunity to talk alone.

'Sam, we've got to watch ourselves here,' said Richard as soon as we were away from our camp. 'Do you believe that story about Bell?'

I shook my head. It was a huge relief to be able to talk. 'This is really bothering me,' I said. 'The way he's behaving – it doesn't make sense.'

'I reckon he killed him when the two of them had an argument,' said Richard. 'He's been really angry about the way Bell's held us up.'

'But we can't be sure,' I said. 'I know he's a rotten bastard, but I can't believe he'd kill his mate.'

Richard shook his head. 'Who knows? Maybe there is a mob of savages round here? Maybe they plan to pick us off one at a time?'

We walked on in silence. I began to feel light-headed and sick with hunger. My brain pounded with every heartbeat, and there was no strength left in my limbs.

We wandered back to the cave around noon. Barrie had gone. 'Probably looking for something to eat,' I said. We walked up hill, scouring the ground. 'Never know what you'll find if you keep looking,' said Richard.

Standing on an escarpment overlooking the valley, we spotted a thin column of smoke half a mile away to the north.

'Don't know what's happening there,' said Richard.

'Could be Barrie cooking up something for himself. Could be these savages he's warned us about.'

He sounded unconcerned. My mind was telling me I ought to be angry with Barrie for finding something to cook and not telling us about it, or frightened for my life because we were so near to natives who might kill us. But in truth, I was so weak I felt only indifference.

'Let's go and have a look,' I said wearily.

'Let's go tomorrow,' said Richard. He sounded even more dispirited than me.

We both sat down. Within seconds Richard had gone to sleep. I nodded off soon after.

When we awoke the sun had sunk so it was closer to the top of the high valley, and I judged it to be around the middle of the afternoon. Our short sleep had refreshed us, and we set off towards the fire we had seen.

We walked on, quiet and fearful. There was a chance Barrie had been telling the truth and we were blundering towards hostile natives.

I knew we were close when the faint smell of burning wood began to reach my nostrils. There was another smell too which I could not at first place. It was a little like pork. Then I remembered where I had encountered it before. It was the smell of human flesh burned in battle.

Richard, who was walking in front of me, stopped dead in his tracks.

I drew breath to speak, but he beckoned me to silence.

Ahead of us in a clearing, by a clump of rocks, was the remains of a smouldering fire.

'Stay very still,' Richard mouthed to me.

We waited. The trees rustled, the occasional bird squawked far away, and the shadows grew a little longer.

When we both began to shiver with cold, our patience ran out. Hoping no one was lurking there we headed into the clearing.

The fire told us little. There was a long charred stick lying half in and out of the black ash. The rocky outcrop near to the fire was bothering me. I just felt in my bones we were being watched. Any moment, I expected a spear to sail across the forest and impale me.

I pointed to these rocks, and the black entrance to a cave inside them.

Richard laughed. 'No point not talking now Sam,' he said. 'If anyone's here they'll have heard or spotted us by now.'

I walked towards the entrance.

Standing at the side I leaned over to peer in, expecting a spear through my head at any second.

Inside there was a faint stench of blood, like a butcher's shop. Fear boiled up inside me, but I stayed where I was. 'Easy Sam, you've been in battle and survived,' I whispered. 'There's nothing here you haven't faced before.' I stood inside the entrance of the cave and waited for my eyes to get used to the dark.

'Richard, come here.'

There in the corner was the outline of a body. 'Help me move him into the light,' I said.

We grabbed an arm each and dragged. He was stiff and awkward to move. We both knew at once it was Bell. He had been shot through the forehead.

There was something else even more horrific. His trousers were missing, and flesh from his buttocks and thighs had been sliced away. There wasn't much more left of him to eat. The rest was as scrawny as a starving dog.

I felt prickly hot and sick in my stomach.

Richard was white as a sheet.

'We can't be certain it was Barrie, can we?' he said.

Then I noticed a line of thread protruding from the clenched knuckles of Bell's stiff hand. I tried to open his fist. It wouldn't budge, and I had to get the knife from my belt to prise the dead hand open. There it was, the button from Barrie's jacket.

'Oh sweet Jesus,' muttered Richard. 'He killed him so he could eat him. Good thing neither you or me went out hunting with him.'

Bell's eyes were still wide open and he had a desperate, imploring look upon his face. At once, I could picture the man's final moments, down on his knees begging Barrie not to shoot, hand clasped to his friend's jacket. And I imagined Barrie looking coldly into his pleading eyes and pulling the trigger on his pistol.

CHAPTER 15

Who's for Dinner?

We walked back in silence. Then Richard said, 'What the hell are we going to do?'

'Keep away from Barrie, that's what,' I snapped. Wasn't it obvious?

Richard thought about this, then he said, 'We don't *exactly* know what happened. Bell might have attacked Barrie. Maybe he didn't mean to kill him. Maybe he killed him in a fit of rage and then decided to eat him because he was dead. We can't just assume he killed him to eat him and we're necessarily his next dinner.'

'Richard. I don't want to take that risk. I think we

should just head off on our own.' I felt convinced this was the right thing to do.

'I don't agree,' he said. He sat down on a rock. 'Let's think this through. He's got a loaded pistol, an axe, and a knife in his belt. All useful for hunting or defending ourselves if the natives ever attack us. We've got a couple of knives, a fishing line and the clothes we're standing up in. If we go back to the camp to collect our tins and blankets, we'll see him there. Besides I want to know where he is and what he's doing. I want to watch the bastard like a hawk. If we run away, we'll be constantly wondering about him stalking us. We'd have to kill him to stop him following us. Could you do that?'

I shook my head. What a choice. 'He's a tough bugger,' I said. 'I wouldn't want to have a fight with him, would you?'

'Only if I thought I'd win,' said Richard. 'He's a brawler, is Barrie. He's probably spent his life scrapping dirty in London drinking dens. Look, let's go back. I think it's best for now. If we can get away from him later, and be sure he won't follow us, then we'll do it.'

Dusk was falling as we approached our base. The events of the afternoon were almost too bizarre to take in, but in my half-starved state of mind I just accepted them. Now I could smell cooking. For one horrible moment I wondered if Barrie had brought back a bit of Bell for us to eat. I was so hungry I had begun to wonder what human flesh tasted like.

Barrie greeted us cheerfully, suspiciously so. He hadn't been this nice for the entire journey.

'Daaah, I was hoping you pair wouldn't come back,' he laughed. 'Then I could have had all this fish to meself.' He was playing the roguish Cockney uncle. 'So how come you two spent two days fishing by the river and caught nothing, and I get two big ones in a single afternoon?'

We said nothing, but our eyes were staring at the fish baking on the fire. 'I've had one of them already – the smaller one mind. This one's for the pair of you,' he said.

My mouth was watering so much I thought I was going to dribble.

Barrie took the fish from the fire, chopped its head off with his knife and carefully lifted away one side of white flesh. Then he peeled away the skeleton in a single movement. 'No bones there, sir,' he joked. 'We aim to please.'

Neither of us knew what to make of this friendly Barrie. We were too hungry to care, and ate the white flesh as slowly as we could bear. We knew it was fatal to bolt your food then choke or throw up.

Barrie asked us what we'd been up to. Richard had his wits about him, and told him we'd been looking for food in a part of the forest well away from Bell's butchered corpse.

We felt stronger after our meal and that evening Richard suggested to Barrie that we move on. 'You got lucky fishing,' he said with plausible logic. 'There's nothing here to eat, so let's carry on east. We're bound to reach the coast sometime soon.'

We all nodded our heads.

Next morning Barrie led and we made brisk progress. I walked behind trying to convince myself that we were doing the right thing sticking with him. If there were any natives out here, I supposed, the three of us being together would make them less likely to attack us. Barrie on his own, or us two boys, would be easier prey.

Three hours later we found another kangaroo apple tree with five fruits on it. It was a meagre crop, as before, but we all ate one then and there, and Barrie suggested we keep the other two for as long as we could stand to. 'We might not have anything to eat for the rest of the day, after all.'

Further down river, late afternoon, Richard caught four small bream while I hunted for plants to eat and Barrie gathered sticks for a fire. That night we slept under a clear sky. It was freezing cold but it didn't rain. We shivered miserably in our blankets despite the fire and the food inside us, our breath curling out of our mouths and noses and into the black sparkling sky.

The next day the river we were following made a brisk turn to the north. We argued sourly about whether to carry on following it, or continue plodding east. I managed to persuade them to stick to our plan. 'We can't be that far away from the sea, we've been walking for ever.'

We crossed the river at a shallow point, wading up to our waists in slow-moving water. I had a vague sense that we were getting more and more hopelessly lost, although I had yet to feel we were going round in circles.

Then our luck ran out. Two days we pressed on, through endless thick bush, our hunger returning to haunt us. We were driving ourselves to extinction. At the end of the second day without food, we found another cave. 'Shall we stop here to rest?' I said. Barrie and Richard both nodded. They looked gaunt and filthy. I imagined I looked the same.

As we gathered wood for a fire, Barrie muttered, 'You and your stupid plan. I knew we should've stuck to the river.'

I looked at Richard for support, but he just shook his head sourly.

I spent a sleepless night shivering in our cave and drifted off just as the sky was growing lighter. That morning I woke to see Richard and Barrie hunched together in animated conversation. They looked a little guilty when they realised I had woken up and was watching them.

'There's a freshwater stream a hundred yards above the cave,' said Richard. I went off to drink, anxious to rid my mouth of the foul taste of starvation.

When I returned Barrie said, 'Richard here seems to have the knack for fishing, so why don't we send him down to the river, and you and me go off and look for food?'

I didn't like the sound of this. 'Why don't we all go off and look separately?' I said. My mind was racing. Had Richard actually agreed to this? What was going on?

'Come on,' said Barrie. 'You're a country boy, you know your plants. I don't know nothing that doesn't appear plucked already and lying on a market barrow. I need you to tell me what's what. Besides, I don't want to go wandering off into the bush on my own. We might meet up with a savage or two. Two of us is going to scare 'em off better than one.'

I looked at Richard. 'Sounds good to me,' he said casually. I felt betrayed. 'You said we had to stick together,' I thought.

We went off, Barrie with his pistol and axe, me with my knife. 'You lead the way,' I said. I didn't want him coming up behind me with that axe and cracking me over the head. I carried my knife in my hand, ready for anything.

'You're a bit jumpy, aintcha?' he chided.

'I'm looking for savages,' I said.

Whenever he grew closer, I tried to get further away. He noticed soon enough, and it began to annoy him. As we walked, a dreadful thought kept entering my head. What was it he and Richard talked about earlier? Had they agreed this together? Had Richard turned against me? If Barrie attacked me and I killed him, would I have to kill Richard to stop him from killing and eating me?

I tried to think ahead, wondering what Barrie was going to do. Would he hit my head with his axe – try to bludgeon me to death? I felt queasy. How many times would he have to hit me before I lost consciousness? Would he hack my head off?

'Here, what are these?' he said, pointing to some berries. I thought he was trying to make me peer down at something and then hit me over the head while I looked at it. I took a quick glimpse. 'No good,' I said. 'I tried those the other day. They taste terrible.'

'You never even looked,' he snarled.

'You don't believe me, try them yourself.'

That shut him up.

Noon came and went, and still we had found nothing to eat.

'Let's stop and rest,' said Barrie. 'Maybe Richard has had more luck? We can sit up there, by that stream.' He got down and began to drink deeply from the muddy water. I thought then, 'Why don't I kill him? Why don't I get out my knife and stick it in the back of his neck while he's down on his belly drinking?' But I couldn't do it. I couldn't kill a man in cold blood. Not even a cannibal who wanted to make me his next meal.

'It's all right, the water,' he said. 'Nice and cool.'

'I'm not thirsty.'

He got angry. 'Go on, have a drink. It'll stop you feeling so hungry.'

'I'm not thirsty.' I was utterly parched. My mouth felt like dried clay. I wanted to drink more than anything else in the world, except dying under a hail of axe blows.

I was standing close by and he leapt to his feet and grabbed my arm so suddenly it caught me off guard. 'Go on,' he commanded. 'Get your face in that stream.'

I backed away. 'Get off me!'

'Here, what's up with you?' He was angry now. 'I just want you to drink so you won't feel so tired and hungry on the walk back.'

I felt cornered. The words spilled out.

'I know what your up to. You're going to kill me!'

That really fired him up.

'You what?' His face twisted. 'What do you mean, yer little shit? Last time I share any of my food with you. D'you think I'd have given you that fish if I was going to kill you?' He was squaring up to me, ready for a fight. I didn't fancy my chances. I played for time.

'We know what you did to Bell,' I blurted out. 'If you kill me, Richard will kill you.'

Barrie's mood changed. Instead of anger, he was icy calm. 'Will he now. Then maybe I'll have to sort him out as soon as I see him.'

I was so taken up with what he was saying I had not noticed him reaching round for the pistol on his belt.

In an instant he pointed at my head and pulled the trigger. Sparks flew in the flintlock, but the weapon made only a muffled bang. It had misfired.

He threw it down in disgust and lunged at me at once with his axe, snarling 'Come on then, let's get it over with.'

I dived to the right and pulled my knife from my belt. I thought to throw it at him, but he seemed too nimble to risk such an all-or-nothing move. Barrie lunged again. I thrust my knife up at him. He rolled over and clutched his side. I had caught him in the chest, under the right arm. Blood oozed out, but it was not a deep wound.

'Come on, have another go,' he leered. We circled each other. 'Wait for him. Wait for him. When he lunges at you, then you can strike.' I knew he had a knife too. 'If he tries to get that out, then you can throw yours.' I was as ice cold as I've ever been in combat. I had to be, and I fought the rising panic that gnawed at my insides with a will I never knew I had.

Barrie began to scrabble around on his belt, trying to

find his knife. It was now or never. I lunged at him but he was too quick and stepped aside. Then things went wrong.

I tripped on a vine and crashed into a tree behind him. When I staggered to my feet he threw a handful of soil straight in my eyes. As I blinked and coughed I felt a heavy blow at the back of my head. My legs went weak and I fell forward, not to the ground but into a yawning black hole. In the distance I heard someone howl in desperation, as I drifted between life, death and agonising pain. It was me making that terrible noise.

I lay on the ground too stunned to move, waiting for the blows that would end my life. But I could hear something else going on. A struggle. Barrie shouting, 'Come on then, you little shit. Come and get a taste of what your pal's just had.'

This must be Richard, come to rescue me. I tried to get to my feet but my legs and arms would not do what I wanted. My head felt like it was going to explode, and a red mist blurred my vision. So this is what dying was like. 'Get it over with. Get it over,' was all I could think.

I heard a dull thud – the sound of a heavy blow falling. Then I remember nothing more.

I came to with a jolt. The back of my head throbbed with hideous intensity, and I could feel a wet trickle down the back of my neck. Three thoughts entered my head. I was still alive. I was in dire peril. Richard had come to help when Barrie attacked me.

I shook my head in an effort to drive away the grogginess, but that just made the pain worse. I tried to get to my feet. I couldn't stand and neither could I move my arms. Was I paralysed? As my senses returned I discovered my legs were tied and my hands bound behind my back. Oh God help me. Barrie had tied me up like a beast for slaughter.

I opened my eyes, dreading what I would see. There was no one in front of me. I rolled over to see Richard lying a few feet away. I wondered if he was dead, but he was making low moaning sounds. Barrie had tied him up too. I rolled around, trying to sit up, and succeeded at last. The bonds were tight and my arms were hurting.

'Richard, wake up,' I whispered as loudly as I dare.

He groaned some more.

Then I heard Barrie's voice behind me. 'I was hoping you might be dead. Good thing I tied you up, wasn't it?' I swivelled round to see him there with his arms full of fire wood. 'Thought I'd have me a feast 'ere on the spot,' he cackled, and dumped the branches and twigs down on a clear piece of rock jutting out through the green and brown forest floor.

Richard gave a cough. He started to retch, spat a sickly green liquid from his mouth, then tried to sit up. His feet had been tied with the belt he wore around his trousers, and thick vines held his wrists. Barrie had done the same to me.

'Just you stay there, the pair of you. Any trouble and I'll bury this axe in your head.'

Barrie busied himself lighting a fire. Which one would he cook? The other would have to watch his friend killed and eaten.

Barrie seemed to relish the situation. 'Now, who's got the most meat on them? I might start with you first, Yankee boy, and save your pal for later in the week.'

Then he started to taunt us, waving his knife inches from our faces. 'Wonder who's the tastiest?

'You look a bit stringy,' he said to me. I said nothing. No point enraging him, and having him hit me again. I needed to be able to think clearly if I was going to get out of this alive.

He was enjoying the power he had over us. I thought his hunger must have turned his mind, for he seemed more of a lunatic than he ever had before. Then he walked off into the bush.

'He's gone for more wood,' said Richard. 'If I swing my feet behind your hands, can you undo this belt?'

We tried. The belt had been tied tight and could be loosened only a little. I wondered where Barrie had learned to tie such a good knot. As I struggled, he came back. 'Thought you'd try something when my back was turned. Well that's made up my mind. It's time to stop messing about. I'll have you now,' he leered at Richard. 'And you can come back to the cave with me for later in the week. Might even give you a bit of your pal to eat, if you behave yourself.'

He pulled his axe from his belt. Richard stared him hard in the face, showing magnificent courage.

It was then I saw a large brown snake with yellow bands along its body, slithering lazily between us – just like the ones we had seen at Charlotte Farm. How could I get Barrie to step on it? I started to shout at him.

'Kill me you scum-sucking maggot. Go on, I'll be far more trouble than him while I'm still alive. Go on, plant that axe bang in the middle of my head. You haven't got the guts have you, you lily-livered bastard.'

I tried to spit at him, but my mouth was too dry.

Barrie stopped in his tracks. He was baffled. Then anger got the better of him. Face clenched in rage he raised his axe high above his head and stomped over to kill me. His foot came down hard on the snake which reared up its head and bit his bare ankle several times. Barrie dropped his axe, yelled 'What the 'ell was that?' then screamed in horror as he saw the snake slithering away through the undergrowth.

For an instant I wondered if he would kill me then and there. But he didn't. He just sat down on the ground resting his back on a tree trunk, a dejected look on his face. I almost felt sorry for him.

'You clever little son of a bitch,' he said with a strange detachment. 'You've done for me, haven't you? We've seen those snakes at the farm. Single bite'll kill a man in an afternoon. Several bites and he's dead in an hour.'

He fell silent. Richard and I looked at each other, then at Barrie. We dare not say anything for fear of provoking him. I didn't want to catch his eye. What was he going to do?

Time passed. Wind whistled in the trees. Sun shone through the dancing leaves, casting a dappled light on the forest floor. The sky looked beautifully blue. I noticed this all with a vivid intensity because I thought these would be the last things I would ever see. Barrie did not move and had buried his head in his hands. I began to think of home, and mother and father, brother Tom and lovely Rosie, and then of my friends on the *Miranda* and my sea daddy, poor dead Ben Lovett. He died with an axe buried in his head too.

My train of thought was interrupted by wild curses. Barrie was working himself into a rage. He started to bang his fists on his temples. 'My head, my head,' he said between clenched teeth, as the poison seeped through his body. He looked up at the sky and bellowed in pain, scrunching his eyes shut tight as if the light were too bright for him.

He lurched to his feet, but the effort was too much

and he leaned against a tree and tried to be sick. Then he staggered to his axe, picked it up and began waving it around. He turned on me. 'You did that didn't you? You thought I'd come over and tread on that snake. You've killed me as sure as a pistol shot to the head.'

'I didn't know the snake was there,' I shouted. 'I didn't want you to kill Richard.'

Richard sprang to my defence. 'He didn't know. How could he? He was looking at you and wondering what you were going to do.' Then he overplayed his hand. 'Let us go and we'll try to help you.'

This enraged Barrie. 'Let you *go*? I'd rather eat my own steaming bowels.' He turned from me and gave Richard a vicious kick. There was some strength left in him after all.

'Well now,' he said. 'I'm reckoning on going straight down to hell, so another couple more corpses to my credit won't make any difference.'

Then he changed his mind, and began to talk half to himself and half to us.

'But what can you do for me? You got any medicine? You got anything on you to stop the poison? You could have sucked the wound, that works sometimes, but you gotta do it straight after the bite. It's too late now. Let you go? No, I'm going to kill you both before the strength goes out of me.'

Richard and I exchanged desperate looks. But then

Barrie's mind began to wander.

'Maybe I'll leave you both tied up. Maybe you'll starve to death or maybe the snake'll come back and get you. That'd be all you deserve.'

'But it isn't all we deserve,' I said. 'Why don't you let us go? We were just trying to escape like you. We've done you no wrong. We've been helping you to stay alive out in the bush. You said you were going to hell? Maybe, before you die, if you spare our lives, God will forgive you. Think about that Mr Barrie, before you do us in?'

I didn't believe it, but it was worth a shot.

Richard piped in. 'Think about it! Kill us now, and you'll die knowing for certain you're going to hell to roast for the rest of eternity. Let us go, and you can go thinking you may yet be forgiven.'

Barrie stopped again, and covered his eyes. 'My head, my poor aching head.' Then he clutched at his stomach, and bent double in agony. The pain passed and he leaned back against a tree.

We waited. I had seen men bad to the bone become meek and pious when death approached. Convicts on the road to the gallows in Sydney, two or three of them sitting in the cart along with their cheap wooden coffins, often sang hymns with great gusto, trying to prove to themselves that they were good Christians after all.

Barrie's breathing became laboured. Every now and then he would twitch in pain or an arm or leg would start to tremble and shake. I feared he would die and leave us both trussed up. I twisted my arms and wrists inside their bonds. There was some slight give in the vines. I could feel them stretch a little. I moved my ankles too, trying to work loose the belt. But it was less forgiving than the vines and the flesh around the belt was soon cut and bleeding.

The wind blew fiercely through the trees. It seemed to rouse Barrie from his stupor. He sat up unsteadily, like a man nursing a brutal hangover. 'I've just been talking with Old Nick himself,' he slurred. 'He just came to see me. Whiffing of fire and brimstone he was. He said, "You do one more job for me Mr Barrie, before you go . . ."' He was struggling with his words. '"You do one more job for me now, and you can come and work for me, down there in the fiery furnace."' He cackled and roused himself. '"Just do in these two conniving little bastards," he said, "and I'll take you all down to hell with me." Won't that be nice?' He staggered to his feet, picked up his axe and lurched over to me.

'I'll start with you,' he said, and brought the axe down on me with all his ebbing strength.

I jerked my body over and rolled to miss the blow. He grabbed me by the shoulder. I was surprised by the strength he still had in his hand. 'Hold still, you little bugger.'

In that final moment before the blow fell, I found the

strength to break the vine shoots around my wrists. I grabbed his hand on my shoulder and bit it with all the ferocity I could muster. Barrie yelled and dropped his axe. My legs were still tied and I could not stand up. As he groped around on the forest floor to pick up his axe I rolled over to snatch a fallen branch and brought it round to land on his head with every ounce of strength in my body.

It made a sickening thud. He dropped face down and stayed down.

'Quick Sam, before he gets up again,' pleaded Richard.

I picked up the axe and severed the vines around Richard's wrists in seconds, and he quickly undid the belt around his ankles.

We stood up and looked at Barrie's sprawled body.

'What shall we do?' I asked.

'If he's still alive we should kill him while we can,' said Richard.

'That snake bite will do for him soon enough. Let's leave him,' I said.

We searched the surrounding bush for our knives, which Barrie had carelessly tossed aside, and took his weapons.

As we left the clearing Richard said, 'I knew he was up to something. He's been toadying with me for a few days now. When he suggested you and him go off to look for food, I thought I'd better follow.'

I wanted to tell Richard I was worried he'd turned against me. But I knew he'd be angry so I said nothing.

We hadn't walked more than five minutes when I was gripped with a terrible doubt. 'What if the poison doesn't kill him after all? What if he comes after us?'

Richard snapped. 'What do you want to do then? Go back and kill him? I couldn't stick a knife into a dying man, could you?'

'No, but we could at least keep him company until he dies.'

'Very pious, Sam,' he snapped.

'But if we're there when he dies, we'll be certain he's dead. Otherwise we'll spend the next week thinking he's going to leap out at us at any second.'

'You're right, Sam.' Richard looked wretched. 'I'm just so hungry, and waiting for Barrie to go wastes time when we could be looking for food.'

'You go and fish, I'll keep an eye on him,' I said.

He nodded. 'I'll meet you back at the cave. Will you remember where it is?'

I headed back. As I approached I began to feel afraid. Was I right to go alone? I reached the clearing and a feeling of horror swept through me. I thought I was going to faint, and began to breathe deeply to steady my thumping heart. His body had gone. 'RICHARD,

COME BACK,' I screamed. The words echoed around the forest, but he made no reply.

Was this even the right spot? I was so exhausted I couldn't think straight. Then I heard the tinkle of water from the nearby stream and felt sure it was here that Barrie had tried to kill me.

I looked around for a cave or crop of rocks, somewhere he might have hidden. The bush around the clearing was so thick he could have crawled into that and be lying only a few feet away. Then I thought of the water again. I was desperate to drink. I went to the stream and knelt down, my knees wet in the soggy moss that grew beside it. The water twinkled in the afternoon light. I could wait no longer and thrust my face into the cool, clear stream. I gulped and gulped, feeling the strength flow back into my limbs and aching head. All I could hear was the sound of my own frantic drinking and the water running down the stream.

There was a sharp crack behind me, the sound of footfall on dry branches. I turned around at once, dreading the thought of another fight. It was Barrie – who else could it be? He was some twenty yards away from me, but I knew at once he would be no threat. His face looked dreadfully haggard, as if he had seen the very fires of hell. Although his eyes looked straight at me, I was sure he couldn't see me.

He staggered then lurched into a thick patch of

vegetation and fell forward. His body twisted on the ground. Then he lay still, face up to the sky.

I watched fearfully from a distance. His legs trembled occasionally, then he made no movement at all. I crept carefully forward and stood awhile watching him for any sign of life. When a fly landed on his unblinking eyelid I knew for sure he must be dead.

Leaning closer to take a final look, I saw a familiar silk cord around his neck. Fearfully, I knelt down and pulled on it, expecting him to flicker back to life at any second. Out popped the ring I had given him to trade with Charlie Palmer for our freedom. He had always kept his shirt buttoned to the top – now I knew why. The sly goat! He had traded something of his own and kept what I had given him. I felt a strong urge to give him a good kick in the guts. Pulling out my knife, I cut the cord and took back my treasure. I left his body to the insects and carrion birds, and walked away.

CHAPTER 16

Adam and Eve

When I told Richard what had just happened he shrugged. I knew how he felt. It was all I could do to gather a few dry sticks for a fire. 'We've got to get something to eat soon, before we die,' said Richard. We both looked like a couple of starving beggars. I kept thinking I should go and bathe and wash my clothes down by the river, but I didn't have the strength to do so. That evening, as we stared into the flickering flames, Richard said, 'I'm so hungry. If Barrie wasn't full of snake poison, I'd eat him.'

Next day we gathered up anything of Bell and Barrie's

we thought we could use, like their blankets and weapons and the sparking kit to make a fire. Then we moved on, staggering through the morning, drinking whenever we could. We had obviously misjudged how long it would take us to reach the coast, but heading there still seemed the best thing to do. The bush stretched out before us, an endless green horizon. Richard and I bickered constantly, but we both knew it was our exhaustion that made us so quarrelsome.

That afternoon we found a bush with black and white fruit which reminded me of raspberries. Richard crushed one in his hand and smelled the juice. 'It's sweet,' he said and tasted it with the tip of his tongue. 'Tastes good.'

We ate what we could find. When he found a particularly big one, he gave it to me. 'That's for being an old grouch,' he said. Even these small berries changed our mood and made us feel better.

We slept out in the open. We both had an extra blanket now, which helped keep out the cold. There was nothing else to do but press on. And now I had something else to worry about – the wound on my ankle from the belt Barrie had used to tie me up was beginning to fester.

That evening I landed a couple of fish. When we cooked them, they tasted a bit like salmon. We ate one then and there, and kept the other for breakfast. We made our camp under a jutting rock and woke the next day feeling hopeful. After breakfast we headed on with something approaching a spring in our step.

Although the sky stayed blue the wind blew cold. There was no more food for that day or the next, and although we always had enough to drink we were growing desperately weak.

In the evening we found a shallow sandstone cave near to a small stream and made our camp. In the morning, hollow eyed and restless, neither of us spoke for a while. When Richard tried to stand up, he fell down again. I got up and felt my legs giving way beneath me, but I steadied myself and went over to him.

'I don't think we'll be going very far today,' he said, his voice barely more than a hoarse croak. 'Let's stay here and look for food and when we feel strong let's press on. It's not as if anyone is following us.'

The idea made sense. 'You rest and I'll go looking,' I said. But soon after setting off, my ankle began to ache badly. It was beginning to resemble the injury that had so fatally hindered William Bell. The skin around the weeping wound was turning yellowy green. Without medical help it would continue to fester and I feared some dreadful infection could set in. I knew this was a painful way to die and the only remedy was amputation. But who was going to do that out here? Richard? With one of our knives or the axe? Besides, how would I even *begin* to survive out here with only one foot?

Soon after noon I stopped by the river to bathe my injured leg, and the cold water brought temporary relief from the constant ache. I hoped Richard might have got up and been more successful in his search for food, but when I returned to our camp he was still fast sleep.

That night neither of us had the strength to gather firewood. We shivered through till dawn. Only when the warm morning sun shone down did we fall into a deeper slumber. I woke again, mid-morning, almost too weak to move. Richard was still asleep, so I lay in my blankets and dozed. Was this how we were going to die? Slowly fading away in our fusty blankets. I wondered how long it would take.

When I saw two figures staring down at us I thought I must be dreaming. They had the sun behind them and a halo of light around their lean bodies.

One of them was very tall and carried a long spear. The other was much smaller and at first I thought it must be a child. But as my vision cleared I could see it was a young woman. I noticed with a jolt that both of them were quite naked. His skin was a dark brown and he had a long, white beard that reached half way down his chest. Her skin was as black as coal.

I stared at them, they stared at me. None of us moved. Then I whispered to Richard, 'Wake up.'

He sat up slowly. The staring continued. I lifted my

hand and waved in a friendly way. The two figures stayed motionless.

'Good day,' I said hoarsely, barely able to speak. 'Please can you help us? We have not eaten for many days and we are very weak.'

They looked at each other and nodded. Then the tall one spoke in a slow, halting manner. His words stunned me into silence, not least because he had a Scottish accent.

'My – name – is – Thomas – Ferring. What – are – you – going – here?'

Now I had heard him speak, I could make more sense of his appearance. Beneath the beard and the deep brown skin his features were European. By the look of him, he was forty-five or fifty years of age.

They came closer. He spoke to the girl, who picked up my mess tin and went to the stream to fetch us water. After we drank, the man gave us a few seeds to chew. As soon as we felt strong enough to talk our story poured out. He took in our tale unblinking and expressionless, but kept saying, 'Slow round'. Perhaps this was some Scottish expression.

Then he spoke again. 'You are not marine or Navy?'

I knew at once what he was getting at. 'No, we've escaped. Are you a convict too?'

He nodded. 'I tell in good time. First, eat more.'

His strange manner of speech puzzled me. I suppose he hadn't spoken English for a long time, and had forgotten many words.

His companion maintained her silence, but Thomas introduced her to us as Tirrike. She smiled warily, her white teeth gleaming against her black skin.

Thomas said, 'You stay, we come back.'

They were gone so long I began to think our encounter had been a figment of my imagination. But eventually they returned with two large watermelons. Thomas sliced them into quarters with a knife and we ate greedily. The sweet flesh soothed our parched throats and gave us the strength to get up on our feet. But what we really craved was meat.

'Follow,' Thomas said.

They walked ahead. I was mesmerised by the sight of Tirrike's swaying hips. The few native women we had seen around Sydney were naked or half-clothed too, but they were usually older and more stout and hefty. And they stank of rancid fish oil. I was told the oil kept away the flies which plagued everyone in high summer. This girl didn't smell of fish oil. Maybe it wasn't so necessary in the winter?

After an hour we came to a small clearing by a sandstone cave. The entrance was partly hidden by a cluster of large rocks. It was a fine hideaway.

Tirrike set about lighting a fire and Thomas bade us sit

down in the sunshine outside the cave. He pointed at my injured foot and said, 'Bad tune.' It took several attempts, with him becoming increasingly irritated, before I understood he meant 'Bad wound'.

When the fire caught Thomas brought two dead lizards from the cave and sat down to skin and gut them. He gave us a stick apiece to cook them on the fire. The meat was leathery and tasted a little of both chicken and fish. Then Tirrike brought us a handful of seeds. She told us a word, which I took to be the name of the plant they came from. The seeds tasted bitter, but not so you would want to spit them out.

Thomas spoke brusquely. 'We trade? Food for you. Tin for me.'

Richard and I carried a mess tin apiece. It seemed a fair exchange that we should give them one of ours. I nodded and handed mine over. At once Thomas set off into the bush, returning minutes later with a small handful of white roots. 'Good haste. Taste like arsenit.'

My father once told me the best way to talk to children who were learning how to speak was not to correct their words, but to simply repeat what they had said in the correct way, as part of a normal conversation. 'You'll make them anxious about speaking if you're constantly correcting them,' he had said.

'Tastes like parsnips?' I said. 'Wonderful. I've not had parsnips since I joined the Navy.'

Thomas went to the stream again, came back with the tin full of water and proceeded to boil up the roots. We ate them and they were good. I asked him if he could show me which plant he had picked. We were fed a succession of small portions and the more we ate the hungrier I became.

'Wait. Give you more later,' said Thomas. 'Too much now, and . . .' he made the actions of a man holding his stomach and being sick.

Tirrike came and sat next to Thomas. She seemed unconcerned by her nakedness. I tried not to stare but I blushed hotly. Perhaps Thomas noticed my reaction, for he put a protective arm around her and they had an animated conversation in a strange tongue. She pointed at my ankle. Thomas nodded and she disappeared into the bush.

I had never heard a white man speak in the natives' own language. I wondered how long he had lived out here, and asked him.

'Tell me first,' he said. 'Tell me again why you're here, and talk slow, so I understand.'

We told our story again, from transportation to our escape with Barrie and Bell, and how we were hoping to reach the white colony four hundred miles to the north. The more we spoke the more confident Thomas became in his own conversation. Several times he asked us the meaning of a particular word, but hearing us speak his own tongue brought his language flooding back.

'I came here on the *Royal Admiral* in October 1792. Didn't like it in Port Jackson. When they had me down for a whipping, I took to the bush. Me and three others. We were heading for China. More fool us. And while I'm about it, there's no colony in the north. That's just a story.'

I stopped listening at that point. *There was no colony in the north?* Then what were we going to do? Go back and face a flogging? We'd be due for a hundred lashes each, at least, and an iron gang for seven years. Maybe we'd be hanged. Going back was not a possibility, but then what else was there to do, other than live out here in the wilderness?

Thomas picked up a small pebble and threw it at me. 'You're not listening.'

I mumbled an apology, then sought to explain myself. 'But what can we do if there's no point going north?'

'Stay a few days, and we'll think about it,' he said. 'There's room in the cave for you to sleep. Now, listen to my story.'

Thomas enjoyed talking in his own language. Only occasionally would he stop and grope for a word. He had an extraordinary tale to tell. When they escaped, two of his companions quickly gave up and returned to face punishment. He and his friend James pressed on for a month. Then James fell ill.

'I stayed with him and did the best I could,' said Thomas, 'but you have to keep moving through the forest if you're going to eat. One night we noticed some natives had lit a fire nearby and I went to look. There were only two, and I ran into their little camp screaming and waving my arms. They fled like a couple of frightened sheep. There was a carcass on the fire, so I brought it back to share with James. Next morning we woke up surrounded by 'em. Long spears they all had. I thought they were going to kill us on the spot, but instead they came up to us and started to feel us all over, like they couldn't believe we were real. Everything we had, our blankets, our knives, our tinder box, our mess cans, our clothes, they took off us. James was so terrified he threw up and soiled himself, and they recoiled from him like he was some sort of evil spirit.

'They marched me off, and left him there to die. At least I thought they did. They took me to a cove where a whole lot of them had gathered, and they lit a big fire and began chanting and dancing. I thought they were going to kill and eat me. Then a woman came up and started to shriek and tear at her hair and her skin. She took me off and gave me food to eat and all these other people kept coming to see me, and poke at me and shriek and tear at their hair. I was terrified.

'But they didn't kill me, they just kept on bringing me food. And that night the woman who had picked me out lay with me as though we were man and wife. So I stayed with them. I learned how to hunt and find food and I picked up their customs and their language. I fathered two children with my new "wife" – Illoura was her name – both tall and handsome girls they are. They treated me well, and when I could talk their tongue I discovered why. Illoura was certain I was the ghost of her warrior husband. She recognised me at once, she said. They believe their dead warriors come back as white people. So that's what saved me.'

'So why didn't you stay?'

He let out a heart-rending sigh. 'I ask myself that question every day. But they're strange people, these natives. They can be very kind. They share everything, and they're very clever when it comes to knowing how to live out here. My friend James, I found out, they visited him every day with food and water until he died. I wish I'd known at the time, because I spent months feeling sick with guilt, leaving him there.

'But they've got another side to them too. Now and then they like to fight with other tribes. Make a big song and dance about it. I didn't want to have anything to do with that, but they expected me to go with them. I was one of their great warriors after all. I've been a bad man in my time, but I was brought up a Christian and I'm not one to kill another man I've got no quarrel with –' He had been waiting years to tell this tale and all his fears and frustrations came tumbling out. 'And their tongue is only spoken by a few of them. I spent years learning how to talk to them but if you walk twenty miles in any direction, they speak a different language. Not even the same words for the sun and the moon. They're not simple these people, they've even got a word for the Milky Way. Don't ever go thinking they're simple. If you want to get on with them you just have to start thinking like they think. There's a poetry in their language. Their word for island, "booroowang" – it's the same word for boat. That makes sense to me.

'But their life – day to day, it just brought me to despair. You know, they have no words for yesterday and tomorrow. Hunt, fish, sleep, drink. Hunt, fish, sleep, drink. They have their ceremonies, but their significance is lost to me, so I didn't get any pleasure out of them. I just had to get away from it, even if it meant cutting myself off completely.'

'So you ran away from them too?' said Richard.

'I did.' Here he paused. 'I did, and I still don't know if I've done right or wrong. Me and Tirrike, we've been living out here three years now. You're the first white people we've spoken to. I've met them before – small groups of bolters, but they run off terrified as soon as they see me. The natives here, we keep out of their way unless there are only one or two. And I'd never bring them back here. Sometimes, they speak with us, sometimes we can't understand each other.'

'And Tirrike, is she one of that tribe too?'

'She was the wife of one of the warriors. Banjura his name was. She's a beauty, isn't she? They never had children, and he was forever beating her because of that. Made him look less of a man, he said. So when I went she came with me. We ran until we dropped. I'd be dead without her. She could find food in a desert. As far as she's concerned this forest is one big larder.'

'So what are you going to do next?' I asked.

'I don't know.' He shook his head in despair. 'Banjura and Illoura would kill me if we returned to the tribe. I suppose I could go back to the settlement. It's been ten years or more since I ran away. They might have forgotten who I am? Maybe I could tell them I was shipwrecked, maybe I could say I walked all the way from China . . .' He trailed off. He would be in for a flogging too, just like us.

I said, 'You'd be taking a risk going back, but you might find they'd be pleased to see you. Someone who knows the natives as well as you do. Someone who can interpret their language.'

His face lit up. 'Aye, they might well. But then they might put me away again. And Tirrike, what would happen to her? It doesn't bear thinking about.'

I could see why he found it a difficult choice. Out

here, he and Tirrike were Adam and Eve in their own little Eden.

'Why can't you stay here?' I asked.

'It's a bonny life in some ways,' he replied. 'But I want to get back to a world where there's something beyond finding the next meal. I want to talk about politics and find out what's happening to the King and Queen of France.'

'They had their heads chopped off,' said Richard.

'Did they now.' His face lit up. 'Just like King Charlie. And have we done the same to King George yet? I'd wager not.'

He took up again. 'I want to get back to Edinburgh and smell the smoke and see my mother if she's still alive and catch up with my brothers and take to the hills in the autumn and walk in the wild mountain thyme and blooming purple heather.'

I thought he might burst into song, but he didn't.

'And Tirrike, will she come too?' I said.

At once he became frustrated and started to shout. 'Will she? If she comes, will she die from one of our diseases, like the natives do? Will she be taken away from me as soon as I go back to the settlement? Will she be looked on as some sort of freak if we go to Edinburgh? She never showed an interest in learning my language. Will she take up with another man? Ahhh, she's half my age at least. But then I can't leave her here on her own, can I?' He let out a long, desperate sigh. It wasn't a good question to ask.

He got up, impatient and agitated. 'You stay here. I'm away to find some supper.'

When we were alone, I turned to Richard and shook my head. 'So much for this colony. I always knew it was a forlorn hope. What are we going to do?' Our future appeared to be a choice of years of danger and isolation in the bush, a flogging followed by seven years in an iron gang, or death on the gallows.

I must have sounded more tearful than I thought. 'Don't give up,' said Richard, trying to be cheerful. 'We could still carry on to the coast, then head on north and see what we can find. Maybe we'll meet some natives who like us and we'll both find a Tirrike of our own?' It was an appealing fantasy.

'Never say die,' I said. 'Let's think about it for a day or two, and see what Thomas has to say about it.'

I brightened up. 'We could always go back to Sydney.' I was feeling bolder. 'See if we can steal aboard a ship. Now we're free of Bell and Barrie we have that choice at least.'

Tirrike returned, carrying something that looked like a caterpillar nest. She stood in front of me with it, and pointed to my injured ankle. I started to blush again and felt very foolish. Then she knelt down in front of me and pulled my foot forward. She shook her head, patted my

275

leg and said a few words. Then she pointed to herself and said, 'Tirrike.' She pointed at me with a look of expectation.

'Sam,' I stammered. Then I pointed to my friend. 'Richard.' I had never been this close to a naked woman before in my life. It was terribly embarrassing, but strangely exciting too. She smiled, said, 'San' and 'Reed', then picked up the mess tin we had given them and went off to the stream.

Richard tittered mercilessly. 'Your face was a picture,' he said.

'I don't know where to look,' I said, half in wonder.

'I wouldn't worry,' said Richard, 'and what the hell is that?' He pointed to the silky nest at my feet.

I shrugged. 'Blowed if I know.'

Tirrike returned with water and a fistful of vegetation. She knelt down and poured water from the tin over my wound. Then she stroked it gently with one of the large leaves she had brought. When the wound was dry she took the nest and carefully prised it open. There were no caterpillars inside it. They had come and gone over the summer.

She placed the nest either side of the wound, then pressed down, moulding it gently round my leg. Then she tied three strands of creeper around it to keep it in place. I watched spellbound, so hot with embarrassment you could have boiled a kettle on my head. When she finished she stroked the side of my face with a single finger, gave me a smile and went back into the cave.

When Tirrike replaced the nest with another one two days later, my leg looked much better. My wound was beginning to heal and my fear of amputation receded.

I told Thomas we were thinking about going back to Sydney and seeing if we could get aboard a foreign ship. He listened carefully, nodding his head. 'You may be lucky. I don't know what else you can do. I'd never survive out here without Tirrike. But get yourselves well and back on your feet before you decide.'

I was desperately grateful for his generosity. In the days that followed Tirrike was amiable and I was amazed how much we could communicate without speaking a word of each other's language. Thomas was gruff but keen to talk. He told me he had read the papers every day in Edinburgh. He was desperate for news of his old city. Did the stage coach still take two weeks to get to London? Was there still a daily coach to Glasgow? I had no idea and the more I told him this, the more impatient he grew. Were the Lowland clearances still happening? I had never heard of them. Had James Watt found any other uses for his extraordinary steam engine than pumping water from mines? Was Robbie Burns still writing his poems? I looked blank.

I tried to change the subject and asked him what had

brought him to these shores. 'My trade is the building of houses and there's plenty of that going on in Edinburgh. I kept the books for the master builder James Raeburn. He built half of the New Town. It bought him a mansion house in George Street and I was still living in a hovel in the old town. Ten years of my life I gave him. He never paid a penny more from one year to the next so I thought I'd help myself to a little of what was coming his way. I should have known better. I was due to hang on 23rd July 1790. But they sent me here instead. I think they thought I'd know something about building. Make myself useful. But I couldn't put a garden fence up, never mind build a terrace of town houses. Balancing books, that's what I used to do.'

My strength returned but Richard grew weaker. Rather than building him up, everything Thomas and Tirrike gave him to eat seemed to go straight through him. Soon he grew so frail I had to help him walk to the midden we had dug away from the cave, and hold on to him as he squatted painfully over it.

I feared for his life, as every day he grew thinner and paler. Thomas told me this was common with starving men. The body had grown too weak to retain nourishment. If we could not cure him, he would die. 'Tirrike will know what to do,' he said with pride. They talked and Thomas called me over. 'She's looking for termites and ants. Go with her to help.'

We set off immediately, she carefully scouring the forest floor. By noon she had found what she needed.

Back at the cave, she emptied two small pouches she had taken with her on to a large leaf. Inside one was part of a termite mound. Once exposed, the creatures inside scurried out and she broke the muddy structure down to a powder. In her other pouch were a collection of honey ants, their insides swollen with nectar. These she carefully removed and crushed into the powder.

We gave it to Richard as soon as it was ready. He complained weakly, but we spooned it down him. Then he drank some water to take away the taste.

We went looking for ants again the next morning. Tirrike stopped from time to time, pointing out berries and other fruits that were safe to eat. Some were hidden by other shrubs or close to the ground where I hadn't thought to look carefully before. It was a useful lesson.

We found our ants and returned to make more medicine. Richard slept for most of the day and night, and then we started to feed him small amounts of fish and green plums. Within a week he was better.

But by then, I started to feel we were outstaying our welcome, especially as Thomas was often gruff and short-tempered with us. As soon as Richard could walk we went fishing. There by the river we discussed our next move.

'She likes having us around. He's worried about that,' said Richard.

'He's worried about having four mouths to feed rather than two,' I said.

'She really likes you,' he teased. 'I can tell by the way she keeps looking at you.'

'Be sensible, Richard.' I was blushing again.

'I think we should go in another couple of days,' I said. 'What's more, I think we should tell him we're going to go. He'll be a lot happier if he knows we're going for certain.'

Richard agreed. 'What do you want to do? Sydney or north?'

'Let's talk to Thomas,' I said. 'Then decide.' I didn't want to think about it. Both carried terrible risks.

We returned to the cave late in the afternoon with three fish. At that moment, more than anything else in the world, I wanted to stay there with Thomas and Tirrike. Everything else seemed too dangerous, too frightening, too hopeless.

CHAPTER 17

Alone Again

I had expected them to be there but the cave was deserted. 'Out foraging, I expect,' said Richard. We lit the fire and cooked our fish, carefully keeping half for our cavemates. But then night fell, and Thomas and Tirrike did not return.

The cave was sparse. Aside from the kangaroo hides that they used to sleep on, and a few clay vessels for storing food, there was nothing in the way of possessions aside from a book made of kangaroo hide that I supposed Thomas had made. It had intrigued me ever since I first noticed it, and now, with them both away, I could contain my curiosity no longer.

It was a journal of sorts and there marking the first blank page was a feather he used as a quill. The writing was cramped and almost illegible, and by the look of their faded and caked appearance, the words were written in blood. Maybe his own, maybe any one of the creatures they killed to eat?

In the flickering firelight I looked through the book, Richard behind my shoulder, hoping to find some clue about us and whether or not they meant us to go. But there was no mention of our arrival in their lives. Instead, Thomas had recorded his hopes, fears and memories.

We began to worry that Thomas would return and find us reading his diary. 'I'll stand outside,' said Richard. 'If they come, I'll give a loud shout to welcome them. I don't think he'd like us looking at this.'

It was an absorbing read, and spoke volumes about Thomas's need to hold on to the life he had left behind. He listed the streets of Edinburgh he had known as a boy. . .

Candlemaker Row
Grassmarket
Cannongate
Leith Wynd
Cowgate
Buccleuch Street

And the plants and flowers in the hills outside the city:

Saxifage
Cloudberry
Heather
Broom
Mountain thyme
Harebell

Although I had never been there I could get a sense of the place and the life he had left behind. The awful loneliness and isolation he felt here was so real I could almost taste it. Leafing through his writings I began to feel guilty, as if I were taking an illicit peep into his soul. On one page he kept a record of his dreams, and especially a recurring dream he had about his capture by the natives.

The savages cavort arond me, shaking their speers in my belly and my fayce. Then they poke with their fingers, looking at me as if I'm some strange anamal. Then their wild music begins and they dance around me in a shreeking frenzy. One takes my nife and cuts my belly and they pull out my guts in a long slithery white rope. Althow I feel nothing I screem and screem and wake up screeming. Tirrike holds me until I stop shaking. I have this dreem several times a month.

On another page, he recorded his feelings for Tirrike and how he had long coveted her before they ran away together. But what disturbed me most was how he frequently felt he was going mad here, alone with this young woman. She had no interest in anything other than their own immediate needs and he wanted to talk about the world. He desperately needed the company of other people, but he fretted about losing her to a younger man.

I felt awkward reading his journal. But it helped me make up my mind about what we should do next. When Richard returned to the fire I said, 'I think we'd get very bored if we stayed out here in the bush.'

'Bored?' Richard laughed. 'We'd end up howling at the moon, stark raving lunatics!'

'We both went to sea because we wanted adventure in our lives,' I said. 'What was it Thomas said? Hunt, fish, eat, sleep. That's pretty much it. I want to get back to England and learn to navigate a 74.'

'You better brace yourself for a hundred lashes then, Sam,' said Richard grimly. 'And seven years on an iron gang clearing roads and sleeping in a wheeled hut. I don't fancy that at all. But you're right. I don't want to stay out here either.'

I shook my head. 'Truth is, I don't know what to do any more than you do. If we carry on north, anything could happen. I'm sure Thomas is right when he says there's nothing there. That friendly colony of white men is a pipe dream. We could be murdered by natives, we could be bitten by snakes or spiders, we could starve to death.'

Richard let out a long sigh. 'We've got to go back to Sydney,' he said. 'See if we can hook up with one of the American whalers that stop by from time to time. We're both sailors and I'm one of their countrymen, so I reckon we've got a good chance of them taking us on. We just have to make sure no one sees us trying to get to the ship.'

It was something to hope for, but I had my misgivings. I wondered what a ship's captain would say to two ragged, stinking scarecrows, clothes in tatters, wispy beards around their boyish faces, coming up to their ship in a stolen boat. I doubted it would be, 'Welcome aboard!'

We slept fitfully. The only thing that was certain about our future was that we should delay our departure no longer.

Thomas and Tirrike returned soon after dawn, both weighed down with all manner of vegetation. Thomas carried three dead lizards at his belt. Their manner was cold and rather distant, even Tirrike, who was usually so warm to us. They had ventured too far to return before evening, Thomas explained. I wondered if they had stayed out simply to get away from us for a while. We were right to be going.

We offered them the fish left over from the previous night and as they ate we told them our plans.

'We've decided to return to Sydney and see if we can pick up a ship,' said Richard.

Thomas nodded. 'Good. We can't feed you forever,' he told us brusquely. 'It's enough to keep the two of us alive out here. You're right to go back.'

'Can you tell us how to get there from here? Maybe draw us a map?' I said.

'I can take you most of the way,' he said at once. I was surprised by how quickly he offered. Perhaps he wanted to make sure we really were going to go, and not come drifting back, begging for food. Or maybe this was a final kindness. We were both pathetically grateful.

We set off that morning. 'Will Tirrike be all right on her own?' I asked.

Thomas shot me a hostile glance. 'She needs to stay to prepare the food we brought in. It needs soaking and boiling and all sorts over several days before it's fit to eat.'

Before we left, I took one of our blankets and gave it to them – I wanted to thank them for saving our lives. Tirrike gave me a broad smile. Thomas seemed indifferent. When we left she was restrained in her farewell to us but gave Thomas a tender embrace. I wondered what he had said to her about us when they were away from the cave? I turned round before we disappeared from view and was surprised to see she was still standing there watching us go. 'I don't envy your future any more than I envy mine,' I thought. Her and Thomas, they were both fugitives living on borrowed time, and something was going to happen sooner or later that would have terrible consequences for one or both of them.

We headed into the bush with a confident stride. I couldn't believe our luck. As we walked Thomas told us we would be heading for a river the other side of the valley which would take us south. Then we would walk a day or so, and pick up another river which would take us to Parramatta. I knew that settlement was a day west of Sydney, and it was simply a matter of following the river east to get back there.

'Once I get you on the river to Parramatta, you're on your own,' said Thomas. 'I'm not ready to go back yet. Not sure I ever will be.'

We stopped that night and made a fire by a cave, as we had done with Barrie and Bell. All day I walked with a greater sense of purpose. It was a wonderful feeling, being with someone who knew where they were going.

The next morning, we came to a wide river and Thomas set about cutting two bark canoes from trees close to the bank. We watched, fascinated, as he skilfully prised a large piece of bark away from the tree trunk with his knife, then carefully sewed either end with a bone needle and twine.

He took one boat, Richard and I the other. Out on the river we felt very conspicuous. Here there was no place to hide. A thin winter wind blew along the water. It was especially cold once the sun went over the top of the high valley and cast a dark shadow over the river below.

We used branches to paddle and, although we had to travel upstream, we made good progress. Sometimes one of us fished and the other paddled. We were remarkably successful with our fishing out in the middle of the river, and by mid-morning we'd caught enough to feed us for two days. 'Not worth catching any more,' I said, 'they'll go off before we can eat them.' It felt wonderful to be able to say that.

Most of the time, Thomas seemed to know where he was going, although there were so many coves and bays and inlets I sometimes wondered if we had taken a wrong turn or gone up a blind alley. It all looked the same to us – steep sides covered in thick greenery with sandstone outcrops. I was amazed at the speed we travelled. We could never have done this without a guide.

Bad weather came and went, but as we were confident about finding nourishment, we felt less need to be constantly moving forward, and we were always prepared for a coming downpour. By the riverbank there were caves for shelter. There was brushwood for fire. It wasn't an easy journey, but in good weather it was bearable.

We saw a few of the natives, distant figures on the far bank of the river or walking along the ridge above the valley. Thomas was as keen to avoid them as us. But my fear of them faded with every passing day. If they really were going to eat us, they would have killed us by now.

After three days our river turned into a stream, then a brook. 'We walk from here,' said Thomas, and carefully hid our boats in undergrowth ready for his return journey. That day we tramped up the steep side of a valley. When we reached the ridge, by late afternoon, Thomas pointed through the thick bush and told us there was another river ahead that would take us down to Parramatta.

We got to a small stream the following evening and walked along its banks until it became navigable. Here we set up camp. While Richard and I made a fire, Thomas fashioned another bark boat for us. As we ate our supper, he told us he would be coming no further. 'I don't even want to see a column of smoke,' he said. 'I want to go back so badly, and seeing you boys has reminded me how much I miss the company of my own people, and being able to talk in my own tongue, but it's not the right time. I can't bring myself to do it, not while Tirrike is with me.'

It was a terrible dilemma, and I could see it was tearing him apart. I wished I could say something to offer him a crumb of comfort, but I could think of nothing worthwhile.

After an awkward silence, Richard said, 'Tell us how to get down to Parramatta from here.'

It was simple enough. We would travel downstream until the river reached a great juncture. 'There's no little tributaries or inlets to confuse you,' said Thomas. 'Just carry on here until you reach another wide river. There you must go east. But beware. You'll soon reach the settlement, and you'll be very easy to spot in the middle of the river. Better leave your boat and walk. Travel by night and keep to the north side of the river. It shouldn't take you more than a day to reach the far side of Sydney Bay.'

That night, troubled by violent dreams, Thomas muttered and moaned in his sleep, constantly waking the two of us. At dawn we said our goodbyes. 'If we hadn't met up with you and Tirrike, we'd be dead,' I told him. To my surprise he gave me a hug. 'I shall miss you boys. Perhaps we'll meet up again back home?' It was the most unlikely thing I'd ever heard in my life. 'Here, I want you two to have this,' he said, undoing a small bag from his belt and handing it to Richard. It was full of nuts.

He stood by the river bank and watched us paddle away. 'What d'you think's going to happen to them?'

I asked Richard.

'I dread to think,' he said. 'He's going to go mad out here, isn't he? Perhaps they'll go back to Sydney, and it'll be a disaster. Or her tribe will find them and kill them both. The best thing that could happen is that she'll run off to another tribe, and he'll come back on his own and they'll give him a pardon because he's useful. Whatever happens, I wouldn't like to be either of them. I'm glad we decided to come back to Sydney and take our chances on a ship.'

The current was strong and we reached the big branch in the river by late afternoon. We could see it parting the thick forest either side of the water. 'This is where we ditch the boat,' said Richard. We paddled to the side and hauled ourselves and our little boat on to dry land.

As we sat on the riverbank getting our breath back in the mild sunshine, my fear returned. What we were about to do was fantastically dangerous. I had not given it a thought throughout our journey back, but now we would have to put our plan into action.

'I don't think we should ditch the boat,' I said. 'It's light enough for us to carry. If we can get back to Sydney undetected, then we can use it to get out to a likely ship.'

'Good thinking,' said Richard. 'Let's eat and rest now, and see if we can get past Parramatta tonight.'

We cooked our fish then dozed into the early evening. The days were getting longer now, and it was mid-evening before we felt it was dark enough to venture further. Sticking close to the riverbank we crept silently onward, taking it in turns to carry the boat. It was light enough to pick up with one hand.

We passed by Parramatta a couple of hours later, its twinkling lights on the far side of the river. We could smell the smoke and the cooking, and hear the low hum of humanity. After all these weeks away from houses and hearths I had a deep yearning to join them. Dark silhouettes moved in the gloom, so we lay still till the dead of night. We had been right not to use the boat for this part of the journey, we would certainly have been spotted.

Eventually the settlement grew quiet and we crept forward once again. Away from the houses we picked up our pace, and Richard said we should try the river again. It was a dark, overcast night and I didn't see why we shouldn't. The river had widened considerably by now. If we stuck close to the overhanging branches of the bank and kept our eyes open for any approaching vessels, we should be able to navigate our way unseen.

The boat was flimsier than I thought. Carrying it had loosened the stitches in the bow and stern and water seeped steadily in. I bailed, Richard paddled. 'Let's hope we don't come across any sharks,' he joked.

Dawn was breaking on the rim of the horizon as the river widened into the great bay before Sydney. The waves grew choppier too, and I worried that our boat would not be able to stand these rougher waters.

We put down on a beach opposite the town. There was thick bush immediately away from the shore, just right for hiding during the day. We cooked again. 'They see a fire, they'll think it's natives,' said Richard, then he peered towards the far shore in the gathering light. I looked over to the houses and towers of Sydney with a lump in my throat. Here was the prospect of capture and awful punishment. But what a lovely life we had had there. And we had messed it up so badly we were having to risk our necks in a foolhardy attempt to escape from the place. I would have given anything to be able to return to Doctor Dan and our little house on the Rocks, and pop into the Sailor's Arms for dinner.

'Tell me my eyes are deceiving me!' Richard shouted. 'That merchantman just starboard of the other ships in the harbour. Is that the Stars and Stripes she's flying?'

I squinted and strained my eyes. We were too far away to be able to say for sure. But when the sun came out later in the morning, we could both just about see that this was indeed an American ship.

Richard could barely contain his excitement. 'I thought we'd be stuck here for weeks waiting for our moment. Let's go now. Come on, let's just chance our arm.' He could scent freedom just beyond his reach, and it was making him reckless.

'Richard, we'd be spotted a mile away. The Navy'd send out a boat full of marines and we'd be in gaol in time for dinner. We've got to wait 'til nightfall.'

'All right,' he said. 'But if she sails today, I'll never forgive you.'

Having been up all night, we tried to sleep. But we were too unsettled. It was a hot day, so we bathed in the bay and washed and dried our stinking clothes. All the while we both kept casting anxious glances towards the American ship. If she sailed, there might not be another one in for months.

When we put our dry clothes back on I said, 'Now when we're seen by anyone, I'm hoping they won't give us a second glance.'

'No chance,' scoffed Richard. 'We still look like scarecrows. Our clothes may be cleaner but they're still falling off our backs. And we need to shave off these scrubby little beards. We look like we've been raised by a couple of wolves.'

I hadn't cared what I looked like in the forest, but now I did. Richard was right. We stood out a mile as the fugitives we were.

I could not remember when time had crawled so slowly. We ate the last of the nuts Thomas had given us, and scoffed down oysters we found among the rocks by the shore.

Eventually the sky began to fade. The cool of dusk settled over us and the lights of Sydney came on one by one. It was a beautiful sunset, but one we weren't at leisure to enjoy. 'Let's go now,' Richard kept saying.

'No. Give it another few minutes,' I urged him. Our tempers were fraying. It was a cloudless night – worst luck – and the half moon was shining brightly.

'Come on, Sam. I can't bear to wait another minute.' Leaving our blankets and weapons behind, we pushed the boat out into the dark water and began to paddle towards the far shore. A stiff breeze blew across the bay and we both shivered despite our exertions. I bailed frantically. This was a river boat, and not at all suited for a great bay.

Halfway across, Richard began to panic. 'Which one is it?' he kept saying, peering through the dark. The ships loomed larger and still we could not be sure which one was ours. My heart was beating so hard I thought my chest would burst.

'Look, there it is,' I shouted, 'I can make out the flag.'

The ship was barely thirty yards off shore from the Rocks. We were close enough to our old home to be able to make out dark figures on the shoreline. I reckoned I could have swum there in a couple of minutes. We drifted closer. 'Let's get right up to the strakes and then

I'll call up,' said Richard. He was absolutely convinced they would take us on board, especially when they heard his voice.

So far, so good. We were close enough now to see the shrouds and ratlines of her rigging. In a minute or two, perhaps less, we would know whether our escape would succeed or not. I wondered what she was called.

Then a voice bawled out from our larboard side, from further across the bay. 'Vessel approaching the *Nantucket*, identify yourself!'

I knew at once they could only be calling to us. Peering through the dusk I could see a Royal Navy cutter in the middle of the bay, probably ferrying supplies from one of our ships to shore.

Richard cursed roundly and said, 'Keep going, the *Nantucket* might still take us.'

'We can't Richard,' I hissed. 'They'll send marines to board the ship and find us, even if the crew agree to take us. We've got to head for the Rocks and hide.'

He didn't reply, but began to paddle for all his worth towards the shore.

CHAPTER 18

Separate Ends?

When we scrambled onto the rocky shore I looked over my shoulder to see the Navy cutter heading straight towards us. She was barely a couple of minutes behind. There was nothing for it but to head for our old home. We didn't even need to say it. I prayed Doctor Dan was still there.

We passed no one we recognised on our frantic journey, and within a minute or two we were outside the house.

'What if he's moved?' said Richard. I knocked impatiently on the door. A voice called out, 'Who's there?'

It was him.

'Dan!' I whispered. 'It's Richard and me. Let us in quickly.'

The bolt drew back. We dashed inside.

'Boys! I thought I'd never see you again!' said Dan. He looked delighted, then, in an instant, alarmed. 'What in heaven's name is going on?'

'No time to explain,' I said breathlessly. 'We've just come over from north of the bay. There's a party of Navy men on our tail. Can you hide us?'

Dan was flabbergasted. 'You must be joking,' he said. 'Where am I going to hide you in this little hovel? We haven't got a cellar or an attic, remember?'

I suddenly realised we were asking him to risk his liberty by hiding us. If the Navy men found us in his house, he would be flogged or worse.

I started to gabble, saying how sorry I was that we were here, but he shut me up.

'Look, listen very carefully. I have some extraordinary news. I heard it from the Governor himself. You are pardoned. Fresh evidence has been unearthed in England. Your ship's Purser, he's been found out. And his son. Can't say I understand it all, but no doubt you'll find out more soon enough.

'Anyway, the Governor has let it be known he is happy to overlook your run-in with Lieutenant Gray and will arrange for you to be shipped back to England. I discovered this a month or so after you were taken away to

Green Hills. I gather the news arrived there the day after you escaped. Yes. I heard about that. I couldn't believe you'd be so stupid.'

'But what of our escape,' I wailed. 'Has that scotched our chances?' This was all too cruel.

Dan looked hopeful. 'Did you kill anyone on your travels?'

'Yes. But only after he tried to kill me,' I said.

'I heard you'd escaped with a couple of thugs,' said Dan. 'Not the best strategy was it?'

We both shook our heads like naughty schoolboys.

'Tell them you were separated and you don't know what happened to those two. They're well rid of them from what I've heard, and they won't be asking any questions. But we need to get you to Governor King's office as soon as possible. I treated his daughter recently, so he owes me a favour. I shall plead your case, and hope he agrees to let you go.'

Silence descended while we took this all in. In the space of a few seconds our lives had been turned around. I felt drained. I wanted to cry, but fought back my tears. 'Doctor Dan,' I said, 'what shall we do now?'

Dan was thinking quickly. 'Look, if the Navy people find you here with me, we'll all be arrested. I want you both to stay here. Hide under the beds. I kept your room the same as it was before all this nonsense. There's no one else in the house. I'm going over to the Governor's immediately.'

'Why don't we come too?' said Richard.

Dan shook his head. 'Oh no. You're not going anywhere in this town without an escort of the Governor's own men. I don't fancy your chances if John Gray's soldiers get to you before you see Governor King. I hear Gray is furious about you being acquitted. Says it's undermining respect for the officers of the Crown. Pompous arse. Now stay here. I'll be back as soon as I can.'

We waited. It was as quiet as it ever gets on the Rocks. We looked around, refamiliarising ourselves with our old home. Then we heard shouting outside. Richard peered gingerly through the window. A small party of soldiers were working their way through the street, along with a Navy officer. He must be one of the men from the cutter. They were banging on doors and searching every house they came to.

We both hid under our beds. Then we realised it was a hopeless hiding place. 'Let's spare Dan the trouble of getting a new door,' I said. 'We'll keep quiet when they knock, but if it looks like they're going to bash down the door we'll just let them in.'

They knocked in a manner that nearly brought the door off its hinges. Then we heard someone say, 'Quinton. Kick the door in.'

We opened the door just as one of the soldiers was lifting his leg to break it down. He looked startled but the other soldiers all swiftly raised their muskets at us. The Navy officer said, 'That looks like them.' Then he talked to us directly. 'You two scarecrows wouldn't be the pair we saw running up from the bay would you?'

One of the soldiers spoke. He had sergeant stripes on his sleeve. 'These are our culprits, sir. They look like they've been brought up by wolves. Come on,' he grabbed me roughly by the arm. 'You're off to the barracks. Who lives here, by the way?'

Richard spoke up. 'We don't know. We just hid in the first house we could get into.'

The sergeant turned to our neighbour Edward Bean, who had come out of his house in his nightshirt to see what was going on.

'Who lives here?' the sergeant asked him curtly.

Edward peered at us curiously. 'Oh, hello lads,' he said. 'Didn't expect to see you for another few years.' Then he looked at the soldiers. 'Daniel Sadler's house that is. But don't blame him. He's out.'

Richard and me were bundled off at bayonet point to the nearby barracks. Here we were thrown on to the floor of a cell with brute force. Ten minutes later the door opened again and Doctor Dan was hurled in with similar brutality.

When he'd dusted himself down he sat on the wooden bench that had been screwed to the wall. 'I thought they'd find you soon enough. Did they kick down the door?'

301

We told him it didn't get that far.

'Good,' he said. 'An open door after dark on the Rocks – there wouldn't be a scrap of furniture left by the morning.'

'The Governor is out, I'm afraid,' he went on. 'Dining with friends out of town, I'm told. I left word with him anyway. Don't worry. I'm sure he'll order our release immediately.'

'Why are you here with us?' I said.

'Picked up on the way back by soldiers. "Harbouring fugitives," they tell me. Apparently I'm due for a serious flogging.'

He didn't seem too worried. As we sat and waited, what he had told us earlier began to sink in. 'Tell us again about this pardon,' I said.

'And while you're about it,' said Richard, 'tell us what day it is. We've no idea how long we've been in the bush.'

'It's the fifth of October,' said Dan. 'You have been leading a wild life.'

I was astonished. We had been gone from Sydney for only four months. It felt much longer.

Just then we heard footsteps outside the cell. 'That'll be the Governor's men now,' said Dan. 'We'll be back in his office in five minutes. Once you're there, you'll be safe.'

The door opened. Five soldiers marched in, bayonets attached to their muskets. They pointed them menacingly at us. Then, a moment later, in strolled an army lieutenant. It was John Gray.

'Off we go,' he said to Richard and me.

'We're staying here,' said Doctor Dan.

Gray grabbed him by his jacket and hauled him to his feet.

'What did you say?'

'These boys are staying here with me,' said Dan. 'They are under my protection.'

Gray sighed. 'Is this the man who's just been arrested for harbouring fugitives?' One of the soldiers nodded.

Gray kneed Dan hard in the stomach. As he bent forward in agony another soldier stepped forward and hit him hard over the head with a pistol butt. He fell to the floor and was roughly dragged to his feet by two other soldiers.

'I demand to see your commanding officer,' said Dan breathlessly. Gray cuffed him around the back of the neck. 'Shut up before you start losing your teeth,' he hissed.

A horrible thought occurred to me. Did Gray know Dan was a doctor and a friend of the Governor? Almost certainly. Doctors were well known to most people in Sydney. If he was treating Dan this brutally, perhaps he intended to kill us all.

Outside the barracks there was a horse and cart, with a load of empty sacks on the back. 'On you get,' said Gray, and all of us clambered aboard.

'Where are we going?' said Dan. Gray took his pistol and pointed it straight in Dan's face. For a moment I thought he was going to kill him on the spot.

'I won't tell you again,' he said. 'Shut up.'

Then he turned to the driver and said, 'Devon Wood.' It was a little way out of town, and we all knew what was going to happen when we got there.

Gray was going to have us all killed. No doubt he would claim we had run away from a patrol and had been shot as they tried to apprehend us. Dan was right about how angry he was about our pardon.

I tried to stay calm, wracking my brains for a way out. Gray was sitting just in front of me, so I spoke up. I didn't care if he hit me, I'd be dead soon anyway. 'Lieutenant Gray, sir. You have no quarrel with Doctor Sadler. Let him go, I beg you.'

Gray laughed. 'What, and let him tell everyone what happened to you two? Another word and I'll have you gagged.'

In my mind's eye I could see what was coming out there in the woods. Gunshots, or glinting bayonets, in the half moon. A cold, dark death. We had cheated fate in battle, escaped our hanging, outwitted our cannibal friend, and now our luck had run out.

As the cart approached the edge of town, we heard the rattle and snort of another horse-drawn vehicle heading towards us. It was an enclosed carriage complete with a detachment of marines marching briskly alongside. Only the Governor would travel in such style. Gray pulled our cart to one side and we waited for them to pass.

Gray hissed, 'Not a word or we'll kill you here on the spot.' The soldier opposite me pressed his bayonet into my stomach, so close I could feel the blade on my skin.

Richard and I were sitting with our backs to the carriage. Doctor Dan was facing it. He sat as upright as he could so his face would be visible over the top of our heads. We saw at once what he was doing and hunched our heads down.

The carriage trundled past. It did not stop. 'Move on,' shouted Gray and we began to lurch forward.

Then I heard shouting. I looked back to see Governor King himself clamber from his carriage. He yelled out, 'You soldiers. Stand down.'

A moment later, King and four of his marine escort strode up to the cart.

'Doctor Sadler? Is that you?'

Dan smiled broadly. 'Your Excellency, I am very pleased to see you.'

King turned at once to Gray. 'Lieutenant, explain yourself.'

Gray seemed unflappable. 'The two boys are escaped convicts. The man here was harbouring them.'

'But this is Doctor Sadler, man,' King said with some exasperation.

'So he told me, sir,' said Gray. 'I am not acquainted with him.'

'So where are you taking them?' said King.

'Sussex barracks, sir,' said Gray. 'The town barracks gaol is full.'

'Well Lieutenant, I can see there must have been a mistake. Doctor Sadler is my friend, and he is welcome to return to my residence with me.'

'Release the prisoner,' said Gray to his men. Dan stood up and jumped down from the cart.

'Now, your Excellency,' said Gray, with icy politeness. 'May I proceed?'

They were going to leave Richard and me with Gray.

'Carry on,' shouted King.

The clatter of horse and cart setting into motion must have drowned out the conversation Dan had with King.

We heard another command.

'Lieutenant, stop that cart.'

King spoke firmly, in a tone that broached no argument. 'These boys have been acquitted of the charges against them by order of His Majesty the King. They are to be released at once.'

That was that. We got out. I could not see Gray's face, but could imagine it. The thought of him grinding his teeth with rage would make me smile for months to come.

We spent the night in the guardroom of the Governor's house, where we were given new clothes, blankets, hot drink and food, and water to wash with. Dan came to see us first thing in the morning. 'Get yourself cleaned up, boys. You're up for an audience with the Governor.'

We were ushered into his office. I was reminded of the captain's cabins I had seen in the Navy. The same polished furniture, glinting silverware and oil paintings.

Governor King was matter of fact. 'I understand Doctor Sadler has already told you of your acquittal,' he said. 'So you are free to return home.'

'Please sir,' I asked, 'can you tell us what happened. Who ordered our acquittal?'

King frowned. Perhaps I was being impertinent. Then he reached into a drawer on his desk and began to sift through a pile of correspondence.

'Here we are,' he said, 'letter from Viscount Neville. I believe you know his son, Robert?'

He put on a pair of spectacles and read it through carefully. We waited awkwardly in the silence. Then he spoke.

'Ah yes – Nathaniel Pritchard, the Purser on HMS *Elephant*. He'd been fiddling the ship's books for years. And his son Oliver – he was the midshipman who deceived the court into thinking you had hidden in the hold, wasn't he? Both of them exposed as crooks. They were sentenced to death. I'm told Oliver made a contrite confession admitting he had falsely accused you both. The court was intending to commute his sentence, as they did yours. But this confession tipped the balance against him. Good for you, not so good for him. Your shipmate Robert Neville has been hard at work on your behalf. His father is a good friend of mine. The family secured you both a full acquittal and ensured news of this was sent at once to the colony.

'Now, I suggest you leave at the earliest opportunity. The New South Wales Corps is not best pleased that I have ordered you to be set free.'

I spoke up. 'Your Excellency, Lieutenant Gray was going to kill us. And Doctor Sadler too, when he tried to protect us.'

King snorted impatiently. 'I'm quite aware of that. Now, I want you to remain here in my house until a ship can take you back home. There should be one sailing in a week or two. I'm sure they'll be able to make use of two experienced Navy men.'

Richard snapped smartly to attention. 'Permission to speak, sir.'

'Carry on,' said King.

'Your Excellency, I am an American citizen. I would like your permission to join an American ship. There is one currently moored in the harbour – the *Nantucket*.'

King eyed him coldly. 'I'm afraid she sailed this morning, but I shall consider your request. Now, for your own safety, I insist on keeping you here. The guardroom's the safest place. You'll be protected by my marines there, and I'll see to it you're well fed and comfortable.'

He nodded. Our audience was over.

I felt I had to say something more. 'Thank you, sir, for saving our lives.'

King turned again and smiled. 'Don't thank me lad, thank Viscount Neville and his son.'

'So you're going back to America,' I said as soon as we were alone in our new quarters.

'I've had enough of the British Navy, Sam. I've had enough of high-born snobs telling me what to do and I've had enough of burgoo and scotch coffee for breakfast. I've had enough of fighting for a country I don't actually belong to. You know a lot of us Yanks are all in favour of the French and their revolution. If King George had lived in America, we would probably have chopped his head off too.'

It was a high-born young man who got us out of this mess, I thought, but I wasn't going to argue. 'I'll miss you Richard. You're the brother I always wanted.'

'Enough of the soppy stuff,' said Richard. 'Anyway, why don't you come back to Boston with me? A bright lad like you. You'd make your fortune soon enough. You'd like it out there, and they'd like you.'

It was an enticing idea. But then I thought of my mother and father, and our house in Norfolk. And Rosie. Had she caught the eye of another boy? Of course she had. She was too pretty and kind-hearted not to have. As for the Navy, I had had enough of burgoo for breakfast too, and the rest of it. The only thing that would get me back on a Navy ship was a press gang.

I said, 'Maybe, one fine day, I'll come and see you in Boston, when I'm captain of my own merchantman!'

'Hey, we aren't going just yet,' said Richard, and for now, we said no more about his leaving.

Doctor Dan brought dinner to the guardroom. He seemed unusually pleased with himself. I supposed he had just been spared from certain death. We told him about our meeting with King and he told us what was happening.

'The New South Wales Corps are a law unto themselves around here. They know it and so does King. Gray has friends right at the top of the Corps, so the Governor won't be questioning him about what he was up to with the three of us last night. It might provoke a mutiny. We should just be grateful King arrived when he did.

'Now I have some interesting news of my own! The Governor has ordered me pardoned and tells me there's need for doctors out in Parramatta, Richmond Hill and Green Hills. I can take my pick. What do you think of that! I think he just wants me out of the way of the New South Wales Corps and Lieutenant Gray. That suits me fine. I've had enough of the Rocks now.'

We were delighted for him. 'You could do worse than Green Hills, that's for sure,' I said. 'It's a beautiful spot. Will Tuck give you any trouble?'

Dan shook his head. 'He's always been very respectful to me. I don't see why that would change. Green Hills it is then. The Governor tells me I should go as soon as I can.'

*　*　*

Dan left to make his arrangements, promising he would be back to see us the following Saturday. In my quiet moments I thought a lot about Oliver Pritchard, how I had detested his sneering face, and how my hatred for him had been part of my determination to survive out here. In a strange way, he had given his own life to save ours. I wished he had been spared. Now he was dead, I could forgive him. I also wondered what had happened to Nathaniel Pritchard's accomplice, John Giddes. He too had almost cost us our lives. Had that strange man been hanged or had he escaped? I would dearly love to find out what fate had befallen him and discover who he really was.

On the Friday, the Governor sent one of his officers to talk to us.

'There's a merchantman leaving tomorrow. The *Orion*, she's called. We've had a word with the Captain, and he's sure he can make use of the two of you.'

'What about me?' said Richard. 'I wanted to get an American ship.'

The officer smiled patiently. 'His Excellency feels that the sooner you are both away from Sydney, the safer you will be.'

'Damn that,' said Richard. 'I'm quite happy to wait.'

The man dropped his diplomatic façade. 'This business with you both and Lieutenant Gray. It's a running sore between the Corps and the Governor. You might have to wait months for an American ship. The sooner you go the better. The *Orion* is stopping off at Coupang, I dare say, so you could pick up an American ship there.'

Richard nodded. 'Thank you, sir.'

So that was that. I was pleased he was coming with me.

'Now, is there anything I can do for you?' said the officer.

'I want to say goodbye to all the people here who've been kind to me, and who I lived with in Sydney.' I especially wanted to bid farewell to Doctor Dan. We could not have found a better friend, and I knew I would miss him greatly. Then there were our neighbours on the Rocks, Mad Bet at the Sailor's Arms, and James Lyons and Orlagh, and all the people at the Navy office.

He sighed. 'Witchall. You don't understand the seriousness of the situation. We're going to have to take you to the *Orion* with an armed escort, probably in the middle of the night. If you go out on the streets, Gray and his men will kill you. There's no doubt about it.'

He agreed to bring me writing paper and envelopes. I filled the last day writing letters of farewell.

The day of our departure arrived. I spent the night thinking of all the people and the things I would miss, Doctor Dan especially. I envied him his life in Green Hills, it was beautiful there. The stories were true. This land was full of promise for anyone with ambition and determination. But then there were the thugs of the New South

Wales Corps, there were the seething resentments among the convicts, there were the natives and their unhappy lot. . . It was a long way off paradise when you stopped to think about it.

We were taken down to the quayside at dawn, and got our first glimpse of the *Orion*, sitting in the bay. She was a large, handsome three-mast vessel and I knew at once I wanted to sail on her.

Our marine escort rowed us over and we were introduced to the Captain, Henry Evison. Towering, unsmiling hands clasped behind his back, he was a forbidding figure. I watched him closely when Richard made it plain he would only be part of the ship's company until Coupang. 'You can stay on ship as long or as short as you like, lad,' he said dourly. 'I'm always happy to have Navy men in my crew.'

Then, soon after noon we weighed anchor. Standing in the rigging, making sail, Richard and I had a splendid view of the harbour as we moved towards the open sea. The sun shone hot on our faces. It was a glorious day. Richard called over to me, 'Psst! Psst!' Then he lowered his voice. 'Look. It's Lizzie Borrow. What's she doing here?'

I looked down on to the deck. There she was, half hidden by her bonnet, come to see the last of Sydney. This was going to be an interesting voyage.

Richard and I were due a rest period that afternoon. We found Lizzie soon enough, out on the deck with her pretty dark-haired maid. She was so delighted to see us she incurred the stern eye of the Captain.

'What are you doing here?' we both said at once.

'You first,' she insisted.

We sat in the forecastle and told her our tale.

'And what about you?' said Richard.

'I called off the engagement to Lieutenant Gray just after the incident that got you sent to Green Hills. I thought he was going to kill you on the spot.'

We told her what had happened when we got back to Sydney, and how Gray had intended to kill us at night in the woods.

'He's angry with me, for refusing him. I don't think he cares about me, he's just lost face. I think he blames you both too. That's why he was so keen to have his revenge.'

The *Orion* passed round the headland and out into the vast sweep of the ocean. Today was the 15th October. If we were lucky, we would reach Coupang in eight weeks, and England by the spring. I would see my parents again, I kept telling myself. But half a year at sea lay between me and home. I had survived so far, but who could tell what storm, accident or misadventure lay ahead?

Fact and Fiction

In Sam Witchall's previous book *Powder Monkey*, all the characters, ships and events were fictitious. Here, in *Prison Ship*, fact and fiction occasionally intertwine.

Sam's ship HMS *Elephant* was a '74' of the period and took part in the Battle of Copenhagen on 2 April, 1801. Among her crew Captain Foley was the actual captain of the ship, Captain Hardy (of 'Kiss me Hardy' fame) was also present, and took a party of sailors out to the Danish line to test the water's depth. Vice Admiral Nelson joined the *Elephant* for the Battle of Copenhagen and is widely claimed to have spoken the words quoted on page 55.

Captain William Bligh also took part in the battle as commander of HMS *Glatton*, as did other ships mentioned in the text, and Vice Admiral Hyde Parker was the commander of the fleet.

In 1801 Australia was known as New South Wales, but also referred to as New Holland and Botany Bay. Matthew Flinders was the first person to call the continent Australia, in 1804, but it took several years for the term to come into common use. Philip Gidley King was the Governor of the colony from 1800 to 1806. Green Hills, where Sam and Richard were sent to work on

Charlotte Farm, was the original name for the town of Windsor in New South Wales. It took its new name in 1810.

The character Thomas Ferring was partly inspired by the 'Wild White Man' William Buckley, who lived for thirty-two years with the Wathaurong people after escaping from Port Phillip in 1803, near to modern-day Melbourne.

Of the old Rocks and old Sydney from this story there is virtually no trace. Among the gleaming glass towers close to Circular Quay and the quaint Victoriana of the Rocks it is difficult to imagine life in the new settlement of 1801. The bush, though, is but a short train ride away from central Sydney, and still alarmingly dense and deserted.

Some Notes on Sources

Although I've tried to base these characters and their circumstances firmly on historic reality, I hope readers more familiar than me with both Nelson's Navy and early colonial Australia will forgive any factual blunders. (In his book *Down Under*, Bill Bryson wryly noted that there was rarely a written fact about Australia that wasn't contradicted somewhere else.)

Most of the information in the Australian section of the story came from books and journals found in the Mitchell Library at the State Library of New South Wales, and in the Royal Australian Historical Society Library. The Museum of Sydney, the Mint Library, Sydney, and Elizabeth Farm, Parramatta, also provided very useful material. In England I'm especially grateful to the staff of the Caird Library at the National Maritime Museum, Greenwich, and the reference library staff at Birmingham and Wolverhampton Public Libraries, for helping me unearth useful sources.

For any reader wanting to find out more about the real history of colonial Australia, I can recommend any of the following:

Transported: In Place of Death (Convicts in Australia) by Christopher Sweeney (Macmillan, 1981). This is a very readable introduction to the topic of convict transportation in Australia.

The Fatal Shore by Robert Hughes (Vintage, 2003). Although some of its content is controversial, this is an evocative and moving account of Australia's convict beginnings.

Pig Bites Baby – Stories from Australia's First Newspaper, Volume 1, 1803–1810 edited by Michael Connor (Duffy and Snellgrove, 2003). A compendium of clippings from *The Sydney Gazette*, it gives a vivid flavour of life in Sydney in the first decade of the 19th century.

Great Convict Escapes in Colonial Australia by Warwick Hirst (Kangaroo Press, 2003). A rollicking good read, it includes a fascinating chapter on 'Wild White Men'.

Acknowledgements

I'm very grateful to Dilys Dowswell for her valuable advice on all my first drafts, and my agent Charlie Viney for his support and encouragement. Thanks also to Peter Rayner, Alex and Louis Costello, and Charlie James for their help.

At Bloomsbury, Ele Fountain patiently steered the story in the right direction, and she and Isabel Ford made valuable improvements to the text. Ian Butterworth created the evocative cover and Peter Bailey's fine line drawings enhance the inside pages.

My trip to Australia to research this book was a wonderful adventure. My landlady, Bobbie Burke, made me very welcome, and Fiona Campbell took me out to visit Richmond and Windsor. On my travels, Ken and Kathy Taylor helped me out when I got lost in the bush, and Lynne Iverson and Stephanie Kaye introducing me to Australian wildlife at Sydney's Taronga Zoo.

Thank you too to Liz Bray, Inara Walden, Karen Bromley and Stephanie Donald for their help and advice. Finally, I'm very grateful to Warwick Hirst, archivist/curator at the Mitchell Library, Sydney, both for the advice he offered when I was researching the book and for his valuable comments on the manuscript.

Writing a novel can be an all-consuming task, so special thanks are due to Jenny and Josie Dowswell for their patience and support.

Read on for a sneak peek at *Battle Fleet*, the conclusion of Sam's epic adventure!

Adventures of a Young Sailor

BATTLE FLEET

Paul Dowswell

CHAPTER 1

Goodbye to All That

We sailed from Sydney on a perfect summer's day, out into the blustery winds of the Pacific Ocean. Richard stood beside me atop the foremast with a huge grin on his face. 'This is a voyage I never thought we'd make again,' he said. 'Certainly not as free men.'

I looked down on our ship the *Orion*, and thought what a handsome vessel she was. Three masts to speed us through the oceans, twenty-four guns to protect us. Despite these guns there was still no mistaking her for a man-o'-war. She had the plump curves of a merchant vessel, and would make a tempting prize for any pirate or privateer who crossed our path. The crew would never pass muster on a Royal Navy ship either.

The *Orion* had visited Sydney to sell – plates, buckles, shoes – rather than buy. She had taken on a small quantity of timber and flax, and us. The crew had also loaded a large number of botanical specimens, each in their own separately marked pot, to be shipped back to England. Then they had stocked up on fresh water, fruit and fowl for the journey. Where there was space beside the plants, the weather deck was packed with caged birds, their constant squawking adding to the general pandemonium.

A voice called up from below. 'Look lively, you urchins on the fore topgallant!' That could only be Lieutenant Hossack, the ship's second in command. We had been on the *Orion* for less than a day, and already I had taken a strong dislike to him.

When we came down to the deck, he was waiting and gave me a swift clout around the ear. 'I'll not tolerate slackers, Witchall,' he said. 'You'll pull your weight on this voyage, or you'll find yourself with some stripes on your back.'

When my duties were over, I went to sit on the fo'c'sle, alone with my thoughts. Evening fell, a beautiful velvety evening, like a warm, starry blanket. A cool breeze cut through the heat and I filled my lungs to bursting. I felt light-headed with happiness. For the first time in perhaps six months I was free from a crushing, ever-present fear of death.

Richard came to join me. We had sailed together since I was first pressed aboard HMS *Miranda* three years before. After fighting side by side at Copenhagen we had been framed by our ship's crooked Purser. Transported together as convicts to New South Wales we had now been pardoned and freed to return home.

He had joined the Royal Navy as his family in Massachusetts believed it would be the best apprenticeship for a boy with the sea in his bones. Now he had had enough. When we reached the East Indies port of Coupang, he planned to hook up with an American ship and work his passage home to Boston.

I was pleased to sit with him, of course, but I felt a twinge of betrayal over his plans to leave. We ought to look after each other. Especially on this ship. They were a rough bunch, the crew, and worse than the merchant seamen I'd known when I first went to sea.

We got some measure of them that afternoon, when there was a tussle on the fo'c'sle. Two seamen started arguing about a harbour girl who had tried to solicit their favour and they began to fight. Several of their fellows gathered around. Rather than pulling them apart, they started throwing stones and other missiles at them.

The Captain, Henry Evison, waded in, banged their heads together and had them both clapped in irons.

'I expect the press gangs have taken the best merchant seamen,' said Richard. 'Half of this lot don't even know their way around the rigging. The other half seem pretty good, though I'd hate to see them with some drink inside them.'

Along with half a dozen passengers, there were only thirty or so men in the crew. They were a curious collection of old salts, chancers, rogues and shirkers. There were colliermen from Newcastle trying their hand at deep-water sailing, a few former slavers, and rogues from the postal packets who boasted openly of their smuggling rackets. Toughest of the lot were the gruff northerners known as Greenlandmen – those who had made long voyages into the Arctic, hunting for humpback and right whales.

They were a breed apart and on that first evening I enjoyed listening to their boastful tales while we ate, especially the stories about escaping the press gang. They were not above a bloody battle when the Navy tried to board their whalers, and would drive them off with harpoon and grapeshot. One of the Greenlandmen, William Bedlington, was a bearded giant – six foot three – as he told us several times.

'So how did you end up at sea?' he asked me.

I told him I'd joined a merchantman at Great Yarmouth and been caught by a Navy press gang.

'I got pressed the once,' he said, 'came and took me from me bunk they did, night before we sailed out of Hull. Before I knew it I were plonked in a boat with a bayonet at me belly and they were rowing for the quay. Soon sorted that lot out. I pressed against the strakes with me back and me feet and broke that boat in half before they realised what I were doin'. Bastards all drowned – that'll teach 'em not to learn to swim.'

It sounded an unlikely tale. Later that night I heard Bedlington claim to have jumped a five-bar gate with his wife under one arm. I wondered if they were still together.

Rough men I could cope with, there were plenty like them in the Navy after all. I hated our cramped quarters though. The crew were packed into a couple of filthy cabins in the fo'c'sle and the stink in there was unbearable. Part of the smell came from the fetid bedding – there were bunks here rather than the hammocks I was used to at sea. Evison was keen to keep the rest of his ship spick and span they told me, but he turned a blind eye to the seaman's quarters. It was so stuffy the candles would not burn for want of air.

Early next day we suggested a good clean up of our cabin, but we got short shrift. 'There's enough bloody scrubbing of the decks to do,' said Bedlington, 'wi'out havin' to do ower own quarters. I like a bit o' dirt meself. Keeps the flux and pox at bay.'

The *Orion* was a creaking, leaky old vessel and Richard and I were quickly put to work caulking the decks and strakes. The ship was rumoured to be stricken with teredo worm too. On a quiet night, it was said, you could hear the dull scratching sound of them gnawing away at the timbers of the hull. I knew there were stormy seas ahead and I hoped the *Orion* would be strong enough to survive them.

Despite our year away, Richard and I still had that Navy sense of discipline and duty – an instinct to do a job properly, for the good of the ship and its crew. When we tended to repairs we would do it until the job was done. This annoyed the other men working along side us who tried to do as little as they could get away with. When I tried to show one of the crew how to do a monkey's fist knot on a rope he was using, I heard oaths that even convicts on a transport ship would shrink from using.

After those first few days Richard and I began to feel increasingly uncomfortable with the crew. They would barely talk to us when we ate our meals, and we would be jostled on the decks or companionways as men walked past. Occasionally one would spit on the deck close to where we were scrubbing it. 'Maybe they're like this with all new sailors?' I said.

Richard shrugged. 'Never mind. We've got each other for company.'

We didn't like the crew but we did like Evison. He was a tall, gruff Lancastrian who spoke with his fists if any man showed disrespect or acted foolishly. But he fed his crew the best he could and treated them fairly. I sensed we were in safe hands.

'I think the Captain's all right,' said Richard. 'Bit of a rough diamond though. Have you heard the stories about him? Spent his whole life at sea. They say he knows neither his exact age or his real name. He was found as a small boy, drifting off the coast of South America, the only survivor in a boat of castaways. Wouldn't like to get on the wrong side of him though.'

I laughed. 'Never mind him, its his wife I'm frightened of.'

'Not as much as he is,' said Richard.

Evison's wife Kitty was a great stout woman, plain in her likes and dislikes. Like him she was also from Lancashire. When we had been brought to the *Orion*, she had been against our joining the crew. 'They're boys, Mr Evison,' she had said to our faces, after we had been added to the muster book. 'You want strapping tars who can do everything they're called on to do, not these. Let 'm travel as passengers, if they've got the means to pay.'

'They're Navy lads, Mrs Evison,' said the Captain patiently. 'I'm sure they'll do us proud. And I'll wager they can do more than most of the other sailors on this ship.'

'Make sure you do, boys,' she said, fixing us with a flinty eye.

Among the other women on board was Lizzie Borrow, the daughter of one of the Governor's officials. She was fleeing back to England after a disastrous engagement to an army officer. This was good news for Richard, who had taken a fancy to her. Lizzie had a maid too – a pretty dark-haired girl called Bel Sparke. Lizzie was occasionally friendly, although she could be haughty too. I had never spoken to Bel, but I felt drawn to her. She had an impish smile and I longed to know more about her.

As we sailed further north, the lush shore began to turn a sickly green as the climate grew hotter and drier. We were making a cracking pace through the breakers and warm wind.

I was surprised how quickly I adapted to life at sea after our year in New South Wales. The food was no worse than what we'd have expected on a Navy ship – the usual salt meat, pease and biscuit – though there was a particularly revolting barrel of salt pork filled with feet and tails still covered with hair, and even the head of a pig with a ring running through its nose.

Our day was little different from that of a Navy ship.

Two watches for the crew, four hours on four hours off. Inspection every Saturday and then the crew exercised with the guns and practised their small arms drill. It was a relief to see they were pretty handy with the weapons.

'D'you know much about where we're going?' said Richard over dinner.

'The Spice Islands? They sound exciting,' I said. On the voyage out here, we had sailed straight from the Cape to the south coast of New South Wales. Now we were heading north to the great ring of islands above the continent and would then bear west to Africa.

'They're excitin' all right,' said John Garrick, the bespectacled ship's carpenter, who was sitting opposite us. 'Excitin' like being chased by a pack of dogs is excitin',' he said in his West Country burr. 'If you don't catch some fatal disease when we pass through, then the pirates will get you . . . not a pretty story. The pirates in these waters come out forty boats at a time and kills every last man, woman and child on a European ship. And you've always got the chance of being killed by an earthquake or volcano.'

I thought they'd be exciting to witness and said, 'We'll be all right if we stick to our ship.'

'Sailed these waters before have you?' said Garrick sharply. 'Thought not. Your earthquakes are followed by giant tidal waves that sweep a ship away in an instant.

The natives call them tsunamis.'

'No matter,' I told myself. What could be more dangerous than going into battle? We'd done that. We were tough enough to take anything the sea could throw at us.

We talked more about the port of Coupang, on Timor Island, where Richard hoped to find an American ship. Garrick was full of gloomy advice here too. 'You'd be better off at Batavia – that's the main trading port around here. You'd have more ships to pick from. But we're not going there, which is a good thing for the rest of us. It's full of Dutch and they say a thousand of 'em die a year from disease.

Garrick really didn't like the East Indies, and there was no stopping him. He was making me feel uneasy and I wished he'd shut up.

'I can't be doin' with the natives round here, either. "They're ugly and strong, and bear malice long" – that's what the Dutch say about 'em. Much rather be doin' business with the Indian or Chinaman. But the Captain don't want to go that way. They say he hasn't got a proper licence – and if the East India Company catch him there'll be trouble.'

I didn't know what he was talking about, and I certainly didn't like the sound of it. He could see the baffled look on our faces.

'East India Company – they've got the sole right to

trade for Britain east of the Cape. You go further than Cape Town you gotta be an East Indiaman. Evison thinks he can beat 'em by trading with New South Wales and the Spice Islands. "Who'll know?" he says. Maybe he's right. There's very little British trade in these islands, so maybe we'll get away with it.'

'What sort of highwayman outfit is this?' said Richard sharply. 'No licence to trade! What will happen if we get caught. Will we get treated like pirates?'

'Don't soil yerself over that, lad,' said Garrick impatiently. 'Evison'll be fined, that's all. Anyway, I'll not have you talkin' about the Captain like that. He's a good man, and he knows what he's doin'.'

I felt a bit bashful about the way Garrick spoke to us. He was a decent sort, and a seasoned tar, but like many of the crew he seemed to have taken a dislike to us. Maybe we were being a bit too cocky?

I was also shaken up by the other things he'd said. A leaky ship without a licence to trade. A pirate-infested sea. A pestilence-ridden land. The chill of impending disaster crept into my bones.

Paul Dowswell

is a former editor as well as the author or co-author of more than fifty acclaimed non-fiction books for children on historical and scientific topics. *Powder Monkey: Adventures of a Young Sailor* was his first work of fiction for young adults. He lives in Wolverhampton, England, with his wife and daughter.

Look for all three books about Sam's exciting life at sea in the

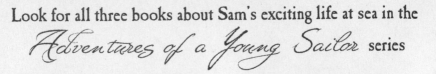 *Adventures of a Young Sailor* series